For my mother, who would have made an excellent queen; and my father, who was the inspiration for His Majesty King Alexander II.

And for Scott Gottlieb, who was left out last time, but not on purpose.

# THE ROYAL
# TREATMENT

# MaryJanice
# Davidson

**WHEELER**
CHIVERS

This Large Print edition is published by Thorndike Press®, Waterville, Maine USA and by BBC Audiobooks, Ltd, Bath, England.

Published in 2006 in the U.S. by arrangement with Kensington Books, an imprint of Kensington Publishing Corp.

Published in 2006 in the U.K. by arrangement with Kensington Publishing Corp.

U.S. Hardcover       1-59722-264-X       (Softcover)
U.K. Hardcover 10:  1 4056 3826 5       (Chivers Large Print)
U.K. Hardcover 13:  978 1 405 63826 5
U.K. Softcover  10:  1 4056 3827 3       (Camden Large Print)
U.K. Softcover  13:  978 1 405 63827 2

The text of this Large Print edition is unabridged.
Other aspects of the book may vary from the original edition.

Set in 16 pt. Plantin.

Printed in the United States on permanent paper.

**British Library Cataloguing-in-Publication Data available**

**Library of Congress Cataloging-in-Publication Data**

Davidson, MaryJanice.
  The royal treatment / by MaryJanice Davidson.
    p. cm.
  ISBN 1-59722-264-X (lg. print : sc : alk. paper)
  1. Princesses — Fiction.  2. Princes — Fiction.  3. Kings
and rulers — Fiction.  4. Inheritance and succession —
Fiction.  5. Alaska — Fiction.  6. Large type books.
  I. Title.
  PS3604.A949R69 2006
  813'.6—dc22                                    2006006825

# Author's Note

I took several liberties with this book, chief of which, Alaska is not a country. Once I made so bold as to twist reality to suit my needs, I changed a few other things as well. I hope the reader has as much fun exploring this new world as I did.

# Acknowledgments

As always, thanks to my wonderfully supportive family for their . . . well, wonderful support. Particularly my sister, Yvonne, who has listened to all my dull story ideas without yawning even once. That's true of my husband, as well. Special thanks to Karen Thompson, who reads my rough drafts without complaint; and Giselle McKenzie, who complains heartily about my rough drafts.

Extra-special thanks to my editor, Kate Duffy, and the generous and kind Lori Foster; they have been unfailingly supportive.

Also, many thanks to two women I've never met: Martha Stewart and Judith Martin. I usually finish a book when my hero and heroine decide to say "I do" and never get to think up a wedding. *Martha Stewart Weddings* and *Miss Manners on Weddings* were invaluable.

# Prologue

From *The Queen of the Edge of the World*, by Edmund Dante III, © 2089, Harper Zebra and Schuster Publications.

Even today, with all the comforts of a peaceful twenty-first century, Alaskans are a hardy group, and none more so than the royal family. There's a saying in this part of the world: Alaskan royals wrestle bears, but only after tea.

This hardiness was vital for a young, vast country. Alaskans had to be tough, not only to break from Mother Russia in 1863, but to then go on and form their own government. It could not have been easy, but the royal family rose to the occasion.

It's precisely this hardiness that occasionally causes trouble. Queen Christina's father-in-law, King Alexander II, was no exception.

Historical records confirm King Alexander adored his daughter-in-law from the moment he set eyes on her. With characteristic impulsiveness, he decided this tough, uncompromising commoner would be perfect for his son, the Crown Prince David.

Of course, convincing His Highness the Prince, not to mention the woman who would eventually become the mother of kings, was no simple matter. . . .

# PART ONE

# *Nobody*

Nobody really knows me, and I don't really know anybody. But that's okay.
— Christina Krabbe

# Chapter 1

"If you *ever* touch me again, I'll pull off your ears and stuff them up your nose."

Christina Krabbe explained this fact of life to her supervisor, who was at the moment rolling around on the deck, cradling his mashed privates.

*Never should have gotten out of bed. Should have tossed the clock on the floor and gone back to sleep.*

But she'd never been late for work a day in her life, and if she didn't crack eight hundred eggs for Friday's rosemary scrambled eggs, who would?

Christina had known there would be trouble, almost from the moment she came on board. Ed had "accidentally" brushed her butt or a breast a million times. Never enough to be called on his behavior, always enough to make her dread the next time she ran into him. She was just surprised her boss had taken this long — almost three weeks — to make his move.

But today . . . coming up behind her and

15

grabbing her boobs like she was a cow to be milked . . . she'd back-kicked and elbow-struck, and then he was on the floor and it was done and couldn't be taken back. Not that she would.

His lips were moving. She bent closer to hear.

". . . fired."

"What?"

". . . fired. You're fired."

"Uh-huh. What's the phrase? You can't fire me, I quit? Is that it? I ought to sue your ass, Ed, you lecherous piece of shit. But frankly, you're not worth the time, the trouble, or the aggravation." *Also, I have no money for a lawyer. But never mind.*

She threw her belongings into a duffel bag while he recovered, climbed painfully to his feet, and shuffled out the door. She didn't watch him go. She'd worry about a reference later.

She marched down the gangplank, flashed her employee badge to the guy counting noses, then promptly dropped it into the garbage can at the end of the dock and fell in line behind the geese.

At least they were in port. If Ed had tried his crap while they were at sea, she'd have had a long swim ahead of her.

One of the tour guides — the line em-

16

ployed several dozen, and she could never keep them straight — was doing Alaska 101 for the geese. Christina eased her way past the throng, half-listening to the spiel.

"— Russia did actually offer Alaska to the United States for sale. As you know, America had the Civil War to contend with, and thus wasn't interested in the purchase at that time, but can you imagine if they had? Alaska would have been the forty-ninth state!"

*And since gold and oil were discovered here, we've been kicking ourselves about that ever since,* Christina thought, smothering a chuckle.

The tour guide droned on while Chris put the gangplank, the ship, Ed, and French Toast Tuesday behind her.

The *Summer's Sweetness* — an exquisitely stupid name for a cruise ship — was leaving port tonight. She had no plans to be on it. She wasn't going near Ed again — he might get the idea in his head that a little payback would be balm to his battered ego. Some men were weird that way. Knock them around defending yourself, and they decide the only way to fix it is to hurt you back twice as bad.

When the ship sailed, she'd still be in port. Marooned in Juneau, Alaska, over a thousand miles from her birthplace. Marooned at the edge of the world, in a place with a famously nutty royal family and more bears than cars.

Great.

# Chapter 2

From *The Queen of the Edge of the World*, by Edmund Dante III, © 2089, Harper Zebra and Schuster Publications.

King Alexander II, head of the House of Baranov, was, as was most of the royal family, a conundrum. Raised to wealth and privilege, he had a common streak. However, he was rarely allowed to "get down and dirty," as His Majesty might have put it, due to his responsibilities, the hovering of his majordomo, Edmund Dante, and his bodyguards.

Often His Majesty would let his beard grow and take a group out fishing. This drove people mad, in particular: (A) his security team, (B) Edmund Dante, and (C) the people in his fishing group. King Alexander was always surprised to be recognized, and once he was, quite a lot of the fun went out of the group. It was difficult for Alaskans to enjoy a day of leisure when they realized their sovereign was the one driving the boat and gutting the fish.

"We're catching tons of fish, but you haven't cracked a smile all afternoon." The captain of the boat plunked down beside her, stretched out his long legs, and stared at the toes of his rubber boots. "What's the matter, kid?"

Christina shrugged.

"Oh, come on."

"Well . . ." She looked at the other members of the fishing party, who were all huddled on the other end of the boat, staring at them. Weird. It had been a pretty jolly group earlier, and now they were walking around like there was glass in their boots. "I'll tell you my problem, if you tell me theirs." She jerked her head in the direction of the group.

"Done."

"Okay. Well, I kicked the shit out of my boss for copping a feel, got myself fired, again, I'm marooned in a strange country, again, and I used my last fifty bucks to come fishing. I mean, how dumb am I?"

The captain looked puzzled. He was a big man, wide through the shoulders, and quite a bit taller than she — and at five-ten, Christina wasn't short. He had bushy, salt-and-pepper hair, an equally bushy beard threaded with silver, and blue eyes that smiled even when his mouth didn't.

"How dumb are you? About which part?"

"The 'spending my last dime on this boat' part. I mean, hello, I could have waited until I found another job, right? Dumb. No excuse." She sighed and stared out at the ocean. "But I just wanted to — wanted to —"

"Do something you loved for a change. I don't think that's so dumb."

"No excuse," she said gloomily. "Work first. Assuming I'll be able to work in this country. I mean, I've got a passport, but — never mind, I'm getting off track. Because the rest of it, not so dumb. I mean, what was I supposed to do? Let him grab? Forget it. He's lucky I didn't kick his balls up into his throat."

The captain was nodding, which cheered her up a little. "Damn right. He got what he deserved. If somebody did that to one of my daughters . . ." His hands closed into fists that were, she observed, the size of bowling balls.

"Right. No mercy."

"*Damn* right."

"Right. We've now established that kicking ass is the way to go. But that doesn't exactly help me out. I've got to find a job. I guess first I have to find out if I can stay."

"You can stay," the captain said.

"That's nice, but I'd better check it out for myself, don't you think?"

He shrugged.

"Right. Uh . . . you look kind of familiar. Have I seen you on TV or something?"

"I've got that kind of face," he said vaguely.

"Oh. Anyway, all my worldly possessions are in a locker at the library, but —"

"What about your folks?"

"My dad took off when I was just a baby, and my mom died when I was in high school. There's just me."

"Jeez, that's too bad."

Now it was her turn to shrug. She certainly wasn't getting into the whole "been on my own since I was sixteen" thing. He seemed like a nice, friendly, older guy, but there were limits.

"What do you do?"

"I'm — I mean, I *was* — a cook on a cruise ship. And spare me the whole 'cruise ships are ruining Juneau' speech — I've heard it before from the townies."

"I've heard it, too. We're working on it."

She stared at him. "Seriously — you look *really* familiar. Are you sure we haven't met, or —"

"What are you going to do when we get back to port?"

"I guess I'll see if any of the hotels needs a caterer or —"

"You can work for me."

"Thanks. That's really nice of you." She was sincere, but being mate on board a fishing boat was not her idea of a good time. It was messy, it was hard work, the pay sucked, and the tourists were annoying. "And I might take you up on it." Beggars, after all, couldn't be choosers. "But I'd better look around myself, first."

"Do you have a boyfriend?"

"Captain, am I going to have to kick *your* ass today, too?"

"Haw! You're young enough to be one of my kids. I'm too old for that shit. But I've got a son, he's a little older than you — what are you, twenty-three, twenty-four? — and I think you'd be —"

She held up her hands like a traffic cop. "No, thanks. The last thing I need right now is a blind date."

"Well, where are you sleeping tonight?"

"Seriously. Am I going to have to kick your ass?"

He laughed again. It was comforting — he had a big, booming bear laugh — but strange. It was like he got a huge kick out of being threatened. Like it never happened to him, so it was funny when it did. Most people did not laugh when she threatened them with bodily harm.

"Take it easy, uh —"

"Christina."

"Christina. I'm Al. Look, I live in a really big place and there's plenty of room for you. And there's always a zillion people around, and all my kids still live at home, so it's not like you'd be — uh — compromised. And I hate the idea of you sleeping on a park bench. I mean, I really fuckin' hate it."

She had to smile at his anxiety. And earnestness. "Thanks, Captain, but I've been looking out for myself for a long time."

He sighed. "Suit yourself, but if you change your mind, just call this number and this guy'll set you up." He fished around and finally extracted a business card. He left a large grease smear on it, but otherwise it was perfectly legible. "It was really nice talking to you, but I guess I'd better get back to it."

He strolled to the back of the boat while she read the card.

*Edmund Dante*
*Chief Secretary to*
*HRM King Alexander II*
*Juneau, Alaska*
*Audentia aeternum audentia*
*763-223-3215*

At first she thought it was a joke — his name was Al, not Edmund. And what was with the Latin? She knew that slogan, she'd seen it on TV or something . . . what was it? Boldness, something. Boldness, ever boldness, that's right. But that was the family — the royal family's —

She watched the rest of the group. *En masse,* they shuffled uneasily when the captain approached.

"Your Majesty," a few of them muttered, staring at the deck.

"Majesty," another one said, slightly louder, and he bowed from the waist.

"Hey, on the boat, it's just Al, okay, you guys?" He scratched his beard. "How'd you recognize me, anyway?"

"Hey!" she yelled, crumpling the card in her fist. *"Hey!"*

"What?" he demanded, turning.

*"The king?* You're the goddamned king of Alaska and you've got *fish guts* under your fingernails?"

"Hey, everybody likes to get away once in a while."

*"Get away?"*

"You call my guy if you change your mind, Christina. We got lots of room —"

"At the Sitka Palace, for God's sake!"

"Well . . . yeah." He grinned at her. She shook her head and scowled at him, but inside, she was smiling. It had been a pretty good joke on her, and that was for sure. Shame on her for not recognizing him sooner, beard or no beard. The guy was on television or in the papers almost every month, after all.

*Assaulted my boss, insulted a king. All in the space of three hours. Can't wait to see what's in store this afternoon.*

# Chapter 3

His Royal Highness David Alexander Marko Dmitri Baranov, crown prince of Alaska, leaned forward and said, "Open up, little lady. You know you want it."

The sleek king penguin, thigh-high to him, opened her beak and wolfed down the proffered smelt. David resisted the urge to pet her. The deceptively cute bird was more than capable of a painful jab if she felt threatened. He had the scars on the tops of his hands to prove it.

He watched the baker's dozen of kings swim and move about the twelve-hundred-square-foot habitat. His home-within-his home. Here David felt truly at peace, here he was able to —

"His Highness, heir to the throne, once again among the waddlers."

"Kings don't waddle, Edmund," he said without turning around. "They're about the only kind of penguin that walks instead of hopping."

"Fascinating, sir. It's only because I'm so

riveted that I'm falling asleep standing. Of course, I dare not sleep talk and suggest you leave your sanctum sanctorum and take a meal with the king and your royal siblings."

"Why would I do that?"

The special assistant to the king sighed. "Never mind, sir."

"So Dad's back from his fishing tour?"

"Two hours ago, sir."

"He got busted again, didn't he?"

"The king remains unaware of his easily recognizable features."

David snickered. It was just too damned funny, the king sneaking off for some private time — how well he understood the urge! And his dad was always crushed when locals recognized him.

"Want to feed the birds?"

"I am overwhelmed at the invitation, but as a simple man, I do not share your family's infatuation with dead fish."

"Smart-ass," David muttered. Edmund Dante had been looking after the royal family since his grandfather's time. As such, while Edmund deeply respected the institution, he had no fear of it.

David's earliest memory was of Edmund bowing deeply and calling him sir, then spanking him for booting Princess Alexandria off the dock and into the harbor.

"Sir, I — ah — hesitate to bring this up —"

"You? Hesitate? Whatever you've been sniffing, can I have some?"

Edmund favored him with a sour smile. He was tall — as tall as the king — but whip-thin. He also had two master's degrees, one in Alaskan history, the other in Alaskan literature. His sisters had given Edmund the nickname "Ichabod Brain." "Your wit is as devastating as ever, sir. I wondered if you were aware the king is . . . ah . . . seeking a bride."

"Dad wants to get married again?" he asked, actually looking away from the penguins. "Holy mother of God, wasn't once enough?"

"Not a bride for him, sir. For you."

"Oh. That whole 'the crown prince needs an heir' thing, huh?"

"I would imagine so, yes, sir."

David shrugged and picked up another bucket of smelt. "Well, he can choose away. I mean, it doesn't really matter, right? As long as she's young and healthy and wants to have kids."

"As you say, sir. Really, the only qualities one would wish for in a wife." Edmund said this with a perfectly straight face and, despite the fact that David narrowed his eyes at him, didn't change expression. Sometimes it was impossible to tell if the man was teasing or not.

Edmund opened his mouth but — thank God — was interrupted when his cellphone/walkie-talkie beeped at him. He pulled it out of its holster and pressed the black button on the side.

"Dante."

"Ah, yeah, Mr. Dante, this is Sergeant Kenner at the east gate?"

"Go ahead, Sergeant."

"Well, there's a girl here — a lady, I mean — and she says —"

"Is that him? Give me that thing." The woman's voice, a faint contralto, suddenly became much clearer. And louder. David straightened from the penguins and cocked his head, listening to the tinny, strident voice. "Is this Edmund Dante?"

"Y—"

"Good, listen, my name's Christina Krabbe and I met the king on a fishing boat today. And don't even say anything — I know how it sounds. But it's true! He was pretending to be the captain and he was wearing what appeared to be a dead muskrat on his face."

"Fascinating."

"Well, anyway, he said I could stay at the palace if I wanted. And he gave me your card. And at first I said no, thanks, but then I said, why the hell not? I know how it sounds."

"Indeed. Ma'am, would you put Sergeant Kenner back on the line, please?"

"Huh? Oh, sure." There was a thud, followed by a crackle.

"Kenner here."

"Sergeant, does the lady in question have shoulder-length blond hair, green eyes, and freckles? And does she come up to your shoulder?"

"Her eyes are kinda more blue than green, but everything else is spot-on."

"And is she as obnoxious in person as she appears over this phone?"

"Well . . . yeah."

"Very well, escort her to the west gate and I will meet her there."

"Right away, sir."

Edmund clicked off and reholstered his phone.

"Who was *that?*" David asked. He forgot to let go of the smelt and one of the kings pecked him. He barely felt it.

"Oh, just someone your father met today," Edmund said airily. "It's of no concern to *you,* Highness."

"Fine, be that way. You'd better get moving. It'll take you at least twenty minutes to walk to the west gate from here."

"Sir, I have told you a billion times not to exaggerate. It will take no more than twelve." Edmund bowed slightly. "If I have your leave, Your Highness . . . ?"

"Like you need it," David grumbled, and waved him off.

Christina Krabbe, he thought after Edmund left. Weird name.

Nice voice, though.

# Chapter 4

From *The Queen of the Edge of the World*, by Edmund Dante III, © 2089, Harper Zebra and Schuster Publications.

To my grandfather, Edmund Dante I, fell the task of teaching the future queen manners, deportment, and all areas of appropriate behavior for a royal. Subsequently, Dante would have known of the king's enthusiasm and would have known, in fact, before Queen Christina herself, the role she was destined to play. So it's likely the entire tone of their relationship was set by their first meeting.

Unfortunately, there are no historical records of such a meeting, so we are forced to speculate what these two strong-willed individuals made of each other. . . .

The sergeant — who'd become perfectly nice once she'd gotten the okay from

what's-his-face, screeched to a halt in front
of a truly gargantuan door. She climbed out
of the golf cart and turned to thank Kenner
for the ride, only to see him check his
watch, nod, and zoom off.

*Well. Sink or swim around here.* That
was just fine by her.

She raised her fist — she figured if she
stood on tiptoe she could almost reach the
middle of the door — when it suddenly
swung open and she was eyeball-to-collar-
bone with one of the tallest, thinnest men
she'd ever seen.

He had jet-black hair, a widow's peak,
and eyes so dark she couldn't tell where his
pupils began. He was dressed in a black
suit, white dress shirt, black tie, and was
deeply tanned. He could have been anywhere from thirty-five to sixty-five.

"Gaaaaaahhhh!"

"Green," the incredibly scary-looking
man said, looking her over. "Not blue."

She put a hand on her chest to slow her
now-galloping pulse. "Wh—what?"

"Good evening, ma'am. Edmund
Dante."

She shook his hand. His grip was firm
and dry. It was like shaking hands with a
plank of wood. "Is every guy in this
country over six feet tall?"

"Yes, ma'am, every single one of us. If you'll follow me?"

"Where are we going?"

"Your quarters, ma'am."

"Oh. Super. And it's Christina, not ma'am."

After six hallways, an elevator ride, and four doors, she was standing in a small suite of rooms.

"Oh . . . man!"

"I trust these will be acceptable?"

"Day-amn!"

"Very well, then."

She flung herself toward the bed, twisted in midair, and disappeared in a billow of down comforters. "Oh, I could get used to this!"

What's-his-name's face appeared above her. This was slightly less startling than the first time. "If you have need of anything," he told her, "just pick up the phone. Tomorrow's luncheon is at one."

"Gotta sing for my supper, huh? Well, fair's fair."

"Would you like to meet Prince David before then?"

"Why?"

"Oh, perfect."

"What?"

"Nothing, ma'am. It's the dry air in

here." He hack-hacked into a closed fist. "It makes me hoarse. I'll attend to it immediately. Good evening."

" 'Bye."

He left, moving like a tall, tanned ghost, and she climbed out of the downy bed — took a while! — and prowled the suite.

Cream walls with gold trim. A zillion windows. A bathroom, a room just for hanging out in, a bedroom. Big windows — bigger than her! — that looked out to an emerald green lawn roughly the size of New York's Central Park. Four phones!

She picked up a receiver, just for the fun of it, and instead of a dial tone heard a cheerful female voice say, "Yes, Miss Krabbe?"

"It's 'Krabbe'," she said, startled. "The 'e' is silent. And, uh, nothing. 'Bye."

She hung up and kicked off her shoes, then flung herself onto the amazingly plush bed again.

*Gotta find the catch. There's gotta be one.*

Before she could figure it out, she fell asleep.

"Did you see her?" the king demanded.
"Fine, Your Majesty, and you?"

"Cut that out, Edmund, you harpy. What did you think?"

"A most . . ." He chose his words carefully. ". . . *charismatic* young lady."

"D'you think David will like her?"

"I —"

"She's just what he needs. She's tough, she's cuter than hell, and she's a no-nonsense kind of gal. She *yelled* at me when she found out who I was. Usually people just sort of . . ." King Alexander made a vague gesture.

"Scuttle out of the reach of your mighty wrath?"

"Oh, shut up."

"Your Majesty, since you did ask my opinion — and as your servant I am most grateful for this rare opportunity to air my views —"

"Spit it out, Edmund."

"— can the prince not choose his own wife?"

"Well, what the hell's he waiting for?" The king jumped up from his seat by the fireplace and paced the room in his agitation. "He's going to be thirty this year and he's not even looking. Hell, he's not even *dating.* That Yank magazine — *People*, is it? He's made their Most Eligible Bachelor issue since he was drinking age, so don't tell me he couldn't get a date if he wanted to. And you've heard him, all this 'as long as she's healthy and wants kids' bull-shit —"

"But that's understandable. Does His Majesty not wish the succession to —"

The king waved that away. "No, no, *no*."

"No?" Edmund teased.

"Jeez, I've got five kids — *one* of 'em's bound to get knocked up, or knock someone up. If David doesn't have kids, Alex's kids can run the country, or the other Alex's, or Kathryn's, or —"

"I believe I see where you're going with this, sir."

"I just want him to *be* with somebody, you know? A partner. A friend. So he doesn't spend all his time mooning around after those smelly birds. When his mom — uh — left —"

"Prince David took the queen's death very hard," Edmund said quietly.

"Anyway, he needs a wife. And if he won't go get one, *I'll* find one for him."

"Lord help us."

"What?"

"Dry air. I'll see to it immediately."

"So, the kid — Christina — she's settled in and all?"

"She was rolling around on the down

duvet when I left her, chortling like a monkey."

"Excellent. And she's having lunch with all of us tomorrow?"

"Yes, sir."

"Good. Make sure David comes, too. It's not a request — tell him the king and he are having lunch, got it?"

"I had it the first time, sir."

"Wise guy. Go away."

"At once, sir. Just one question . . . I confess to consuming curiosity —"

"What a gigantic fucking surprise."

Edmund sniffed disapprovingly at the language, but didn't comment. "I take it you have abandoned your peace-making attempts with Her Majesty the Queen of England?"

"She won't answer my letters," he said gloomily. "Her secretary's been writing back, how's that for a diss? Uh . . . no offense, Edmund. When I have you write back for me —"

"It's because you can't be bothered — yes, sir, I know. So England remains implacable?"

"Too damn right. Jeez, an honest mistake, and we're all banned from Buckingham and Sandringham for life."

"The honest mistake being when you

mistook one of her prized corgis for a raccoon and chased after it on horseback?"

"I thought it had rabies," the king whined. "You know all the problems they've been having this summer. I was going to kill it for her."

"As a gesture of good will."

"Well . . . yeah."

"A fortuitous beginning that would cement relations with her house and yours."

"Exactly!"

"Instead you merely chased her beloved dog to exhaustion, causing it to succumb to dehydration."

"Hell, it didn't *die* or anything. Just needed to see the vet. For a few days. Okay, a week."

"Um-hmm." Edmund passed a hand over his immaculate hairstyle. "Thus, we can forget about a marital alliance with the House of Windsor."

"Pretty much."

"So we've resorted to picking American commoners off the street?"

The king jabbed a finger the size of a sausage in Edmund's direction. "Never mind that snob bullshit. My great-grandma was a nobody and she turned out to be the greatest queen this country's ever seen. Bloodlines don't mean shit up here.

It's what you *do* that counts."

"Yes, Your Majesty."

"Christina's got the goods. David doesn't care. And I want them hitched. So that's that."

From *The Queen of the Edge of the World.*
*And that, as they say, was that.*

# Chapter 5

"Maps," the blonde said, hurrying into the dining hall. She saw the steps too late and instead of skidding to a halt, simply sailed over them and landed lightly on her feet. She was wearing khaki shorts, a short-sleeved, powder blue sweater, and loafers without socks. "Maps in the rooms."

"What?" the king said. "What's the big deal, kid? Lunch at one, third floor. Easy."

"There are *three* dining rooms on this floor," she snapped, eliciting gasps from the servants and grins from the royal siblings. "Say it with me — *maps.*"

"Well, excuse the hell out of me. Next time I'll have Edmund escort you."

"Swell," she muttered, sitting down at the empty seat beside David. "That won't scare me to death."

King Alexander cleared his throat. As were his children, he was dressed in denim and khaki. The watch on his left wrist was worth eighteen thousand pounds, English Sterling (a gift from Queen Elizabeth before relations deteriorated), and he had a rubber band on his right wrist, which was worth about eight cents, Alaskan. "Everyone, this is Christina Krabbe."

"It's pronounced *Crab,* not Crabby. The 'e'," she said, turning to David, "is silent."

*"Anyway,"* the king continued loudly, "she's sort of stranded in our country for a while, so let's make her feel at home."

"America didn't want you, huh?" the youngest boy said, and laughed.

"Shaddup, Nicholas," the king retorted, drawing on his formidable store of child psychology. "Christina, this is my oldest son, David, my oldest daughter, Alexandria, my other son, Alexander the Third, my daughter Kathryn, and my youngest, Nicholas."

"I know," she said. "I mean, it was nice of you to introduce me, but I read a newspaper occasionally. Also, you were all prominently featured in *People* magazine's Wild Royals issue."

David snorted before he could lock it back.

"The press," Alexandria announced, "plagues us. Plus, could they have published *less* flattering pictures? Blurgh."

"Oh, quit it," Nicholas said. "You know you're gorgeous, so no more whining about all the bad pictures, 'kay?"

"Pipe down, twerp," the princess retorted, but she looked pleased.

"I'm so glad you shaved," the commoner explained to the king. "That whole 'dead animal on the face' thing was just . . . yech. Also, as a disguise, it was pretty lame."

Now the Alexes were elbowing each other and snickering into their napkins while the king scowled.

"Look, let's just have a nice lunch, okay, brats? Okay?" The king, David could see, was trying not to plead. His brothers and sisters, like wolverines, could smell fear.

The first course, fresh oysters on the half shell, was brought out. David sucked the first one down while keeping half an eye on the woman beside him. She was really something — adorably cute, with bouncy blond hair and freckles sprayed across her nose and cheeks. Beautiful green eyes, the color of forest moss. She smelled terrific, like soap and wildflowers. And the mouth on her! If she was intimidated to find herself lunching with the royal family, she sure didn't show it. Most people sat stiff as a board and barely touched their meal.

"So, there's not a lot of bowing and scraping around here, I noticed," Christina said, eyeing the oysters with a neutral expression.

"Bowing and scraping
Is discouraged by Papa
Plus it takes too long."

"What was that?" Christina, completely befuddled, asked Prince Alexander.

Prince David leaned close and murmured, "My brother's in this phase right now. He only speaks in haiku."

*"Why?"*

"He lost a bet," Princess Alex said. "Anyway, back to the bowing and scraping. Our father discourages it." She drained her water glass and, the second she set it down, a footman glided over and filled it again. "We weren't really raised to bow when the sovereign enters, bow when called, bow when he leaves, bow —"

"Big damned waste of time," the king said with his mouth full.

"And this *is* Alaska. We usually have more pressing matters on our mind than royal protocol."

"Unlike *some* royal families," David said, looking down his long nose.

"Don't blame the Windsors
Locked into their traditions
They are prisoners, too."

"That is amazing," Christina announced.

"You can just — come up with those on the fly? You open your mouth, and poetry pops out? I couldn't write a poem to save my life."

Prince Alex smiled at her. Women were not usually impressed with his haiku. Or his fanatic interest in the period films of George Lucas.

"Kid's right — don't be slamming the Windsors," the king said, salting his lox. David thought it was a miracle his father didn't have a cholesterol level of eight hundred. "They can't help it. They've been doing the same shit for fifteen hundred years. Like Alex said, they're prisoners as much as any poor slob in jail."

"That's nice. Umm . . . where's the cocktail sauce?" Christina whispered to Edmund, who had taken up his post by the window, four feet behind her.

Edmund leaned forward. "I beg your pardon, ma'am?"

"The cocktail sauce," she said loudly and slowly, as if speaking to someone developmentally delayed. "For. The oysters."

"It comes with a vinaigrette," David explained. "Try it, I think —"

"*I* think I'll barf if I have to suck down raw oysters without cocktail sauce. You know those annoying people who have to put ketchup on everything?"

"Like the king?" Edmund asked snarkily.

She ignored that. And David found he had to bring his fist up and rest it below his nose to hide the grin. "Well, I'm one of those people who have to put cocktail sauce on seafood."

"Jeez, what's wrong *now?*" the king complained.

"Well, hell, my rights are being stomped on!" said Christina.

"Your rights as an illegal alien?" Princess Alexandria asked, and she did not trouble herself to hide *her* grin.

"Alexandria, we're trying to be nice to her," the king sighed.

"Matchmaker!" she coughed into her napkin by way of reply.

"*Match*maker?" Nicholas repeated, delighted. He barked shrill, boyish laughter.

"For crying out loud," David muttered.

Completely unfazed by the current discussion, their guest continued. "I mean, Jesus, you guys are lucky I'm even willing to *eat* these things." Prince David jerked his head back, narrowly avoiding Christina's waving hands. "The first guy who ever ate a raw oyster was a fearless — or desperate — son of a bitch, I can tell you that right now. Let's call a spade a spade, here — it looks disgusting. I'm sorry, but there it is — ow!"

A roll sailed across the table from Princess Kathryn's side, beaned Christina in the forehead, then fell into her plate with a plop. Oyster shells rattled and Christina looked up, but the princess in question was wolfing down her oysters and didn't return the gaze. Christina stared at her suspiciously for a long moment, then added, "So, cocktail sauce?"

Prince Nicholas had disappeared under the table, the better to muffle his laughter, which was piercing, to say the least. The king was resting his head on his hands, and Edmund was stonily silent.

Martha, the senior server, had reappeared and was holding a silver tureen brimming with, David prayed, cocktail sauce. She set it before Christina, smiled, and moved away with her usual silent, speedy efficiency.

"There! Cocktail sauce. Well, *thank* you." She twisted around in her seat to glare at Edmund. "Was that so damned hard, Jeeves?"

"Edmund."

"Whatever."

David joined his little brother beneath the table.

After lunch, Christina wandered around the castle, guidebook (*The Official Sitka Palace Guidebook, revised edition 2003*) in hand. Lunch might have been weird, with a yelling king and giggling princesses and a weirdly silent crown prince who later ducked under the table with his little brother, but the palace was pretty swell; the Cinderella Castle at Disney World had been modeled after it.

Eventually, after many turns and stairwells, she found herself in a long room lined with portraits. The floor-to-ceiling curtains were drawn, to protect the paintings, she figured, but the room was filled with soft lighting.

Here was the king as a little, sneery boy. That pony didn't look too happy, either.

Here was the king's mother, a kindlooking, white-haired woman — look at all those curls! — with the king's laughing blue eyes.

Here was the king's great-grandfather, Kaarl Baranov, who helped break Alaska away from Russia, and won a crown for his trouble.

Here was his great-grandmother, the legendary Queen Kathryn, who was a chambermaid in the king's house when she caught his eye. Funny to think of a regular woman helping run the country. Well, they did it in America all the time.

Here was . . . whoa.

Here was a woman, imposing and beautiful and frightening, all at the same time. Her waist-length hair was deepest black, and her eyes, green as poison, glittered from the portrait. Her dress was made of deep blue velvet and she wore a necklace of sapphires as big as Christina's thumbs. Her skin was creamy white, unblemished and perfect. Her nose was a blade — Princess Alexandria's nose. Her mouth was blood red. Her teeth were very white, and looked sharp. The mouth of a passionate lover . . . or a woman who would bite when she was angry.

"She was something, eh?"

Christina jumped, then replied, "She sort of reminds me of the wicked queen in *Snow White*. You know . . . she was beautiful, but it didn't stop her from being bad."

"Hmmm."

She turned — and jumped again when she recognized David. "Oh, shit! I just insulted one of your relatives, didn't I?"

"My mother," he said.

She clapped her hands over her eyes.

"Aaarrgghh! I thought she looked familiar! Jeez, I'm really sorry. It's been so long since she — um — jeez, this isn't going to get any better. . . ."

"Well." She felt him gently grasp her wrists, and pull her hands away from her face. "You're right, you know. She was beautiful. But she had her terrible side, too."

Christina couldn't think of a single thing to say to that, so she just stared at the prince. He was pretty easy to stare at, truth be told . . . he looked a lot like his father, had the same thick black hair and piercing blue eyes, the same build, almost the same height. She felt small next to him.

And his mother! Queen Dara had flaunted her affairs to the press and the king, respectively. Rumors of divorce had been thick, but then fate intervened. The queen had been killed in a car crash, during a rendezvous with her lover *du jour.* She'd apparently been applying lip-liner and had accidentally driven off a cliff. It was horrible and funny at the same time. A field day for the press.

David, if she recalled her modern history, had been seventeen at the time. Nicholas, the youngest, had just been born. And there had been nasty rumors about

51

that, hadn't there? About Nicholas maybe being only *half* royal . . .

"Your family," she said, because she had to say something, "is really — uh — special. You got a gorgeous sister, a teenage sister who's gonna be gorgeous but who in the meantime doesn't talk much, a cute younger brother who only talks in poems — and the boy really needs a milkshake. What's he weigh, a hundred pounds? And he's six feet tall? And another brother who hangs out under the dining room table to yuk things up. And they all look the same except Nicholas, who has a head full of curls I would die for! Never a dull moment, huh?"

"I've come to ask you something," David said abruptly.

"Right. I'll go pack."

He smiled at her. His teeth were even and very white. He'd inherited his mother's mouth, if not her less desirable qualities. Christina would kill for the name of his orthodontist. He had a dimple in his left cheek. He was really very yummy, if a little standoffish, but that was —

"— like it here?"

"Huh? I mean, yeah, it's great. Your dad was really nice to let me come over and stay."

"He's a sucker for hard-luck cases."

"Is that what I am?" she asked, amused.

"But I'm getting off track. Christina . . . I was wondering . . . would you consider becoming my wife?"

She laughed. "I thought you just asked me to marry you. The acoustics in here!"

"I did."

"I — what? Oh." She considered for a long moment. "You mean it? You're not teasing?"

"No." He took her hand, rubbed the knuckles gently with his thumb. "I'm not teasing."

"Get married, live here forever, be the queen someday?"

". . . yes."

"No, thank you." She added, at his look of surprise, "But you were super nice to ask."

# Chapter 6

"No? What the hell do you mean, she said no?"

"No. *Non. Nyet.* She said no. Well, that's that. A pity, to be sure, but plenty of fish in the sea and all —"

"Freeze, Edmund! And you, too, David." The king noticed his son had started sidling toward the doorway. "Get back over here. Now. Did you do it right, with diamonds and roses and violins and shit, or did you blurt it out the first time the thought popped into your head?"

"Blurting might have been involved," the crown prince admitted.

"Jeez, Davey, that's no way to woo!"

"To what?"

"This is a classy broad. You know, under all the swearing and yelling. She's American, they're born romantics, you've gotta woo her. Because they don't have princes, they fantasize about 'em all the time."

"How disturbing," Edmund commented.

"She's not like one of the girls up here,

super practical and likely to say yes because she sees the big picture."

"I'll admit," David admitted, "it wasn't the answer I was expecting."

"See? See? Can I pick 'em, or what? Now on top of all her good qualities —"

"Which are?" Edmund asked.

"— we know she's not a gold digger. You offered her a crown and more money than God and she says thanks, but no thanks." King Alexander drove his fist into his palm. "We gotta change her mind! This is the woman I want running the country when I'm gone. You know, along with you, Davey."

"Thanks for that."

"This is the mother of my grandchildren!"

"This," Edmund muttered, "is a royal pain in the ass."

"Proof! Proof! Edmund doesn't like her."

"Didn't you like my mother, Edmund?" David asked.

Edmund blushed, a rare and wonderful thing, and became unusually quiet.

"Well, I suppose I could try again." In fact, he was impatient to try again. Christina was . . . unexpected. And his father was a pretty bright guy. There were worse things than listening to the king's advice. Also, she had really cute freckles. "She isn't leaving anytime soon, is she?"

"She's got nowhere to go, poor kid." The king pointed a finger at him. "You. Go woo. Now."

"Majesty," David said, grinning, and dropped into a classroom-perfect bow.

"Cut the shit."

"As my lord and king commands," he said, and backed out of the room, still bent over in a bow.

"Nicky, you little brat, if you don't give that back *right now* . . ."

"That's no way to talk to a prince," His Highness Prince Nicholas, fifth in line to the throne, complained.

"I'm going to smack the crap out of a prince if you don't take my bra off your head this second. It doesn't fit you and besides," she added coaxingly, "it's my last clean one."

Nicholas, who had been fascinated by the new guest, not to mention the new guest's undergarments, crawled out from under Christina's bed. He had the bra fastened over his head, the snaps tied under his chin, and looked not unlike a mouse with large white ears. He had inherited his grandmother's hair (probably), and looked up at her from a mass of blond curls. "I was only fooling," he said by way of apology.

She snatched the bra away, almost strangling him. "Try it again, and they won't find the body, get it?"

He laughed at her. "Nuh-*uh*. You wouldn't. 'Sides, it's against the law in this country to hurt a member of the royal family."

"So? If it means I keep my underwear to myself, prison is a small price to pay," she admitted. "What are you doing here, anyway? Don't you have — I dunno — prince lessons or something?"

"Not on Sunday, dummy."

"Nice way to talk to a guest!"

"Are you going to stay for a long time?"

"I don't know. I mean, there's only so long I can live on your dad's charity."

"It's not charity," the prince said, shocked. "It's totally not. Dad likes you. He has guests over all the time."

"Yeah, yeah. Listen, I *have* to get a job. Maybe I could get one here!" Why hadn't she thought of that? And why was she confiding in a seventh grader? Oh, well. "I should go find the kitchens, talk to the chef . . ." They might be able to use an extra cook. At the least, she could make sure they never ran out of cocktail sauce.

"Um . . . Christina . . . I don't think Daddy wants you to *work* here . . . exactly . . ."

"Well, tough shit. Sorry. Don't repeat that."

"I'm twelve, not two. I've heard that word before. 'Sides, the king uses it all the time."

"I'll bet," she snickered.

*"All the time,"* David announced from a doorway, "is a minor exaggeration."

Christina jumped. "Don't you guys ever knock?"

"The door is wide open," he pointed out. "Get lost, little prince."

"Awwww, David! It's so *boring* here. An' don't call me that. I'm almost as big as Alex, and *he's* six years older."

"You are not. And as the king might say, tough shit."

Grumbling, the boy prince took his leave.

"I hope he wasn't bothering you," David said, closing the door as he entered the room.

"He's a cutie, with a disturbing yet healthy interest in women's underwear. Uh . . . what do you want?"

"Have dinner with me."

"I think I'm supposed to have dinner with all of you again tonight." She started peeking under pillows and checking drawers. "Damned schedule's around here somewhere . . ."

"Never mind the schedule. Have dinner with *me*. Whatever you want."

"Scrambled eggs and bacon?" she asked brightly.

He frowned at her. "I'm offering you anything you want, and you want eggs?"

"I love them. I, like, *crave* them. Scrambled, fried, poached, over easy, over hard —"

"*Why* won't you marry me?" he blurted, then smacked himself on the forehead.

"Whoa! Easy on the self-flagellation, there, dude."

"I'm supposed to woo you," he explained.

"Well, don't waste the woo on me. Not that it's not a really nice offer. Because it is!"

"So. Why won't you?"

"Because, frankly, being queen sounds like a gigantic pain in the ass."

"I offer you a country and you tell me it's a pain in the ass?"

She stared at the ceiling, then nodded and said, "Yeah, um . . . yeah. I'm going to stand by that."

"But you don't have anything!" he exclaimed. "My father said you're all alone in the world and you — uh —" *Don't have anywhere to go, and are entirely dependent on the kindness of strangers.* Never mind. That wouldn't do.

She jabbed a finger in the middle of his chest. "I've got *myself,* pal. And that's more than a lot of people have. Why should I submerge my identity with your family's? *I* can hop a boat or a plane and go anywhere in the world, for as long as I want. You know, if I had any money. Can you?"

"Theoretically." After the king approved, and the bodyguards were lined up, and the arrangements made, and security triple-checked everything, and —

"Right. Pass. No offense. But thanks for asking. Again."

"Well, you can at least have dinner with me. You know, to let me down gently."

She laughed. "Sure, you're soooo crushed. You don't even know me! Another excellent reason to say no, by the way. But all right. We'll have dinner."

"Scrambled eggs and bacon. And oysters with cocktail sauce."

"You can skip the oysters. And I like ketchup on my eggs."

He managed to conceal the shudder as he bowed, and took his leave of her.

"Hey!" she yelled after him. "I'm not gonna have to curtsey, am I?"

"We don't curtsey in Alaska," he called back. "We only bow."

"Well, good."

# Chapter 7

Christina started to get a bad feeling when the smell hit her. Bird droppings and dead fish. The last time she'd smelled that, she was in Boston visiting the New England Aquarium.

But in the palace? What the hell? Sure, she was on the farthest west end of the palace . . . much farther and she'd be out on the lawn, but that smell . . . ugh!

She tapped on a door marked *P, P,* for *P* and at David's "Come!" entered cautiously.

"I knew it!" she said as the smell assaulted her anew. "You've got penguins in here!"

He straightened up from where he'd been leaning and tossing fish into the water. He was dressed in navy shorts, belted at the waist, a billowy white shirt open at the throat, and sandals. His big blue eyes gleamed at her in a friendly way, and stubble bloomed along his cheek. It was almost enough to distract her from the reek.

Almost.

"Hello again. Forgive my appearance, but I had the distinct impression you wouldn't mind if I wasn't in a suit. Aren't they charming?"

"Bleah, *no!*"

He froze in the act of dropping another dead fish, and nearly lost the first two fingers on his left hand to a particularly hungry penguin. "What?"

She threw up her hands. "Jeez, Dave, you are *so* spoiled! This whole crown prince gig makes things really easy, doesn't it?"

"I have no idea what you're talking about, but in five minutes you won't notice the smell. Now, I'm having our dinner delivered up here in ten minutes, but there's champagne in the —"

"Ugh, we're eating in *here?* Amid messy birds and fish scales? What is *wrong* with you? A normal guy would never, ever get away with this. But you can bring girls to this stinky room and they actually pretend to be into it, don't they?"

He cocked his head — just like the penguins were doing! — and said sharply, "Pretend?"

She folded her hands over her breasts and looked adoringly at him. "Oh, Your Highness, they're so cuuuute! And they swim so fast! And look, they're eating right out of your manfully royal hand! And they don't smell like fishy shit or *anything!*" She fluttered her eyelashes at him, then had to stop when it made her dizzy. "Seriously, Dave. That whole, 'Hi, I'm going to be the king of Alaska someday . . . how *you* doin'?' thing works pretty well for you, doesn't it?"

"What is wrong with a hobby?" he demanded, wiping his hands on a nearby towel.

"Hobby! There's gotta be a hundred of the little buggers in here. So you, like, *kidnapped* them from Canada or wherever —"

"Antarctica," he said sourly.

"— then shut them up in your little palace of horrors —"

"I did not!" He angrily shook his head. "By that I mean, they have plenty of room, they're happy, and they're in no danger of being devoured by a killer whale or a walrus in here."

"No, they're just in danger of making guests pass out from the stink. But I guess that's okay."

"Well, I'm not getting rid of them," he shouted, "no matter how many freckles you have!"

"What?"

"Never mind."

"Well, *I'm* not eating in here."

"You certainly are, Christina!"

"Oh, that's supposed to be a royal order or something? Fact check, Prince Penguin, *I'm* an American citizen. You can't make me do shit."

"Then go away," he snapped.

"In a New York minute, pal! If I see one more bird shit on those rocks, I'm going to yark. Not that you'd notice the smell. And what's P, P, for P?"

"What?" He was *very* red, but took a deep breath and seemed to recover enough temper to answer the question. "It's Privacy, Please, for the Penguins."

She stared at him for a moment. "Oh, I'm gonna puke right now," she finally decided, and let herself out.

The moment she left, David hurled the contents of the last bucket into the water, and watched moodily while the cleverest, most charming creatures on the planet devoured the last of the fish.

"Well," Edmund coughed, emerging from one of the storage areas, a hose coiled over his shoulder, "that went well."

David nearly fell into the penguin pond. It was absolutely uncanny the way Edmund popped up and disappeared, never being heard or seen unless he chose to. "What are you doing here? If the rocks need to be washed off, I'll take care of it."

"I was merely anticipating your needs, sir, as any good assistant —"

"Eavesdropper!"

"— would do. It's just as well."

"What?"

"Well, the last thing in the world you need is a wife and partner who will tell you the truth, no matter how unpleasant. You need a flatterer, a panderer, a —"

"— woman like my mother, no thanks." He stared gloomily into the water for a long moment. "Well, I'm not getting rid of them, and that's that."

"As crown prince, you don't have to do much you don't wish to."

"The biggest lie of all," he sighed. "But I suppose you're right. She's — well, refreshing, at the least." He thumped his chest with a closed fist. "And she got me right here — I *have* had other girls up here, and they've seemed to go into raptures about birds that eat fish but can't fly."

"Fascinating creatures," Edmund conceded, "but not that fascinating. Ah, supper for two," he added as a footman rapped on the door and wheeled in a prodigious amount of food.

"Take it to the gallery," David grumbled. "I'll be there directly. As soon as I'm sure I can talk to her without strangling her."

"The gallery?"

"That's where she probably is."

Edmund cocked an eyebrow at him. "And how does His Highness know that?"

"Oh, she loves it in there. I think she likes looking at all the relatives. Because she doesn't have any, you know." He hurried to the sink in the far corner and washed his hands. "This is assuming she hasn't left the palace in disgust."

"Oh, if only."

"What?"

"Dry air." Edmund coughed, and coiled the hose neatly on a rock, and followed the prince out the door. "I've still got to look into that, I suppose."

# Chapter 8

"What the hell is wrong with me?"

"I have no idea," Princess Alexandria replied truthfully. She was seated at the far end of the galley, an easel in front of her, her denim workshirt and cargo pants spattered with primary colors. She was shoeless, and her toes were small and pretty, and French manicured. She appeared to be painting the scene outside the window, which was interesting, because the curtains were drawn. "Frankly, we've all been wondering."

"Har, har. I mean, your brother, a perfectly nice guy — if a little obsessed with flightless waterfowl — asks me not once, but *twice* to marry him, and I blow him off like I can do better. I mean, what the hell?"

"Maybe you can," the princess suggested, shoving her brush into Caribbean Blue and smooshing it around. The brush spread into a fan shape and the blob of color on her palette doubled in size. "Do better, I mean. I love my brother, and he's quite cute, but there's plenty of other fish in the sea."

"Not at the rate he's feeding those penguins."

Alex snickered, but didn't comment.

"Are you doing that devil's advocate thing?" Christina asked.

"No, I'm doing the polite conversation thing. Frankly, I don't know what you're waiting for. He's nice, he's cute, he's rich, and you're the first female he's shown any interest in forever."

"Sure, ramp up the pressure, see if *I* care." Christina flung herself into the chair nearest the princess. "How about you? Any marital prospects?"

"Plenty," she replied, drawing a bold blue stripe across the easel, "but they're all fortune hunters. And boy, did they come flying out of the woodwork when I turned eighteen. It's enough to make a girl renounce the marriage market. At least Kathryn's spared that for a couple more years."

"Didn't I read something about you and Prince William . . . ?"

She sighed. "I wish. He's perfect for me — good house, good manners, good bloodline, great body. And we're exactly the same age. But it was tabloid fantasy, unfortunately."

"That's tough. And never knowing if they like you or your title — that can't be much fun, either."

"Mm-hmm." The princess looked at Christina sideways and cocked a dark eyebrow. She, like her older brother, shared the king's coloring. Even casually dressed, the princess was breathtaking, with blue-black hair, dark blue eyes, and a porcelain complexion. Sitting next to her, Christina felt like the village frump. Which she probably was . . . if the royal family was any example, Alaska's general populace was ridiculously good-looking. "I suspect that's why my brother is anxious to reel you in, so to speak."

"Enough with the fishing metaphors."

"Fine, I'll put it this way. Your indifferent, uncaring attitude is a breath of fresh air." The princess managed to say this without the tiniest bit of irony.

"So, not giving a shit is a big selling point, huh?"

Alexandria snickered. "I'm afraid so." She shoved a hank of dark hair off her forehead and sobered. "Let me level with you, Christina, woman-to-woman."

"Or princess-to-commoner."

"My brother hasn't cared about much of anything since my mother died in that stupid, senseless accident. He was focused on school, and duty, and occasionally penguins. Now all of a sudden he's chasing you all over the palace. My father's all for the match. And you, pardon my bluntness, have nowhere to go. So what, exactly, is the problem? There are about a zillion worse things than eventually being the queen of Alaska."

"Mmmm. A zillion, huh?"

"So marry him, or don't. But in my so-humble opinion," she added, "it's rude to enjoy my father's hospitality when you have no intention of giving anything back."

"I knew there was a catch," she muttered.

"A rather large one," the princess agreed.

"Accept an invitation to lunch and now I've gotta be a princess."

"It's not so bad. All right, that was a lie." Christina laughed unwillingly.

"Maybe it would help you to consider what your parents might have wanted for you." A yellow stripe joined the blue one, followed by a shaky red one. The painting looked like a fucked-up rainbow. "If they were still around, what would they say about it?"

"Well . . ." Christina leaned back and

stared at the ceiling. Which, in addition to cherubs, gods, and goddesses, had a large rainbow on it . . . so *that's* what she was painting. "I never knew my dad. And my mom worked pretty hard most of her life . . . she usually had at least two jobs. We had to move around a lot . . . I never really got to make any friends. It was just the two of us. And then — and then it was just me. So, there's really no contest. She would have told me to go for the brass ring, and kick the crud out of anybody who got in my way."

Alexandria pursed her (perfect, pink) lips and nodded. "Well, then."

"Except . . . what makes me different from the rest of the throng, if I take your brother for the dough?"

"The very fact that you're asking that question makes you different. Also, we all enjoy it enormously when you yell at the king, so you simply must linger."

"What am I, the court jester?" she grumbled.

"No. But you might be a princess."

"Great."

Still. Alexandria was certainly giving her a lot to think about. She was beautiful, and sly . . . asking the *what would your mama say?* question clinched it. Her mom would have been overjoyed, thrilled, ecstatic. It would have been worth putting up with the pomp of a royal wedding just to see her mom's face light up.

So was it stupid to do something to please her mother lying in her grave these ten years? Or was it the beginning of compassion?

"Okay."

"Okay, what?"

"Okay, I'll do it. I'll marry you."

David accidentally ran the cart into the wall. Silver platters flew everywhere with a clang.

"For crying out loud," Christina said, watching scrambled eggs soar through the air, "maybe I should have broken it to you more gently."

She'd met him just outside the gallery — in fact, he'd nearly run over her foot with the damned cart.

"I'm just — surprised, that's all. Happily surprised," he added hastily. He moved to her to take her hand, slipped on a piece of bacon, and she ended up steadying him. "You won't regret it, Christina," he gasped, leaning on her for support. "You've made me a very happy man."

"We'll see, Penguin Boy," she said. "And

listen — if it gets too weird — not that *that* could *ever* happen — I'm outta here, and the engagement's off, got it?"

"Oh, yes. Yes, of course. And, of course, that applies to me, too."

"Sure, that's fine."

"Well, no. That was a bluff. I could never break our engagement."

"Okay." Weird. "I guess . . . should we kiss? Sort of to seal the — mmph!"

The guy was a mind reader! Or he'd slipped again and fallen on her mouth. Either way, they were sealing the deal. And it wasn't bad at all. He either hadn't spent enough time in the penguin room to reek, or she'd gotten used to it. All she could smell was bacon, and his own clean scent. His mouth was firm on hers, his hand on the back of her neck was wonderfully strong — normally she didn't care for that, but with David it was like she was protected rather than smothered.

"— my father right away."

"Mmmm — huh?" Nuts. All done kissing. She stared at his mouth. Really, truly all done? Yes, dammit. Worse, he was still talking.

"— said, let's go tell my father right away."

"Oh. Okay. Uh . . . but maybe not the

rest of the world? Right away?"

"As you wish." He grinned at her, his blue eyes twinkling, grabbed her hand, and they ran through the spilled food.

# Chapter 9

From *The Queen of the Edge of the World*, by Edmund Dante III, © 2089, Harper Zebra and Schuster Publications.

As one can imagine (and if one has been paying close attention to this tome), the king was as overjoyed at the news of the crown prince's engagement as Edmund Dante was appalled.

Princess lessons were to begin at once, designers and planners were commissioned, and a date was set for five months hence . . . April the second. Normally that would be a shockingly short time for a royal engagement, but the general consensus seemed to be to "get it done" before the bride-to-be could change her mind and flee the country.

But first, Edmund Dante was to try one last time to talk the feisty commoner out of her wedding. It is difficult to tell if he did it for his own sake, the country's, or the future queen's.

And Queen Christina's reaction to this attempt gives historians another tantalizing glimpse into what drove this foreigner of uncommon strength to take a crown.

"Miss Krabbe . . ."

"Call me Christina. Or Chris. Anything but Tina . . . yech. My mom hates her name her whole life, and what does she do? Slaps it on the end of *my* name. Nice!"

"Miss Christina, are you sure you have considered this *very* carefully?"

"And by that he means, congratulations," the king said, glaring at Edmund from his seat.

Edmund forced a smile, which disappeared as quickly as it formed. "You haven't been in the country a week, you barely know His Highness, and frankly . . . ah . . . frankly . . ."

"I'm not the princess type?" She tucked her legs beneath her and grinned at him. "Tell someone who *doesn't* know."

"Edmund . . ."

They were in one of the sitting rooms, and the king had called for beer to celebrate the announcement of their engagement. He'd downed two in rapid succession and apparent relief. Christina had taken a sip, masterfully concealed a shudder, and handed her glass to David.

"Your Majesty, please. It must be said. And it appears to have fallen to me."

"Who says?" the king whined. "You're gonna queer the deal, and then I'll be forced to break both your legs."

"A lively ending," the prince commented, "to an unparalleled career."

"It isn't fair," Edmund said quietly. "Look to the House of Windsor if you don't believe me. She must be warned."

"Fine, fine, but get it out of the way. And don't *bug* her, for Christ's sake."

"Too late," Christina sang. David, in the act of sitting down beside her, barked surprised laughter and fell to the sofa with a thump.

Edmund turned back to Christina. He towered over her like a tree dressed in fine linen. His hands were clasped — clenched — behind his back. "I — *we,* rather, wish to be sure you know what you're getting into. It's not all palace living and cocktail sauce."

"It's not?"

"As a member of the royal family, not only will the eyes of the world —"

"Not to mention *People* magazine."

"— be on you, but you'll have heavy responsibilities. Also —"

"Also," she interrupted yet again, "my children will never have to worry about their next meal. They'll never have to pay taxes, they'll never have to worry about how to afford to send their kids to college. They'll always have the option of a solid roof over their heads, and three squares a day. There will always be people around to look after them and protect them. They'll never, never be alone. And if they see something wrong, they'll have the power to fix it."

Dead silence.

"That about right?"

"Yes." David nodded, studying her intently. "That is exactly right. All that, and more. And all that goes for your children's children, and your children's children's children."

"Well. All right, then." She smiled, and instantly felt like she'd jettisoned ten pounds of stress. Maybe twenty. "If there's nothing else, Edmund, let's get this show on the road."

# PART TWO

# *Lady*

Getting married's probably not so bad.
It's all the screwing around before-
hand that gives you a migraine.
— Lady Christina of Allen Hall

# Chapter 10

"Ah, Lady Christina, I'm not sure how to ask this . . ."

"Well, first off, I'm not a lady," she said.

"No kidding," David said, grinning. He stopped grinning when one of the royal wedding designers forced a pointed black shoe onto his left foot. "Uh, can we try one that's not so — er — Machiavellian? Also, I can't feel my toes."

"I mean," Christina said, flipping through one of eighteen sketchbooks, "it's not my title or anything. I'm just plain old Christina."

"Not true," David grunted, trying to free himself of the shoe.

"Oh, so I've had a title all these years that I never knew about? Hmm, let's think about this; do you think I inherited it from my truck driver dad or my waitress mom?"

"With due respect, my lady, the king tells me your title is Lady Christina of Allen Hall."

She nearly fell out of her chair. "Since

when? And where the hell is that? And do ladies wear blue jeans? Because, if nobody's noticed, jeans make up about ninety-eight percent of my wardrobe."

David snickered. "Allen Hall is the part of the palace where Dad lets me keep the penguins."

"Oh, ugh! Very fucking funny. Remind me to kick the king in the slats when I see him next."

"Looks better on the invitations if you've got a title, even if it's minor. I thought you'd be happy."

"Then you haven't been paying attention the last two weeks, boy-o."

"You're right," he admitted, shrugging into the black silk coat held by another designer. "I didn't really think you'd be happy. But you know Dad . . . once he's got his mind made up . . ."

"Oh, yeah, he's not like *anybody* else I know." Christina glared at David for good measure, completely overlooking the fact that she could be talking about herself. "Now, what were you asking me, Harry?"

"Horrance, my lady. And I was asking — ah — if your dress — your wedding gown, rather — if it — ah —"

"White," she said firmly.

"Right, then," Horrance said hurriedly,

clapping a sketchbook shut and unwrapping a fresh one. He squinted at Christina and started sketching broad swoops across the paper.

"Reeeeeally?" David asked with a friendly leer.

"Sure," she replied evenly. "It's my first wedding, isn't it?"

"Ah . . . hmm." The six people in the room could easily read the MYOB vibes Lady Christina was giving off, so David acted the gentleman and changed the subject. "What d'you think of this suitcoat?"

"I think it makes you look embalmed."

Horrance whimpered.

"Hey, it's nice and all," she added, backpedaling madly, "but it's just not him. You know what you should wear? White. It'd really set off your hair." *Your gorgeous, thick, black-as-sin hair . . . mmm . . .*

"The bride wears white," Horrance's assistant — what was his name? Jerry? Jerkin? — said firmly.

"Well, were you in the military? Because you could wear your uniform —"

"No. I was busy getting my doctorate in marine biology."

"Oh, yeah?"

"Alaska doesn't require military service from its royals."

"Whatever. So, on top of everything else, you're an egghead. Well, I can overlook that." Was it Jeremiah? Julian? "Fine, don't wear white. But don't wear a tuxedo, either. I hate the penguin look. No offense, Dr. Prince David of the Penguins."

"Mock all you will . . ."

"Okey-dokey!"

". . . but I remind you, you'll be Mrs. Dr. Prince David of the Penguins."

"Oh, barf. Is there time to cancel this thing yet?"

She heard a light tap at her door and groaned into her pillow. After a moment, she rolled over and said, "Nicholas! It's after midnight, you little twerp! Enough of these weird, late-night excursions! Go to sleep!"

A head poked into the room. Not Nicholas's. "Remind me to have a talk with the royal twerp," David said. "Although I can hardly blame him for being unable to stay away. May I come in?"

"What *is* it with you people? Don't any of you need sleep?"

"We take long naps in the morning." He stepped into the room. "Interesting day today, hmm?"

"If you say so. But if I have to look at

one more *peau de soie* shoe, I'm going to barf. What the hell is *peau de soie,* anyway?"

"You're asking me? And there's no way your shoes are going to be less comfortable than mine."

She laughed as he sat down on the edge of her bed, and propped herself up on her elbows. "Since I plan to wear flats — and I thought the designer dude was going to cry when I told him — I'll give you that one. And d'you know what's worse? This was just, like, preliminary stuff. We're going to have meetings and meetings, every day. Flowers, shoes, dresses, food, cakes, time, place, shoes —"

"While we're on the topic of fashion . . ." She could see him a little better now, in spite of the room's gloom, and once again wondered if his hair would feel like it looked . . . like coarse silk. "What's this about a white wedding gown?"

"Oh, are we gonna do *that?* Because the time to do *that* was before you asked me to marry you."

"I'm just curious," he said mildly.

"Sure you are. Let's put it this way: I'm not a virgin, but I'm not a slut, either."

"You can't know," he said, perfectly straight-faced, "how relieved I am."

"Listen up, wise guy — I can count the number of partners I've had on one hand." She paused and added pointedly, "Can you?"

"Ah . . . not on *one* hand, no . . . in fact, I think I might need a third hand . . . maybe . . . and possibly a few of my toes . . ."

"Hypocrite!"

"Well, I *am* six years older than you. Oof!" He said "oof!" because she'd swung her pillow, sidearm, into his face. "Ah-ha! Now the truth comes out — you're going to be an abusive wife, I can sense it."

"Sure I am. Look, if you really want chapter and verse, we can do that. I mean . . . you're right, it's a fair question. But I expect reciprocation."

He shook his head. "No need."

"Chickenshit."

"No, it's like I said, I was just curious. It's in the past, it has nothing to do with me, or us, and besides that, it's your own personal business. That's not the main reason I came in here, anyway."

"Yeah? Other than keeping me from much-deserved sleep, what are you doing here?"

"I like teasing you. It's . . . something different. Your reaction, I mean."

"Super. Listen, not that this isn't fascinating and all . . ."

"*You're* fascinating." Was he leaning in? He was! The lean-in! Oooh, prelude to a kiss. Their *second* kiss. Excellent. She'd been ready to make a move herself if he wasn't going to. "I didn't expect that. I knew you'd be pretty, but . . ."

*He's really got to work on this romantic prince thing. Because he just sucks at it. Well, maybe princes don't have to try as hard.* "Thanks."

". . . but I didn't expect . . . the sheer excitement . . . I think it's the force of your personality . . ."

"David. Will you shut up and kiss me?"

". . . it's really extraordinary, you fairly vibrate with life . . ."

"David. Seriously."

". . . and — ack!"

He said "ack" because someone had grabbed him by the shirt collar and hauled him off the bed. A very large someone, even broader than David. In fact, it was —

"Ah-*ha!* Trying to get some nookie before the big day, eh?" The king shook the prince like a terrier would shake a rat. "Nice try."

"Al!" she said furiously. "Get lost! Go to bed!" *On top of being weird, they're all in-*

somniacs . . . *bizarre!* "Don't make me kick your big butt out of here."

"Save it, sweetie. And you . . . time to go to your *own* room. I'm a modern guy —"

"A modern idiot is more like it," Sweetie snapped.

"— but I can't have premarital royal sex going on under my rooftop."

"It's none of your damned business if I want to have sex with a *duck!*" she screeched.

"No," Prince David said, extricating himself from his father's grasp, "but it's mine." He straightened his shirt and jerked his head, tossing his dark hair out of his face. "Oh, and my lord king, if you ever yank me away from my fiancée again, I'll break out all your teeth."

"Whoa," the king and Christina said in unison.

David treated them to a frigid bow. "Good night."

"Did you hear that?" the king cried as the door slammed. "He threatened felony assault!"

"He's not the only one."

"On his sovereign! Awww, they grow up so fast." He tapped his chest, which was currently covered with a T-shirt that read, I'M THE KING, WHO THE HELL ARE

90

YOU? "Gets me right here."

"*I'm* going to get you right there. Go away."

"Calm down — I'm going, I'm going."

*What a bunch of nutjobs,* she thought, lying back down. *I must be out of my mind.*

*Sure you are. Then how come you can't wipe that silly grin off your face?*

Sleep was hard in coming; she spent entirely too much time thinking about the lean-in, and replaying the look in his eyes. For the first time, she didn't worry so much about what she was getting herself into.

# Chapter 11

"Look, Eddie —"

"Ed*mund.*"

"— don't take this the wrong way or anything —"

He sighed. "I am bracing myself, because you always say that before coming out with something thoroughly offensive."

"Cracked my code, eh? Anyway, I'm going to be the princess, right? So who cares what fork I use when? I mean, I'll be . . ." She snorted a giggle through her nose. He fervently hoped she would get over the habit of laughing like a loon whenever she contemplated her future station. ". . . royalty, and all."

"Exactly why you must set an example."

"Me?" He noted she nearly fell out of her chair in surprise. "Set an example?"

"I admit," he said, admiring the way the sunlight bounced off her shoulder-length waves, making the blond strands look like beaten gold, "it pains me to speak of it."

It was fortunate she had excellent hair,

because there was a truly unpleasant expression on her face at the moment. In fact, her dimples had entirely disappeared. They were, he privately thought, her best feature. They made her look mischievous and charming at the same time. "Edmund, I've got a real news flash for you. People don't give a crap what fork royalty uses."

"I beg to differ."

"Ed — they totally don't."

They glared at each other and then Edmund, who had battled the king for years, switched tactics. "Of course, if you want people to disparage His Highness because he chose a commoner who refused to rise above her station —"

"Whoa, *whoa.* You're saying David will have to eat shit if I'm not a good princess?"

"In a word, yes."

"Well, son of a bitch!"

"On the contrary, my mother was an extraordinarily patient and kind woman."

"Uh-huh." She grabbed a hank of hair and chewed on it. A loathsome habit he needed to break her of before she appeared in front of television cameras. "Hey, Edmund, can I ask you something?"

"You mean, something else?"

"Yeah, yeah. How come you're doing

this? Aren't there, like, a zillion underlings here in the palace who could be doing this? Tell me you wouldn't rather be just about anywhere else." She added in a mutter he heard perfectly well, "God knows I would."

"I lost the coin toss," he said, striving for the right note of cool disdain. She really was quite something. He had seen instantly why the king had been charmed, and why David had dropped his I-don't-care-who-I-marry pose. She would be a splendid queen, if he could get her to lend an attentive ear.

And naturally, such a vitally important job could not go to just anyone. He would oversee her education himself. Even if it killed him. "Now. Again — oyster fork, soup spoon, marrow scoop, fish knife, entrée knife, main course knife, salad knife —"

"— fruit knife, dessert spoon, dessert fork, and a partridge in a pear tree!"

He stared at her, completely surprised. "Oh. Oh! Well, that's very good. Ah . . . if you understood all along, then why . . . ?"

"Well, I'll tell you . . . I just can't resist yanking your chain." She tipped her chair back (French Louis XIV, circa 1860, listed for $972 Alaskan at Sotheby's) and grinned at him. "What do you think of that, Eds?"

"Edmund."

"Whatever. What's next on my agenda from hell?"

"You have a history lesson in thirty minutes with our palace historian."

The legs hit the carpet with a thump. "History lessons?"

"If you are to be a member of the royal family, it's important you know something of Alaskan history."

"Can't you just pick up that fruit fork and stick it in my eye instead?"

"It would be improper before dessert is served, my lady. After history, you'll be meeting with Horrance, your wedding gown designer. We try to use local artisans whenever possible," he added, pretending she was remotely interested in an explanation, "to aid the economy."

"Super. As long as he doesn't stick any pins in my ass. Then?"

"Then lunch with the prince and the king. Then a meeting with the caterer. Then the florist. Then —"

"Eds, how come *I* have to do all this stuff? (A) where's David, and (B) *you'd* be so much better at it."

"(A) David is in Allen Hall, doing the

morning feeding, and he will be joining you, and (B) that's very true, but it's not my wedding, is it, my lady?"

"Don't call me that, I hate that. Call me Chris."

He looked down his nose at her. "I think not."

"Fine, Chris-teen-uh then. Anything but My Dork-o Lady."

"My lady jests, pretending she will not have a title all her life."

"Also, it really creeps me out when you talk about me in the third person. Seriously. Don't do that."

For the first time all morning, Edmund cracked a smile. "Nobody likes it. Thus, I do it as often as I can."

"Well, how would Edmund like it if I talked about him in the third person? Doesn't Edmund think that's fucked up?"

"No. Edmund doesn't. Now, if my lady has tired of etiquette lessons, why don't we cover something you might find more relevant?"

"Yeah, why don't we? What's on your fiendish mind, Eds?"

"Only this." He paused delicately. Christina's eyebrows arched, disappearing under her bangs, a gratifying sign of her full attention. "You must always be wary of the name Domonov."

"That's Queen Dara's maiden name."

He could not mask his surprise. "You know?"

She yawned behind her palm. "*Us* magazine."

"Ah. Well, contrary to the lurid interpretations of the American press —"

"Whoa, whoa, easy on the America bashing, pal."

"— Her Majesty the Queen was not a bloodthirsty cannibal with a stone for a heart."

"I think 'bloodthirsty cannibal' is redundant."

"At any rate, the queen's family is slightly . . . unreasonable . . . on the subject of His Highness Prince Nicholas."

Her eyebrows arched still higher. "Oh-ho."

"Furthermore, they have no love for their king and have tried many times to strike at him, any way they can."

She frowned. "Um, okay, that sucks, but how come Al doesn't toss them in the clink?"

Privately, Edmund thought that was an excellent question. "The king would, but as he is still very fond of his late consort, his heart is soft toward her family and the Domonov in question is soon released.

Also, the king may have said something along the lines of, 'I can take care of my own damn self — I don't need the courts to help me.' "

"Yeah, that sounds about right. So, okay, anybody introduces themself to me as Mr. Domonov, I kick his ass. Got it."

"It's not entirely that sim—"

"Later, Eds. I have to go check something out. Thanks for the Princess 101 stuff. I guess." She waved distractedly over her shoulder and practically ran out of the drawing room.

Christina screeched to a halt in front of Queen Dara's portrait and once again studied the proud, amazingly beautiful features. Then she sidled down a few feet and looked at the painting of the king's grandmother.

*The queen's family is slightly unreasonable on the subject of His Highness Prince Nicholas.*

Idiotic notion. They believed the rumors of all the lovers the queen took. Believed Nicholas belonged only to the queen, that there was none of the king in him. And wanted to steal him for themselves. It was sad, because grief did horrible things to people, but it was stupid, too.

"Morons," she said to the empty gallery. "Anybody can see the kid looks exactly like his great-grandma. On his *father's* side."

*You must always be wary of the name Domonov.*

"Okay, okay!" Amazing. The guy was twenty-three rooms and two floors away, and he was still droning in her head.

She heard footsteps and whipped around, already feeling the goofy grin on her face, a grin which instantly dropped off when she saw the visitor wasn't David.

"Oh. It's you."

"Nice! I could have you deported, kiddo." King Alexander snapped his fingers, which, she couldn't help but notice, were filthy. Gardening? More fishing? Digging in the dirt with his youngest son? Who the hell knew? With this guy, it could be anything. "Like that!"

"Sure. Like you're going to let me get away that easily."

"True enough," he said cheerfully, wiping his dirty palms on his blue-jeaned thighs. "You're stuck here. We all are!"

"I was just looking at your family's portraits."

"Yeah." The king stopped and squinted at Queen Dara's likeness. "Boy oh boy, what a woman. When they made her they broke the mold. Then they beat the living shit out of the mold-maker."

She burst out laughing.

"Well, it's true. And if it isn't, it oughtta be. She was — you have no idea." The king ran his fingers through his hair, leaving a smudge of dirt on his forehead. He looked distracted and sad. Her heart broke a little, seeing him like that. Plenty of women had tried to entice the royal widower. Everyone had failed. He so obviously still carried a torch for the dead queen. "Some days I wanted her to be at my side all day long, and others I had to actually resist the urge to strangle her."

"I've heard she was . . . uh . . ."

"Well, she was. But she was exciting, and beautiful, and things were never dull when she was around. You know what happened? How she died?"

"Uh . . ." Some of the more lurid headlines popped into her brain: *Alaskan queen killed in car wreck en route to lover's hideaway. Queen Dara dead in crash outside lover's house.* "Well . . ."

"She was on her way to her hairdresser and wasn't paying attention, and got in a crash."

"Oh. That's . . . uh . . . a little different from —"

"She was on her way," the king said with deadly quiet, "to the hairdresser."

"Sure. Everybody knows that."

His shoulders relaxed. "I s'pose I should have insisted she use a driver, but that shit didn't help Princess Diana, did it?"

"I guess not." She paused, then added, "I still remember exactly where I was when I heard Diana was dead. I was so upset . . . didn't cry, but . . . I just couldn't believe it, and I was so bummed. Which was weird, because I'd never met her. But I was really sad about it, for a long time."

"Well, I *did* meet her. And you never met a more charming lady. She was about the only one at Buckingham who didn't make me feel like I had straw in my hair and cowshit on my heels."

"Is *that* what's under your fingernails?"

They laughed together, like family.

# Chapter 12

"— and while our ancestors were happy to make new lives for themselves in the formidable Alaskan wilderness, Russian law forbade permanent settlement by Russian citizens."

"Bummer," Christina said, concealing a yawn behind her palm.

"It was, really, because a man would bring his family over, start trading in fur or logging or what-have-you, and then, when he started to make headway against the wilderness, when his family was settled, when they had made a life for themselves, they would have to pick up and leave."

"So David's great-great-grandpa decided that sucked the root?"

"Yes. In fact, it was as close to a bloodless coup as possible. Russia had offered Alaska for sale to America —"

"Oh, wait, I know this part — America was hip-deep in the Civil War, and the last thing they wanted was to cough up a bunch of dough for a new state. They were having enough trouble controlling the states they already had."

"Quite right. And Alaska hadn't worked out for Mother Russia as they had expected. The primary goal of taking Alaska was to feed Russia. But farming was difficult — crops didn't take, or were devoured by mice and squirrels, or the Russians weren't terribly enthusiastic farmers. Meanwhile, the natives, while befriending the Russians actually living and working the land, resented the mother country —"

"Understandably. They were here first."

"Well, yes. Something the royal family has kept in mind —"

"Is that why all the native Alaskans — the *true* natives — get all that money from the government?"

"Yes. And they are allowed to continue the lifestyle of their forebears for as long as they wish. Millions of acres have been set aside for their use. But we're getting off topic."

"Typical white-guy attitude," Christina commented.

"At any rate," Edmund continued, annoyed, "when Kaarl Baranov rallied the troops, so to speak, and prepared to break away from Russia, Russia let them go with surprising ease."

"No bloodshed?"

"Minimal bloodshed. But it was obvious Mother Russia's heart wasn't in it, and we — Alaska — quickly won. And rather than setting up a Tsar and Tsarina of Alaska, they decided to cut ties still further, and became King Kaarl and Queen Kathryn."

"My," Christina said. "What a long story."

"My lady, we've only been talking —"

*"We've?"*

"— for five minutes."

"Well, I've pretty much got the picture. And it sure explains a lot."

"Explains . . . ?"

"About the royal family. I mean, you have to admit, they're an independent bunch."

Edmund cracked a smile. "Yes. I have to admit that."

Prince David, intent on his late-morning observations of the residents of Allen Hall, never saw the arm that snaked around the doorway, effectively clotheslining him. In a flash he was on his back, and being dragged into a small, dark sitting room. He got a whiff of wildflowers and decided not to resist.

"The thing is," his fiancée told him,

straddling his chest, "I appreciate you buying the cow and all, but I think you ought to get some milk for free."

"Are you feeling all right?" he gasped. One minute he'd been wandering the halls, minding his own business, the next — attacked!

"Oh, sure, it's just — I'd be crazy to plan on spending — what? — fifty, sixty years with you? Without . . . you know. Sampling the merchandise."

"If I understand you," he said carefully, "and I'm not at all sure I do, you're proposing we — may I have my shorts back, please?"

"In a minute," she said, and then she was nimbly unbuttoning his shirt and spreading it open.

"This is really too —" and then he forget where he was going with this as her soft, hot mouth touched his mouth, his throat, his nipples, and now she was actually licking his nipples, and he brought a hand up and fisted it in her hair, and she nipped lightly, which made him yelp, and then he was tugging at her shirt, her shorts, they were writhing together in the dark, his hands were everywhere, relishing the touch of her smooth, warm skin, her curls were in his face and he breathed deeply of her natural perfume. Being with her was like being in a dark garden.

He felt her hand clasp him —

"Oh, *my*. How many vitamins do you eat a day, Dave?"

— and groaned, felt her fingers slide up and down with delicious friction, and had trouble remembering the fact that ninety seconds ago he'd been wandering down the hallway, fully clothed and thinking about *Aptenodytes patagonicus.*

She had straddled him again and was all smooth, nude skin. She was humming something and in a minute he placed it — it was Bad Company's "Feel Like Makin' Love."

She was still gripping him, and now she was easing herself down on top of him, and he instantly felt his I.Q. drop another thirty points.

"Wait," he managed, feeling for her soft pelt. "It's too soon, I don't want to hurt —" He found her slick folds and realized she was more than ready for him. "Belay that," he added, and she laughed, and eased down on him, and oh, it was — it was exquisite. He put a hand in the middle of her back, feeling her muscles flex, and sliding up into her was like sliding into the best dream he ever had.

It was a tight fit, but she didn't seem to mind, and God knew *he* didn't mind. He had thought it was the pinnacle, it was the finest, it simply could not get any better, and then she began to rock against him.

He pulled her down, found her soft, sweet mouth, and kissed her while she rocked, rocked, rocked, still humming that excellent tune.

He broke the kiss and groaned again, then managed, through gritted teeth, to say, "I have — very bad — news —"

"Oh, I know," she teased, leaning back and tickling his balls. When she leaned that far back, her curls brushed the tops of his thighs, and he shivered. "That's okay. My turn next time."

"Deal," he gasped, and then came so hard he felt his eyes roll back in his head.

"You tried to kill me," he accused, when he had his breath back.

"Oh, sure," she said. They were on their sides in the nameless, dark little room; he'd cuddled her against him like two spoons in a drawer. "That was my fiendish plan all along."

"It's the only explanation I can think of," he said, and puffed against the back of her neck, parting the hair so he could kiss the

exposed skin. "I hope you don't think —
that is to say, I enjoyed it *very* much —
very much — but I wouldn't want you to
think —"

"Relax, Penguin Boy."

"Please don't call me that after coitus,"
he grumbled.

"Please don't ever call it coitus. And I'm
well aware of what happened — didn't I,
what d'you call it — instigate the whole
thing?"

"That's true," he said, cheering up. "I
was just an innocent victim of your lust."

"Right. Anyway, I know it was too fast
for *me*. But not for you. Right?"

"Right. Next time," he said, testing her.

"Right," she said, yawning into his
forearm. "Next time. Fuck the king."

"I'd rather," he said, "fuck you."

"Such dirty language from a prince . . . I
bet that's the first time you ever said 'fuck.'
Um, don't we have a meeting or something?"

"Yes, but I have to check on the penguins first."

"Ooooh, you're getting me hot all over
again. I love it when you talk about flightless waterfowl after boinking me! Now talk
about dead fish."

"Christina . . ."

"C'mon, I need to hear it!"

"You're impossible," he grumbled, sitting up and groping for his shirt.

"And you're stuck with me," she said, sounding indecently satisfied.

"Yes," he said, feeling more than a little satisfied himself. "I suppose I am."

At Lady Christina's insistence, they combined the meetings with the florist, the caterer, the gown designer, the protocol officer, and about twelve other people into one efficient meeting.

Well, as efficient as such a meeting can be . . .

"No, no, *no*. No wedding announcements."

The royal protocol officer, a woman who bore an uncanny resemblance to Shania Twain, gaped at her. "But my lady . . . we have to . . ."

"Invitations are enough. Look, we all know announcements are just a greedy grab for more presents. And we're going to get tons of stuff, anyway. Right?"

"But it's not a — not a greedy — ah — greedy grab —"

Edmund's hand dropped to the protocol officer's shoulder. "It helps if you close your eyes and think of a happy place," he said in her ear. Then, louder, "Very well, my lady. No announcements . . . except to the press."

"Well . . . okay. They're gonna find out anyway." Christina stretched. She felt pleasantly sore. Tackling David had been educational *and* fun. The man had a dick on him that wouldn't quit. She couldn't wait to get her hands on it again. For compatibility's sake, of course. Not because she craved his company or anything. "And *where* is David?"

"He's coming, my lady."

*Again, you mean.* "Hip-deep in penguin crap, no doubt."

"No doubt, my lady."

"And while we're on the subject —"

"Of penguin crap?"

"— who's paying for this shindig? I've got my last paycheck, and that's it."

"I'm paying for it," the king announced, entering the large meeting room. "Sorry I'm late. Last night's pizza is *not* agreeing with me."

Edmund closed his eyes, as if in great pain, and Christina giggled.

"I guess that's my cue to protest," she said, "but since this is a royal wedding, I guess a royal guy has to pay for it."

"You just show up. If you do that,

we'll all be happy."

"Really? That's all I have to do?"

"Sit down, my lady," Edmund said sternly. "The king exaggerates."

The king slumped into the tattered blue La-Z-Boy at the head of the table, and hit the recline lever. His feet went up and he sighed. "So, where were we? And where's David? Jenny, you don't look so good."

"I'm fine, Your Majesty," the protocol officer replied, trying a game smile.

"Put your head between your knees," the king ordered.

"It doesn't help," Edmund said. "Trust me."

"Sorry I'm late," Prince David said, hurrying in. He looked gorgeously out of breath, and flashed her a secret grin. She had to put a hand over her mouth so as not to grin back.

*Gorgeously out of breath?* Had she really thought that? What was *with* her lately?

"What'd I miss?"

"No wedding announcements, just invitations," Christina said. "And your dad's got the runs."

"That makes good sense. The first part, not the latter. Dad, how many times do I have to tell you to lay off the pizza?"

"You might be the crown prince, but

you're still a punk," the king snapped. "I'll eat what I like."

"Fine, enjoy your week in the bathroom." David took the seat next to the bride, bending to drop a careless kiss to her forehead as he did. It was not lost on Edmund that she blushed for a moment and her eyes got very bright.

"Well," Jenny began, "I think we need to pin down the wording of the invitation. I was told that the lady's parents are deceased?"

Christina nodded. "Completely deceased."

"Well." She cleared her throat. "Protocol dictates that only the living can issue invitations."

"Well, duh. I don't want my dead mom to be inviting people . . . yuck!"

"Perhaps the king can invite guests on behalf of both parties," Edmund suggested. "It's a little unorthodox, but . . ."

"That will be fine," Jenny said gratefully, crossing an item off her list. "And I'll meet with the engraver this afternoon, so —"

"What? Engraver? Come on, that'll cost a fortune. What's wrong with just using a printer?"

"Happy place, you're in your happy place," Edmund reminded Jenny.

Christina appealed to the king. "Seriously, Al, come on — d'you really want to spend a zillion dollars on the *invitations?* What's the alternative to engraving?"

"Raised print," Jenny said in the same tone someone would have said, "A cobra under the bed."

"Well, do that. What's wrong with that?"

"Chris, hon, I can afford it," the king said gently. "It's no problem."

"I know *that,* but why throw your money away on something David and I don't care about? Right, Dave? You don't care, right?"

"I don't care," David admitted.

"All right, then. Next!"

The other wedding experts had managed to bunch themselves into the far corner of the meeting room, suspiciously close to the window. As they were meeting on the first floor, escape was plausible.

"Come on, come on," Christina said impatiently. "What's next?"

"L-location?" Jenny ventured.

"What's wrong with here?"

There was a tense moment, then the group relaxed, *en masse.* "The palace would be a fine place. We can have the ceremony in the main ballroom, and have the reception on the grounds."

"Better have a Plan B," the king warned, propping his feet up on the table. "What if the weather's shitty?"

"I will work on a Plan B," Edmund promised, making a note on his clipboard. "Very well, then. Next?"

Emboldened, the dress designer stepped forward. "Horrance Tyler, my lady. We met the other day."

"Hi, Horrance. Whatcha got?"

The stuff, Christina later thought, nightmares were made of.

"No. I'd disappear in that thing. My goal, on my wedding day, is not to look like a big-ass meringue."

"But it's so flattering to your coloring —"

"Big-ass meringue, Horrance. Sorry. That one, too," she said, pointing to a perfectly lovely dress with a scalloped neckline and, yes, a rather large, full skirt and eight-foot train. "I don't want a dress ten times as big as I am. And *no* train. Have you ever walked in a train, Horrance? Don't answer that. Anyway, I haven't, and the day a zillion people are watching me? Not a good day to start. Next."

The flipping of sketchbook pages lulled the king to sleep, and soon his gentle snores filled the room as Christina worked through the sketches.

"Nope. Too nunlike."

"Too much lace."

"Not enough lace."

"Too Amazonian — what's with the silver belt? Am I fighting crime after the reception?"

"Too pretty."

"What are you talking about, *too pretty?*" David said, jerked out of his own near-slumber.

"It's too pretty for me. Too fancy, I guess is what I mean." She pointed. "Look at it — silver shoulder straps! And diamonds on the bodice. I'm a Wal-Mart girl, get it? Hey, Horrance, it's not personal, okay?" she said to the designer, who was manfully fighting tears. "They're gorgeous dresses, they really really are. They're just . . . just not me, get it?"

"I get it," Horrance said, slightly mollified, as he grabbed the seventh sketchbook.

"Too plain. It'd be great for a regular dance, but not for a wedding gown. It's very pretty, though," she added hastily.

"Nope. Train."

"Not much of one, my lady, it's —"

"It's a train, Horrance. A beautiful train, but a train. Choo-choo. Next."

"Neckline's too high. I'd be tugging at it

all day. On camera. It's probably just — what's that?"

Frozen in the act of slamming the last book shut, Horrance said, "Those are my sketches for a bridesmaid's gown, my lady."

Christina pulled the book toward her and stared hungrily at the page. It was an A-line gown, strapless, with an inch-wide ribbon around the middle, right below the breasts. It was ice-blue, and came with a floor-length, off-the-shoulder cape in the same color.

"That."

"That?"

"That's the one. That's what I want." She couldn't look away from the sketch. It was glorious! Plain, but beautiful.

"In — in that color?"

"Yes. Don't change a thing."

Prince David chuckled. "So. *Not* white."

"Drop dead, white bread. I just like the color, is all."

"Oh, but . . . a princess of the realm really should be married in white —"

The king snorted and woke up. "Eh? What's up now?"

"The lady Christina wants to get married in blue," Horrance tattled.

King Alexander blinked. "Um . . . I

dunno, kid, that's kind of . . . different . . . even for us . . ."

The protocol officer stepped in. "Actually, Majesty, the tradition of wearing white wedding gowns was started in England. By Queen Victoria."

"And everybody jumped on the bandwagon. The *English* bandwagon," Christina added.

"Well, screw that!" the king said loudly. "Alaskans do things their own way, dammit. The kid wants blue, it's blue. Let the House of Windsor chew on *that.*"

"Thanks, Al." *Thank you!* she mouthed to the protocol officer, who smiled graciously.

"It's nice," David said, looking at the sketch. "It'll bring out your blue eyes."

"Her eyes are green," Jenny protested.

"You guys, focus, please? And my eyes are hazel — blue-green. Besides, I've already given up forty-five minutes of my life I'll never get back. What's next?"

"Well, the shoes should be —"

"Forget it. I'll pick out a pair of nice flats the next time I'm at Payless."

"I beg your pardon — you certainly will not," Edmund said.

"Watch me. Next!"

"Bridemaids' gowns?" David asked,

scooching a little closer to Christina, the better to help her fend off Edmund's strangling hands.

"Oh. Was I going to have some of those?"

"Er . . . what?"

"Christina moved around a lot as a kid," David explained. "She doesn't have a lot of close friends."

"We were thinking the princesses," Edmund said.

"Which is fine," Christina said, turning to David, "but does your sister talk?"

"Kathryn, you mean?"

"She hasn't said two words to me the whole time I've been here, but she keeps throwing stuff at me!"

"She likes you."

"So," Edmund said loudly, "the princesses."

"And Jenny," Christina added.

Jenny's mouth popped open. "Oh, my lady, I couldn't! It wouldn't be appropriate, it —"

"No, I want you to, Jenny. You're going to work like a dog on this — why shouldn't you get some of the glory?" Besides, the woman had really saved her bacon, stepping in with that tidbit about Queen Victoria. Talk about a true (if brand new) friend!

"Well, I — I would be honored, my

lady." Jenny was flushing to the roots with pleasure. "Really, I — my mother will be so pleased."

"Okay. You can tell Mom later. So, bridesmaids — Princess Kathryn, Princess Alexandria, Jenny. Are there any — um — does your mom — I mean, the late queen — anybody in her family that you might like —"

"No," David said firmly.

Long silence.

"Okay!" Christina said brightly. "Bridesmaids' gowns, right? Right. Whatcha got, Horrance? Come on, don't be scared. You can do it."

"Well . . ."

"Nope. It's those high necklines again . . . yech. And the color! They look like they're wearing steel."

"It's gray, miss. The new black."

"Black is the new black, Horrance. Um . . . this is close," she said, tapping a picture. "But too sparkly. And that looks like heavy material . . . it'll be June, not January. No bridesmaids passing out at the altar, please."

"No ballerinas, either."

"Or waiters."

"No."

"Sorry."

"She looks like a bell. A pretty bell, but a bell. No."

"Perfect."

"Perhaps if we — what?"

"That one," she said, stabbing a finger at a midnight-blue, square-necked sheath gown. "It's gorgeous — they can wear it again, and it'll look good on everybody because all three of my bridesmaids could stand a few milkshakes, get what I mean? Anyway, that one."

"What do you think of the hat, my lady?"

"*No* hats. She looks like she's going to start tap dancing any minute."

"Very well," Horrance said, making notes with a now-shaking hand, "no hats for the maids."

"No hats, Horrance."

"Let me just show you a few things," he coaxed.

"You're a brave man, Horrance," Prince David commented.

"Thank you, Highness. How about this?"

"Why would you want me to look like a Rockette? Look at all those feathers! No, thanks."

"Nor do I want to pretend to be Humphrey Bogart."

"Or the Cat in the Hat."

"No hats," Horrance surrendered, slapping the book shut. "I think we can postpone our jewelry discussion for another day?"

"I'll take care of that," Prince David said.

"Oh, yeah?" Christina said, raising her eyebrows.

"I do have some talents besides acute knowledge of flightless waterfowl."

"It's nice to find out unexpected things about future husbands," she said cheerfully. "Which reminds me, what are *you* going to wear?"

"All the men in the royal family will be in standard tuxedos," Edmund announced.

"Oh, yes!" Horrance said, clapping enthusiastically. "You'll all look so dashing!"

"Ugh," the bride commented. "Penguins."

"Nothing wrong with looking like a penguin," David said, sneaking a peek at his watch.

"Says the obsessed! Look, do you really want to be mixed up with the waiters at our reception?"

Horrance giggled. David glared. Christina just raised her eyebrows and waited for an answer.

"Ah — my lady, Your Highness — tell

me what you think of this." Horrance extended yet another sketchbook, and Christina and David looked down at it. It was a double-breasted tuxedo, but while the jacket and pants were deepest black, the waistcoat was a cheerful herringbone, and the tie was deep gray. "We could match the ties to the bridesmaids' gowns," he suggested.

"Actually, it's great the way it is. That whole matching thing — I never got it. What are we, in a parade? I think this looks great."

"I do, too. Nice work, Horrance."

"Next?"

A plump, matronly woman with brutally short, salt-and-pepper hair and an intriguing eggplant-colored pantsuit stepped forward, cheeks bulging with chewable antacid.

"This is Marge Sims," Edmund said into her ear, nearly making her leap out of her chair. "What she doesn't know about flowers isn't worth knowing, so for God's sake, go easy on her."

"Okay, okay! You're acting like this is fun for me. And leggo." Christina wriggled until Edmund's skeletal fingers fell away from her shoulder. "Got news — this is about as much fun as commercial fishing.

In fact, I would rather *be* commercial fishing."

The florist swallowed and, when she spoke, her breath was redolent of Tums. "Margie Sims, m'lady."

"Hi, there. Nice to meet you. Well, let's get to it, Margie m'girl."

"Yes, my lady," Margie said, slumping across from Christina as if going to her doom. "I've brought several photos of my past — what's that noise?"

"The king fell asleep," Prince David whispered. "Again."

"Oh." Marge lowered her voice. "If any of these catches your fancy, Lady Christina, we can — uh — perhaps if you looked a little more carefully, you might find . . . um . . ."

Flip. Flip. Flip. "No — tulips will cost a friggin' fortune that time of year."

"You mean spring?" David asked doubtfully.

"You hush. This is pretty, but it's too delicate for me — has it escaped anyone's noticed that I'm a blond hulk?"

"Now, my lady, that's just not so," Marge said kindly. "You're slender and quite lovely. But you are of striking height and coloring, and you're quite right, no one would see such a diminutive violet bouquet."

"Hear that, Eds?" Christina said triumphantly. "Marge says I'm right! Eh? No, these are all too small. And this is too Thanksgiving-ish. Oooh, now *this* I like!" It was a large cluster of old-fashioned roses in a rainbow of pastels. "Except for the colors. Oooh, this is nice, too!" Again, a cluster of roses. "Except it's in a heart-shape — hello, cliché, anyone? You know what I like, Margie?" she asked, turning to the woman, who now had beads of sweat on her upper lip. "I really like irises. Dark purple irises. Which would go with the dresses. And if we could stick some big red roses in there . . ."

"Easily done, my lady."

"But don't make it too heavy. I'm gonna have to lug it around all day, okay?"

"Yes, my lady."

"Okay. Next?"

"The caterer," Horrance whispered, terrified.

"Great," David muttered. "We'll be able to settle on a menu by sundown, at the latest."

"This is Don Musch, my lady," Edmund said, bringing over another tall, strapping Alaskan, this one with blond hair caught back in a ponytail. He looked like he'd be more at home splitting timber than whip-

124

ping up soufflés. "He'll be the head caterer."

Christina slapped the last sketchbook
closed and cleared her throat. "Okay, Don-o,
listen up. I want nice, light drinks . . . real
lemonade, some sherbet punch — orange
sherbet, not lime or pineapple — maybe a
nice honeydew punch, too — and use
frozen fruit for ice cubes, or it'll be a
watered-down mess before we get to 'I do.'
And I'd like Bellinis, please — that's champagne with apricot nectar, to you non-
Americans. *Not* orange juice — mimosas
are such a cliché. Plus, I had to make
about a zillion a day on the ships . . . I'm
not having them at my reception.

"For hors d'oeuvres I want a nice variety
of open-faced sandwiches, maybe some cucumber and watercress, cream cheese, and
you can dress it up with caviar, sesame
seeds, whatever. Some nice crostini would
be good, too, but make sure the tomatoes
are ripe . . . I don't want a bunch of red
potatoes served with the mozzarella.
Actually, yellow tomatoes would be really
great with that, if you think you can get
them. They're so pretty. And fresh basil,
please, nothing out of a jar.

"Some asparagus, maybe steamed and
served with a really tangy vinaigrette,

would be good, too. No need to go for the white — green asparagus will do fine. And shrimp cocktail. I love shrimp cocktail, and I bet you guys could get a great price.

"Now, for entrees, let's do some poached salmon — no halibut, it's too friggin' expensive — and serve it with a nice home-made mayo, maybe some cukes, too. Do *not* make a salmon mousse — I don't expect the guests to choke down whipped fish. I'd also like to do a couple different pasta salads, one with meat, one without. I mean, there's gonna be some vegetarians there — be nice if they had something to eat, too.

"A cheese course would be good, but only if you can protect it from the heat . . . nothing worse than sweaty cheese."

"*Nothing* worse?" David asked, managing to get a word in edgewise.

"I'd also like lots of fruit — I love fruit. Minted melon balls, strawberries, and a really good fruit dip — try two parts cream cheese to one part marshmallow fluff — that's good stuff. Melon wrapped in prosciutto would be good, too — yum! Oh, and lots of crusty bread, and I've got a great recipe for strawberry butter. It sounds weird, but it's actually very good. Especially if you can keep the rolls warm."

Don, the caterer, was managing to take rapid notes, while everyone else's jaws were hanging open. Even the king had awakened and was paying attention.

"Now, dessert. I do not, repeat, do *not* want colored Crisco on the wedding cake. Real butter cream, please. I want a multi-tiered cake, and I'd like each tier to be a different flavor. Chocolate, vanilla, strawberry, mocha, lemon. Something for everybody. Fillings can be fruit, mousse, whatever, but again, no colored Crisco. And I'd like a pearlized fondant to decorate the cake, and have each layer be a different color. You know — blue, orange, pink, green, yellow, whatever. You can pipe swirls over the fondant to create a what-d'you-call-it? — a Wedgewood effect. My mom," she finished defiantly, "loved Wedgewood."

"Gaaaaaaah," Marge said, trying and failing to articulate her startlement.

"Oh, and I've got a great idea for Penguin Boy's groom cake . . . we could do a chocolate cake with white fondant icing and cut out black fondant in the shape of playing card symbols — you know, decorate it with aces, hearts, spades, clubs. It'd be really dramatic and kind of fitting, too, because of the black and white, you know?

Anyway, we can have that the night before, and on the big day, the tiered cake. And a Croquembouche. It's so pretty, and so good. I love cream puffs. I know it'll be a pain, but I'll help.

"Anyway," Christina said into the dead silence, "those are my ideas. And whatever David wants to eat, too."

"Of course!" David burst out. "She's a chef!"

"I'm a cook," she corrected. "Chefs go to school."

"This — this is all very fine, my lady," Don said, still scribbling furiously.

"Nice and specific, you mean, you lucky bastard," Marge muttered.

"Okay. And don't worry, Don, I'll help."

"My lady, that's really not —"

"Oh, I want to! With the cakes, at least. What's left? All this food talk has me starving."

"Me, too!" the king said. "I'm ready to go for some of that croakembooch right now."

"Just some minor details . . . transportation —"

"Where? I thought we agreed the wedding would be here."

"Yes, Lady Christina, but the people will want to see you," Edmund explained. "I

128

thought we could use the royal carriage —"

"Forget it."

"How come?" David asked. "It's romantic. Isn't it?"

"Trotting behind a steaming horse butt? Pass."

"I, uh, never thought of it that w-way," David said, his voice almost breaking on "way" as he choked back a laugh.

"And on that note," Edmund sighed, "I suggest we adjourn for the day."

"Good call," Christina said. "I'm missing *Jeopardy.*"

# Chapter 13

She had no idea where they were — closets weren't as big as living rooms, right? But what other room was bulging with coats on hangers? Anyway, they were groping and she heard a seam tear and then she was clawing at the clothes for purchase, finding the pole beneath the furs and hanging on for dear life as David's tongue parted her lower lips and slipped inside her. He was on his knees in front of her, his big hands on her thighs, spreading them apart, as he licked and teased and kissed and stroked, and she thought she was going to scream.

She must have made a sound, some sound, because he said, "Shhhhh," against her slick flesh, and she whimpered in reply. His tongue sped up, no longer leisurely licking, finding the quivering button that was the very center of her, sucking it, licking, stabbing at it, and her uterus clenched as her orgasm bloomed within her, as fire raced down her limbs and she let go of the pole, tumbling to the floor of the closet in a heap of furs.

His mouth was instantly on hers and she tasted herself; she was groping wildly for him, found him, felt him sliding inside her with delicious slowness, came again as he started to thrust, cried out in his mouth. They still had their shirts on (and their shoes) but his hand found her left breast and squeezed it through the cotton, and through it all his mouth never left hers, not once, and he shuddered above her when she came again, as if he could feel it, as if they were reading each other's minds.

"Is it me, or is it sort of depraved to do *that* before we go see a minister?"

"Oh, it's just you," he said seriously, then laughed when she tickled his ribs.

"Are you sure you wouldn't rather go find that closet again? Those furs felt awesome! And a cedar closet! Yum! What floor was that, anyway? We've got to make a mental note of that room . . ."

"We've defiled it enough for one day."

"Nice! Defiled! Hey, I'd prefer to do it in a bed like a regular person . . ." A rather large lie. David was fiendishly inventive in closed spaces. ". . . but if we did, we'd give Nicholas a real education. Or one of your sisters. Or the king would burst in, or —

131

yech! — Edmund. Or Jenny. Or —"

"I," David said loftily, "always excelled at hide-and-seek as a child."

"You were the prince. They let you win."

"Possibly. But we're getting off topic again. Come along, Christina, we promised to go."

"I think 'we' means 'you'," she grumbled.

"Look at it this way," Prince David soothed. "Lots of people get premarital counseling before the big day."

"Do I strike you as 'lots of people,' Dave? Come on, this is a big waste of time."

"Oh, you'd rather be shoe-shopping with Jenny?"

"No, I'd rather be —"

He grinned. "Don't change the subject, minx. Because Jenny told me she's been trying to pin you down for two weeks —"

"Fine, let's go see the minister."

"Actually, he's coming to us," David said, not quite apologetically. He glanced at his watch. "In fact —"

"The Reverend Jonathon Cray to see you, Your Highness, my lady."

"Swell," Christina muttered as Edmund escorted a short (finally!) man in a minister's collar and sober dark suit. He wore glasses, behind which merry blue eyes twinkled, was bald as an egg, and had the full cheeks and slight paunch of a man who didn't miss many meals. His cheeks were rosy and there was a bounce in his step as he crossed the room.

"Your Highness," Minister Cray said, bowing. "My lady."

"It's nice to meet you, Minister Cray." David put a hand on her shoulder, the better to keep her from fleeing. "This is my fiancée, Christina."

Christina actually looked around for a second — *fiancée?* Yep, he was talking about her. She stuck out a hand. "Pleasedtomeetcha," she mumbled. Small he might be, the minister had a grip like a starving anaconda. She extricated her mashed paw with difficulty.

"Thanks for coming up to the palace," David said, and she barely restrained a snort. Sure, like anybody was going to say no to the crown prince! Well, why should they? She sure as shit didn't. Well, she did, but he snuck in under her defenses and weakened her. Bum. And *now* look at how she was spending her time. Making florists cry and getting her fingers broken by men of the cloth.

"Why don't we get started? I'm sure you

both have a thousand details to tend to."

"Don't remind her," David said wryly.

"If you'll just fill out these question-naires, we'll go from there."

"Oh, great! A test!"

"Yes," Minister Cray said, handing her a stapled set of papers. "But I will give you candy when you're done."

"I see you've been briefed on the lady," David said, accepting his own set of paper-work.

"Extensively," Cray replied.

"I foresee problems ahead," Cray said forty minutes later.

"It was a hard test," Christina whined.

"Mm-hmm. My lady, I see here for question number one, you do not appear to know your fiancé's full name. You've written, *'It's David something something something Baranov, and there's probably an Alexander in there somewhere.'*"

"Well, I was close, wasn't I?"

Prince David stopped in mid-snicker when Minister Cray added, "And you, sir, don't appear to know the name of anyone in your fiancée's family."

"But they're all dead!"

"They still have *names,*" Christina hissed.

"And, my lady, in answer to question six, *'How will you go about fulfilling your duties of a wife?,'* you have written, *'By keeping my head down and spending a lot of time hiding from my in-laws.'*"

"That was a joke," she said weakly.

"Har-har," the prince replied.

"And, sir, *you* have replied to question six, *'By letting my wife spend as much time as she wants in the kitchens.'*"

*"What?"*

"Because you're a chef!" he shouted, fending Christina off with his questionnaire. "Not because I'm a chauvinist!"

"It appears," Minister Cray said loudly, before a real fight could begin, "that you two know very little about each other."

"I know everything I need to know," Christina grumbled. "Jerk."

"Shrew," Prince David coughed into his fist.

"This is problematic," Cray added, distracting Christina with a Charms Blowpop, "as you're getting married in two months."

"God, is it really two months? Already?"

"Ah, it seems like just yesterday you were an illegal alien, sponging off my father and eating all the cocktail sauce in the palace," Prince David said, wiping away an imaginary tear.

"Shut your face, Penguin Boy."

"Now I really *will* cry."

"Look, Minister Crepe —"

"Cray, my lady."

"What difference does any of this make? We're each getting married for our own reasons."

"And that," Cray said, "is exactly why I'm here."

She ignored this. "He's healthy, I'm healthy, and, thank God, the king's healthy. We'll have, like, forty years to get to know each other. And lots of time before we actually have to, you know, do anything."

"Hopefully so, my lady, but that's not the end of it. You both come from — ah — that is to say, both of your parents — no offense to the late Queen Dara, or your mother and father, my lady, but — ah — that is to say —"

"Cough it up, Cray."

"He means neither one of us grew up close to a happy marriage," the prince said. "Your dad left and my mother was a terrible wife."

"Yes," she said, "but she looks dynamite in a painting."

"Thanks. But the question is, how can we know how to make a happy marriage on our own?"

Christina was silent, except for the crunch of her teeth breaking into the lollipop to get at the succulent bubblegum center.

"So, two months." David cleared his throat and plunged in. "Well, let's get to it. Uh, Christina, my full name is —"

"Crown Prince David Alexander Marko Dmitri Baranov," she said, still crunching. "Also known as the Prince of the Penguins, the Dork of Allen Hall, and my black-haired nemesis."

Cray's eyes widened so much she feared his glasses would fall right off his face. "My lady, if you knew —"

"She likes to mess with people's heads," Prince David said, not quite able to keep the grudging admiration out of his tone.

"Also, we've been in here an hour. Can we do this another time?"

"Oh, yes, certainly. In fact, I strongly recommend we all take a break."

"Cool. 'Bye." She handed the lollipop stick back to the minister and exited the drawing room, snapping her gum.

"Ah . . . Your Highness . . . a word, please . . ."

Prince David sat back down, resigned.

Christina, he was gratified to see, was

waiting for him. "What's that?" she asked with faux casualness, popping a bubble and pointing to the small piece of white paper in his hand.

"It's a prescription," he replied grimly. "You've broken the minister."

"Oh, come on. Broken?"

"Broken. As in, he doesn't want to counsel us anymore. As in, he thinks we both need professional help. And by 'we' he means 'you.' So now, instead of talking to a kindly minister about our hopes and dreams, we'll be talking to a shrink."

"Oh, shit."

"My sentiments exactly."

# Chapter 14

From *The Queen of the Edge of the World*, by Edmund Dante III, © 2089, Harper Zebra and Schuster Publications.

Alaskan royalty has never had much trouble dealing with international and local press. The reason is simple: Alaska is 656,425 square miles, over twice the size of Texas. And quite a bit of it, even in this century, is difficult to get to. Thus, any time the royal family has wanted privacy, they could disappear into the wilderness, and no one — "Not even God with a telescope," as King Alexander was fond of saying — could find them.

Thus, there wasn't the hostile relationship between the House of Baranov and the press that was sometimes seen with other countries' royalty.

For example, England is a small island. It's difficult to hide there. Alternatively, there wasn't the manipulation of the press that was sometimes credited to Princess Diana, King William's mother.

What does this mean? It means that "scoops" were often more a case of a reporter being in the right place at the right time than the result of endless royal-stalking.

The greatest day of Don Cook's life started out horribly. The Check Engine light went on as soon as his car started, his boss ripped him a new one for missing his deadline the night before, and his mother left him a voicemail telling him she was coming to stay with him for the rest of the winter.

The lead reporter for *The Juneau Empire* decided to flee his life's problems by going out into the bitter cold to buy an extra-large coffee, extra cream, lots of sugar. And while he was waiting patiently in line at the coffeehouse counter, he happened to glance across the street and see the crown prince's fiancée, and the palace press officer.

Even better, they were entering a psychiatrist's office.

"Holy God," he replied when asked what he would like to order, and immediately fled the line.

Later, Don was to say, "It was pure chance I saw her. Thank God I had my camera in the car. And she was just — even before she was queen, there was something about her. A no-nonsense thing. And she was just so pretty, even in blue jeans and a T-shirt. Plus, she gave me a helluva quote. Probably got in big trouble for it, too. Not that she would have cared. She wasn't like that. Not at all."

"For the record," Lady Christina announced, "this is a big waste of time for both of us."

"It's a pleasure to meet you, too," Dr. Pohl replied. She was a woman in her late fifties, with curly white hair, piercing brown eyes, and bifocals that made her look like a kindly grandmother instead of one of the country's leading psychiatrists, with a high triple-digit I.Q. and a brain like a razor.

Her office was decorated in Modern Duck. They were all over the place . . . duck prints on the walls, duck decoys on the credenza, even a duck pencil holder on the woman's desk. "I appreciate you taking the time to see me."

"Hey, Doc, let's cut the shit, all right? We both know this wasn't *my* idea. That minister's got it in for me." *What's the term for fear of ducks? Duckophobia? What would she do if she had a patient who was scared of waterfowl? Redecorate? Treat them at home?* "He, like, hates me."

"I doubt that very much, my lady."

"Okay, if I'm gonna have to sit in here for fifty minutes — and get charged for an hour, and don't think I didn't notice how fishy *that* is — you're gonna have to stop with the 'my lady' stuff right now. Chris is fine."

"Very well, Chris. Why do you think Minister Cray sent you to me?"

"Because he hates me and is evil?" she guessed.

"Close, but not quite. He's concerned about your motives in agreeing to marry Prince David."

"The king didn't care why, and the prince doesn't care, but that's not good enough? Now I have to justify myself to a shrink?"

"Do you think you need to justify your actions?"

"Shrink talk," Christina muttered. "Are you going to be like that cool shrink in *Good Will Hunting*, or the annoying shrink in *Girl, Interrupted*?"

"That raises an interesting point . . . have you noticed that Robin Williams seems compelled to play brilliant, yet misunderstood, men? *Good Will Hunting*, *Patch Adams*, *Dead Poets Society*, *Awakenings?* I wonder what he's trying to tell us."

Momentarily startled — whoa, the doctor actually sounded like a real person for a second — Christina replied, "Actually, his new thing is playing psychos. *One-Hour Photo*, *Insomnia.* Like that. He was great in *Insomnia.*"

"I agree. It's interesting, the choices people make."

"Oh, here we go. By the way, you're about as subtle as a brick to the forehead."

"Thanks — I went to school for many years and learned just how to swing that brick. But we were talking about choices —"

"Speaking of choices," Christina interrupted, "I read up on you."

"I'm flattered, yet alarmed."

Her mouth twitched, but she refused to give the shrink the benefit of a smile. "Yeah, well, I read that you did your master's thesis on the royal family. And you're considered an expert on them. So who chooses to spend their life studying *other* people's lives?"

"Someone with no life of their own," the doctor said cheerfully. "You can't annoy me by saying things that are true, you know."

"Oh, yeah? Well, give me a chance. How about —"

"Do you miss your work?"

"— the way you — hmm?"

"Your job with the cruise line. Do you miss it? You've been staying at the Sitka Palace for a few weeks now. And my understanding is that you and the prince will live there after your wedding."

"We will?"

"That's what I was told," Dr. Pohl replied carefully.

"Well, we'll see about *that.* Although I guess there are worse things. Anyway, my job — no, I don't miss it. When you cook for that many people, it's hard to be creative. Do you know how many loaves of bread I went through on French Toast Tuesdays?"

"No, I —"

"Six hundred and forty-two."

"That's a buttload of bread," Dr. Pohl observed.

"Tell me! So, no, I don't miss it. I have the run of the kitchens at the palace — let me tell you, that really weirded out the kitchen staff. Took 'em a while to come around."

"Well, you very likely will be queen someday," Dr. Pohl pointed out. "They probably prefer you to stay out of the kitchen."

"Tough. They were all, 'This isn't your place,' and I was all, 'I'll be the judge of that,' and they were all 'We're telling Edmund!' and I was all 'Fine, see if I care.' And they did! They ratted me out to that skinny weirdo. But we get along okay now," she added hastily. "Once they saw that Eds couldn't make me quit cooking."

"You traveled quite a bit for your work?"

"Different port almost every day, sure. Great way to see the world for cheap."

"Difficult to make friends, though."

"Well, you know. We were all pretty busy. The geese — I mean, the passengers — come first."

"That's very interesting to me. Do you know why?"

"Because you have no life?"

"Not only that. I was told that you moved around a lot as a child."

"My, my, they're like a bunch of fish-wives over at the palace, aren't they? Yeah, we moved a lot. So? My dad took off when I was a baby, and my mom bounced around the country, chasing work. She had a kid to feed."

"Uh-huh. Probably not much fun for you. Growing up that way, I mean."

Christina shrugged.

"What's interesting is, you've chosen one of the few professions that also makes it impossible to set down roots. In essence, you've duplicated your childhood."

Christina opened her mouth, but nothing came out.

"You can see how, as an impartial observer, that would be interesting to me."

"So, what?" Christina said defensively. "You're saying I like to be alone?"

"I'm saying we choose what's familiar, for good or ill. And now you're going to be a member of the royal family."

"Which is deeply meaningful how?"

"My understanding," Dr. Pohl said, "is that a big reason you agreed to marry His Highness is because you want your children to have roots. But I think you may have overlooked the fact that you, also, will have roots. At last."

"Well, what if I did? I mean, what if that's my big reason? So now I'm a nutjob?"

"Good heavens, I hope not. I'm not equipped to treat nutjobs."

"Well. You know your shit, I'll give you that much."

"Dare I hope you will return?"

"I have to," she said gloomily. "David and Jenny and I made a pact. They'll get me out of most of the rest of the wedding meetings, and in return I come here."

"That seems like a fair deal."

"You have *no* idea."

"So, how did it go?" Jenny stood the moment Christina entered the room, and slung her purse over one shoulder. "You didn't break this one, too, did you?"

"Hardly. She looks like a sweet old lady and she's as sharp as a shuriken."

"A what?"

"Never mind. I'd have an easier time breaking a steel girder. She was okay. Not too shrinky. I guess."

"My heart! Can it stand the strain?"

"Ho-ho, I'm convulsed with laughter."

"Do you want to grab a bite before we head back?"

"I can't," Chris replied glumly, following Jenny out through the entryway. "David's going to show me how to feed the penguins today."

"Oh."

"Yeah, I know, *très* lame, but he really

wants me to, and it's, like, the thing he thinks is the most interesting thing in the whole world, so I guess it wouldn't kill me to go back in the penguin room. You know. Once."

"So you've crammed all your — ah — less — um — desirable errands —"

"Into one never-ending, hellish day, yes."

"Good practice," Jenny predicted. "And speaking of undesirable errands —"

Christina groaned.

"— has anyone spoken to you about Boston?"

"You mean from a historic standpoint? Do they want my thoughts on the Big Dig?"

"His Highness gave quite a bit of money to the New England Aquarium, and they're anxious to show their appreciation. He'll be going late next week, and he thought it might be nice if you joined him."

"David did? David asked if I could come?" That changed everything! "Because if he wants me to go, I'll go. Y'know, if I don't have anything else on my schedule."

"Well, perhaps we could discuss it with him when we get back."

"Yes, perhaps we could. New England

Aquarium, huh? Wait a minute . . . aren't there, like, a thousand penguins in that exhibit?"

"I don't know," Jenny said seriously. "I never counted."

"Remind me to kill you one of these days," she grumped.

Jenny laughed, which made Chris laugh and, still giggling, they shrugged into their coats, and when Jenny pushed the door open they both heard the *snap* of a camera shutter.

"Lady Christina! This way, please."

Poor guy had less of a life than Dr. Pohl if taking *her* picture was part of the job description. "Why don't you take a picture? It'll last longer. Oh, wait, you just did."

"Don Cook, *Juneau Empire.* Are you seeing a psychiatrist, Lady Christina?"

"Don," Jenny said, exasperated, "you know perfectly well we've got a press conference set up next —"

"Yes," Christina replied. "I am."

*Snap!* "Why?"

"Because," she said, feeling absolutely evil but deciding to go with it, "the pressure of marrying into the Alaskan royal family has turned me into a drooling psychotic."

"Chris!" Jenny nearly howled.

"I hope you'll send me a copy of the story," she added sweetly, grinning for the camera and then walking away.

"Don . . ." Jenny said pleadingly.

"Sorry, Jenn. Does the Sitka Palace have anything to add about our future queen's rampant psychosis?"

"Don, please."

He was smirking. "Give me a break . . . if you were me, would you go with it?"

The press officer clutched her head, then hurried up the street after Christina.

# Chapter 15

"So, how'd it go?"

Wrinkling her nose at the stench, Christina said, "It was okay." She decided not to mention her comments to the reporter. David would find out soon enough. "When do *you* have to go?"

"In another hour. C'mere, I want to show you how to feed them."

"Can't we spend this time playing, um, hide-and-seek?"

He smiled at her. "This is important to me, too, Christina. Although, admittedly, not as fine as feeling your —"

"Okay, okay, I get the gist. It doesn't actually involve touching the dead fish, does it?" she asked, gingerly crossing the room. Her voice practically echoed off the walls; the penguin palace was a cavern. A zillion of the funny birds were walking and swimming and preening and shitting all over the place.

"Says the cook!"

"Hey, if we're talking a nice fillet or

maybe a decent gumbo or chowder, I'll touch the dead fish, all right? But unless you've got some butter and flour in that little cart of yours . . ."

"Sorry. Just hoses and buckets."

"Oooh, sexy."

"Now, just toss it lightly — it's a little early for them to start eating out of your hand."

"Years too early." She picked a smelt or whatever the hell it was out of the bucket and tossed it. One of the penguins snatched it out of the air. Yeesh! Carnivore birds who couldn't fly. But who came up to her knee and could make lunch out of her patella. This got better and better. "Well, this has been fulfilling and all, and I've certainly learned all sorts of new and interesting things about you —"

"Nice try. How about another one?"

"How about not?" But she grabbed another smelt, and threw it at a penguin about three yards in front of her. "So, this is what you do all day?"

"Not all day. Some days I have to go see a shrink because my fiancée is really stubborn."

"You're a real fucking comedian."

"Are you nervous about Boston?"

"That was a subtle subject change.

Actually," she said, tossing another fish, "I just heard about Boston."

"Jenny?"

"Yeah, she asked me. But you know, David, *you* could have asked me." She was trying hard not to pout.

"Well," he said, looking faintly surprised, "I put it on my list and delegated it to Jenny. She wouldn't have asked you without my say-so. So it really was like I'd asked you."

Christina sighed. "David, David, David . . ."

"What?"

"Never mind. To answer your question, I'm looking forward to it. Except for the penguin angle. I seem to be totally unable to get away from penguins in my new life."

David laughed and gave her a quick hug, which she enjoyed entirely too much, given that this was a marriage of convenience. "Sorry about that. But they've been talking about opening the new wing for quite a while, and I didn't want to put them off any longer."

"You're a prince. They'll wait."

"Well, yes. But why should they have to?"

"Good answer."

"Anyway, now that they've expanded their exhibit, they'd like me to come down for the dedication ceremony. It's what Jenny and Edmund refer to as a fluff job . . . no real pressure, no tough questions, just smiling for the cameras, cutting ribbons, and looking appropriately modest. Piece of cake, right, Christina?"

"I guess." She still had a hard time believing she was news, but supposed her fellow Americans needed to be distracted from their economic woes. More, she loved Boston, and was anxious to get out of the palace for a few days.

And she kind of liked the idea of traveling with David as a couple. Weird, but there it was.

"If you get nervous," he was saying, "just hold my hand really tightly and smile."

She had planned to do that anyway.


"Well, well," he said the next morning, looking considerably less amused, "if it isn't my fiancée, the drooling psycho."

"Uh . . . good morning?" She looked up from chopping chives for her scrambled eggs. "Want something?"

"Yes, but I doubt it's anything you're going to actually do."

"Oh, sit down. And calm down." She watched as he stalked across the large palace kitchen and slapped the paper down on the chopping block, nearly upsetting her chive pile. It didn't escape her notice that the kitchen instantly emptied of the few servants who had been there. Apparently the prince in a temper was a rare sight, and nobody wanted to be around for it. "Hmm, not a bad picture. You can see my teeth. Probably nobody knew I had teeth."

"The picture is fine. More than fine," he added grudgingly. "It's the headline we're all having a little trouble with."

"Yes," she said, taking in *ROYAL FIANCÉE TREATED FOR RAGING PSYCHOSIS.* "I can see that. By the way, I never used the word 'raging.' "

"Really, Chris." The corner of his mouth twitched, but he still looked severe. Severely cute! His dark hair tumbled across his forehead and he looked like he'd thrown his clothes on. He hadn't shaved yet, either. Yum. Someone had clearly hauled him out of bed and tossed him the morning paper. "What possessed you?"

"The devil?"

"That's what Jenny thinks. She's been lying down with a cool cloth on her forehead all morning."

"Oh," Christina said, feeling fresh guilt. She didn't mean to make Jenny's job eight times as hard. It just sort of happened naturally. Like acid rain. "I'll go see her, if you want."

"That would be nice. Do you know what *else* would be nice?"

"No," she said humbly, "but I can guess."

He gave in and laughed. "Christ! I just about wet my pants when I saw this."

"What'd your dad say?"

"Never mind," he said, getting stern all over again, so she knew the king had thought it was hilarious. Sometimes she thought David was more Edmund's son than King Alexander's. "Look, just try to ignore these impulses toward wickedness, all right? For all our sakes."

"Well, I'll try," she said doubtfully.

"Thank you." He snatched her plate — onto which she had just piled her three scrambled eggs with chives and cheddar — and her fork. "As penance, I'm going to eat your breakfast."

"That'll learn me." She cracked another three eggs into the bowl. "Sorry about the rude wake-up call."

"Why didn't you tell me yesterday?"

Christina deduced that Jenny hadn't ratted her out, and made a mental note to do something especially nice for the woman. Maybe even (ech!) go shoe shopping with her. "There just wasn't a good way to bring it up."

"Try harder next time," he said sourly.

"I will," she promised, shutting off the burner, "for a kiss."

He looked around, seeing the now-deserted kitchen. "I'll give you more than a kiss, you little —"

Shrieking, she darted away from him. He caught her in one of the dry goods cupboards, which they promptly defiled.

# Chapter 16

Christina watched the mountains below. No matter how often she was reminded of Alaska's beauty, it knocked her out every time. It was like living in a postcard. It gave her hope for the rest of the planet . . . if they could keep this place nice, they could probably —

"My lady . . ." The flight attendant, wearing a navy blue blazer with the royal family's crest, paused by Christina's seat.

She stopped in mid-slurp. It was hard to make a perfect Bloody Mary; most people put too much Tabasco in them. Why not just add too much battery acid? Anyway, this one was perfect. It was also her third.

She had thought riding in the royal family's private jet would be cool. Instead, it was weird. The thing was practically empty, except for the crew, Jenny, and the prince. And Jenny was lying down in the rear of the plane, fighting off another migraine with Advil and cold cloths.

She'd tried to distract herself with the

view, but that didn't last very long. And now here was a flight attendant with news of their doom.

"My lady?"

"Eh? We're crashing? It's okay. You can tell me. We're crashing, aren't we? I promise I won't get mad. Just tell me."

"No, my lady. The prince would like to see you in his room."

"The prince wants to see me?"

"Yes."

"But we're not crashing?"

"Correct."

"So I can unbuckle?"

"Yes."

"Okay, then. But I'm taking my drink." She unlatched her seat belt, cautiously stood, then walked toward the rear of the plane. She knocked on a small door where the bathrooms would be on a commercial plane, heard David's "Come!" and poked her head in.

And nearly fell on her ass. "Wow!" Instead of a cramped bathroom, it was a medium-sized bedroom, with a desk and laptop in one corner and a queen-sized bed in the other. There was a pitcher of ice water on the bedside table, and a bowl of oranges. Her stateroom on the cruise ship hadn't been nearly as nice as this.

David looked up from the computer and smiled, absently brushing his dark hair off his forehead. She really ought to suggest he get a haircut. Later. "Hello. Thanks for coming back. I wanted to make sure you were handling all this okay."

"All this? You mean, your super-secret private nookie room?"

He laughed. "I usually use this plane for business, and I can safely say there has been no nookie gotten here." His dark blue eyes took on a gleam she hadn't seen before. "Although . . . since you're here . . . and we *are* engaged . . ."

"And I'm tipsy on three drinks . . . good bartender, by the way."

"Why are you drinking? I don't think I've ever seen you take a drink. Come here and sit down. What's wrong?"

"Nothin'." She walked four feet forward and sat on the end of the bed. He got up from the desk and sat beside her. She got a whiff of what she was beginning to classify as "Dave-smell". . . crisp cotton, light aftershave, and his own clean scent. Yum. "It's just . . . this is just kind of weird, you know. And frankly, it just doesn't seem right not to spend an hour standing in a security line at the airport. Not that I'm complaining. Because I'm absolutely not.

But it's still weird. Jeez, I've been saying and thinking weird a lot in the last few minutes. But, there it is."

"Well, we'll be in Boston in a few more hours. Why don't you take a nap, relax."

"In here?"

"Sure, in here. This is as much your room as it is mine, now."

She laughed unwillingly. "Ah, no. I don't think that's right at all." Just as much hers? What had he been smoking? He was the prince; this was his dad's jet. She was a mongrel nobody.

Still . . .

She looked longingly at the bedspread, which was the same color as the flight attendant's blazer. "It would be weird . . . damn, there's that word again . . . sleeping on a plane while actually being comfortable."

"God forbid you experience anything weird," he said. She looked at him narrowly, but from his innocent expression she had no idea what he truly meant by that. "Here, come on. Lie down."

She crawled toward the head of the bed, felt him pull her shoes off, then flopped beneath the covers and sighed. "All right. You're right. This is very relaxing." She drained the last of her Bloody Mary while lying down, then set the empty cup on the bedside table.

He slipped into bed beside her and she settled comfortably into the crook of his arm. Instantly she was no longer relaxed. Instead she was tense and almost . . . nauseated?

"You know, my father didn't come along on this trip," David whispered, making all the hair on her left arm stand up.

"Uh-huh."

"And it's just the two of us in here."

"Picked up on that, did you?"

"I'm a Ph.D," he said solemnly. "We're very observant."

"Unfortunately, there's a problem with that."

"Oh?" He was rubbing her shoulder with his right hand and nuzzling her ear. Under ordinary circumstances, that would be delightful. "What's that?"

"The thing is, if you grab my tits, I'm probably going to throw up."

He let go of her like she was hot. "Oh."

"Sorry. Too much to drink, too tense, too weirded out."

He sighed. "That's all right."

"Not that I don't want to join the Mile-High Club with you. But while we lust to reach that peak, I probably shouldn't be

162

struggling not to puke."

"I agree. It's a good rule of thumb for any romantic occasion, actually."

"I mean, I'm gonna be really pissed at myself later. Because, frankly, since the cedar closet, I've been dying to —"

A sudden pounding on the door. "Your Highness! My lady! Stop it at once!" Jenny's voice, sounding harassed. "The king made me promise! No touchy!"

"For heaven's sake," the prince muttered, while Christina giggled. "Come *in,* Jenny."

The protocol officer fairly burst into the room. She had her hands tightly over her eyes. Her lips were curved into a grimace. "I'm very sorry to interrupt. But His Majesty made me promise. Could you please get dressed now?"

"Jenny," David said, exasperated, "open your eyes."

She slowly pulled her hand away and cracked one eye open. Then they both opened. "Oh. Oh! Very good, then."

"It's nap time," Chris explained. "Not nookie time. Really, Jenn. You've got such a filthy imagination."

Blushing harder (if that were possible — Christina feared the woman's head would soon blow up), she said, "I'm very sorry.

Of course, you're tired . . . the trip . . . the preparations . . . the . . . uh . . . I'm going now. With your leave, Highness."

"Leave," David said.

Jenny bobbed a quick bow and practically ran out, shutting the door behind her.

"Gotcha," Chris said, giggling, then moaned and clutched her head.

"Remind me to put a lock on that door," he muttered.

"I'll put it on my to-do list from hell."

"Go to sleep."

"Is that on my list, too?" Before she could add something more sarcastic, she was asleep.

". . . thanks to a generous endowment from Prince David, our feathered friends will have more room to play, interact, and do all the things we all love to watch them do."

"We?" Christina muttered out of the side of her mouth.

"Don't start," David muttered back.

"So, without further ado, I'd like to introduce Prince David and his American fiancée, who I understand *loves* the city of Boston —"

Wild applause. Cheers.

"— Christina Krabbe!"

"The 'e' is silent," she sighed. Then she stood with the prince and grinned like a monkey and waved like a fucked-up prom queen while about a thousand flashbulbs went off in her face.

They were outside the New England Aquarium, but as it was cloudy, all the photographers had brought their flash packs. So she stood and smiled and was privately amazed . . . didn't these reporters have anything better to do? Sure, they were entertainment reporters, but shouldn't they be tracking down Tom Cruise or Johnny Depp or Jennifer Aniston?

"Miss Krabbe! Miss Krabbe! Darrell Hanson, Fox News. How does it feel knowing you're going to be the queen of Alaska someday?"

"It's unbelievably alarming," she said into the microphone. There was a burst of laughter from the press corps, and out of the corner of her eye she saw Jenny had started rubbing her temples again. She cleared her throat. "Actually, David and I want the king to live a long, long time. We'd love it if we were never in charge of the country. He's great, and he does a terrific job."

Abruptly, Jenny stopped rubbing. She and the prince traded a glance. The prince was smiling. "Actually," Jenn said in a low voice, "that's — that's okay. That's . . . it's very nice, actually. Keep her up there."

"Alison Smith, Miss Krabbe, *Entertainment Weekly.* When's the wedding?"

"A few more weeks. I guess all your invitations got lost in the mail, because we want tons of reporters to be there," she added wryly.

More laughter.

"Mark Spangler, Channel 10 News. Where are you honeymooning?"

"New York."

The prince's eyebrows arched in surprise, but he didn't say anything.

"*Entertainment Weekly*, Miss Krabbe . . . you could go anywhere in the world . . . why New York?"

"Are you kidding? Some of the best restaurants in the world are in New York City." She rubbed her hands together with glee. "And we're gonna try 'em all!"

"Miss Krabbe —"

"Christina."

"Christina, is there pressure on you and the prince to provide an heir to the Alaskan throne?"

She shook her finger at the reporter from MSNBC. "Now, now. How the hell is our sex life any of *your* business?" But she said it with a smile, and it was the lead in all their stories that evening. Along with the picture of the future princess yawning with her fingers over her mouth during the prince's speech.

"That was really nice, what you said about Dad."

"It's the truth." They were touring the aquarium, along with about sixty thousand other people. The security team was, as usual, as tense as cats in a dog pound. "I don't want to be queen. And come on, do you *really* want to be king? Wouldn't you rather be a prince forever?"

Frankly, he had never thought about it before. It would never have occurred to him to think about it in those terms. "It's my duty."

"Nice, but I notice you didn't answer my question."

He felt a stir of impatience, and quelled it. It had been a long day; no need to take it out on the pretty blonde at his side. She hadn't been born to duty, as he had. She still had the luxury of questioning fate. "That's because it's an irrelevant question. It's my duty. It will be your duty. For what it's worth, you'll be a fine queen."

"Thanks. For what it's worth, I don't

like it when you tell me I'm being irrelevant."

He blinked in surprise. She didn't sound
like she was kidding. "Noted."

"Chris! Christina!" A strong baritone
reached them, and then a piercing whistle
split the air. "Hey! Krabbe-with-a-silent-e!"

She stopped in her tracks and he nearly
stumbled into her. "Stop!" she said, seeing
the security team all twitch toward their
handguns. "Let him through. I know this
guy."

David watched as the blond, broad-
shouldered man in jeans and a black T-shirt
with the logo FREE MARTHA worked his
way through the crowd.

"Christina, who is that?"

"Kurt Carlson." She was waving furiously at the stranger. "You remember how
I told you I could count all my lovers on
one hand? That's number two. Kurt!" she
cried as he finally reached her. Her feet left
the ground as he picked her up in an exu-
berant hug. "How the hell are you? What
are you doing here?"

"You kidding?" David could hear California surfer in the man's voice, although
he had to be close to thirty. "I had some
leave from the department coming, and I
read in the papers you were gonna be in

Beantown. So I hopped a plane and here I am."

Christina looked disturbingly thrilled. "You came all the way out here to see me? You big dummy, you should save your vacation time to see your mom."

"She's in Greece with Stepfather Number Six. Hey," he added casually to David. He didn't bow, which was entirely appropriate, as the man was American. Americans, since time out of mind, did not bow, curtsey, or obey any sovereign on earth. Still, *some* acknowledgement of his station would have been nice. Anything instead of, "How's it hanging, guy? I'm Kurt. Chris and me go way back."

"He was supposed to take a cruise with his mom," she added, "but she stood him up to honeymoon with Stepfather Number Three. So we got to know each other. It's so *great* to see you!"

"Nice to meet you," David said, interrupting another hug by sticking his hand out, forcing Kurt to shake it. "I've heard . . . well . . . nothing about you."

"Oh, that's Chris for you. She never volunteers shit if she can help it. But boy, dynamite tattoo, eh?" The peasant actually elbowed him in the ribs.

*Tattoo?* What fresh hell was this? "I

169

wouldn't know," the prince said thinly. *Though I mean to find out.*

"Oh, quit it, you guys," Chris snapped good-naturedly. "Jeez, it's like watching the Discovery Channel. So, Kurt, you're in town a couple days? Can you hang out?"

*Ugh.* The prince avoided "hanging out" if he could at all help it.

"Sure," Kurt said. "I've got two weeks leave coming up. I was planning to hang around here, but if you guys have something else in mind, I could tag along."

*Oh, splendid.*

"It's so great to see you," Christina said for the third? — fourth? — time. "I can't believe you came all this way to see me."

"You kidding? You're in all the papers out here. It's big news when a Yank lands a prince. How could I not look you up?"

And he had the gall to drop David a wink.

# Chapter 17

"You're killing me, kiddo. You're god-damned killing me!" The king slapped the newspaper down on his desk. She could read the upside-down headline easily enough; the print was over an inch high. *FUTURE PRINCESS CLAIMS SEX LIFE NOBODY'S BUSINESS.* "I'm on my second bottle of Pepto-Bismol this morning — you happy now?"

"Hey, Al, guess what? My sex life *isn't* anybody's business."

"Sure, go with that, see where it gets you. Nice yawn, by the way."

"Give me a break! Look, I'm sorry, but David was going *on* and *on* for, like, an hour and a half, and I was really —"

"Hung over," David said dryly. "And my speech was six minutes and twenty-eight seconds long."

"And what's this about bringing an American cop back with you? You don't like the Alaskan cops? You had to kidnap one and haul his ass back to the palace?"

"Oh! Right, forgot to tell you . . . he's an old friend of mine, and David invited him to come back and stay with us for a while — wasn't that great?" Smiling, Christina squeezed David's arm, then dropped it. "His name is —"

"Kurtis J. Carlson," Edmund said from his corner.

"Uh, yeah. And he's a —"

"Homicide detective with the L.A.P.D."

"Edmund, you're creeping me out again. What'd you do, instantly run a background check the second we got here, or something?"

"Yes."

She blinked at that, then said, "Anyway, speaking of Kurt, I'm gonna see if he's all set up in the guest wing. Okay if I take off?"

King Alexander waved her away, and she practically skipped out of the room. David turned to follow her, but stopped short at his father's, "Freeze, boy!"

"Don't start, Dad."

"Bet your ass I'm gonna start! First, you don't care if you get married or not. Then you flub proposing to Christina. Then she finally — miracle of fucking miracles — says yes, but won't decide on a ring. Then she drives half the wedding staff to nervous breakdowns. Then — then! She runs into an ex-boyfriend and you decide to bring him *here?* Are you *trying* to get out of your engagement?"

David sighed. "I realize on the surface it looks a bit bone-brained —"

King Alexander snorted. "Not just on the surface, boy-o."

"— but you should have seen her face light up when she saw him. I think she's been a little overwhelmed here, and it did her good to meet up with an old — uh — friend. She was so — well, I invited him to join us on the return trip and stay for a bit. You should have seen how happy that made her. She — well, she was quite pleased."

The king was rubbing his temples, much the way Jenny did. "Cripes, the two of you are going to drive me to an early grave."

"Your Majesty, if I may, this actually solves the security problem revolving around Lady Christina," said Edmund.

"Yeah? Howzat?"

"As you know, she doesn't feel she needs a security team when she leaves the palace —"

"And she's wrong, yeah, we know that. Had to put my foot down on that one, and she didn't like it one damned bit. Got a headache from all the yelling."

"— so rather than have bodyguards dogging her heels, lately she has elected not to leave the grounds at all."

"It's why she was so excited about visiting Boston," David added.

"But traveling with a police officer, one licensed to carry a firearm —"

"Yeah, but can he shoot? Will he?"

Edmund crossed the room and tapped the file on the king's desk. "See for yourself, my king. He enjoys an outstanding reputation within the police force; he's their top detective. He's also killed four men in the line of duty, either to save lives or to apprehend killers. Detective Carlson's superior was quite frank with me. He referred to Detective Carlson as 'the number one gunslinger' in the Los Angeles Police Department."

The king opened a desk drawer, then leaned back in his chair and rested his feet on it. "Huh. I getcha. Let her run around with what's-his-face — she can go wherever she wants and have fun at the same time."

"Exactly, sir."

"So, throw her together constantly with an ex-boyfriend."

"Lady Christina would not forsake the

prince for another, not at this stage. She's an honorable woman."

The king nearly tumbled out of his chair. "Whoa, my heart! Can it take the strain! I thought you said something nice about her."

"It's the dry air in here."

"Well, shit, I guess I don't care, if Davey doesn't."

"*I* don't care," his son lied.

The king studied his heir for a long moment. *Fuckit. This might be what finally gets the kid to shit or get off the pot. He's been way too laid back about all of this.* "Fine. So, the cop's Christina's new bodyguard."

"Fine."

"Indefinitely? We clear that with his boss back home?"

"Yes, Your Majesty. His captain realizes this is good publicity — for a change — for the L.A.P.D., and has extended Detective Carlson's paid leave indefinitely."

"Well. That settles that, I guess."

"I guess," the prince said distantly.

# Chapter 18

Kurt still couldn't believe the size of his room. He'd expected . . . he didn't know, something like what he got when he stayed at Motel 6. A really nice Motel 6. Instead, he was worried that Edmund guy had given him the king's room by mistake.

Heck, the whole place was beyond amazing. The country was gorgeous — it all looked like Northern California, except (bad Kurt!) maybe a little better. The people were unbelievably nice. The palace was ultra-cool.

Yep, Christina had really gotten herself a sweet deal. As usual, the crazy cutie had fallen face-first into a pile of crap and gotten up covered with diamonds.

Except . . . she wasn't happy here. Couldn't be. No way — not the Chris he knew. For one thing, look at this place! Everything was a priceless antique.

For another, check the fiancé. Chris so totally did not dig the I'm-not-as-stiff-as-I-look-okay-I-guess-I-am type. Even if he was supersmart. And richer than God. And was gonna have his own country someday.

Nope. He'd done the right thing, coming to Boston. He would — he would save Chris from herself!

Or, rather, he'd save her for him. She was the li'l chickie who got away.

Totally his fault; he knew it then, he knew it now. They'd been going out pretty heavily and then his roving eye had caused trouble and she'd shown up at the same party as his roving eye and some other bim whose name he couldn't even remember.

There had been harsh words, followed by a flying lamp and a mild concussion. He'd told her to take a hike. She'd told him to perform an impossible act on himself. He'd told her he'd rather do that than choke down another omelet she ruined by sprinkling thyme or whatever into it. She told him it'd be a cold day in hell before she made an omelet for him without spitting into it. Then she'd left. And he thought that was okay; he thought he was happy, he thought his concussion would heal up in no time.

They'd made up the next year, when time had softened her heart and woken him up to the colossal mistake he'd made.

He didn't do anything about it then, because it was kind of a new thing, a nice thing, being friends with a woman who wasn't a cop, or a stripper. And he had time; they were both young.

He'd always planned to hook up with Chris again, knock her up, have her squeeze out a few li'l chicks, hang out, get old, all that good shit. Y'know, after. After he sowed some more oats and got ready to settle down and shit. Chris was a great gal and all, but not exactly a demon in the sack. He wanted to see a bit more of the world before settling on a single ice-cream flavor.

Then: the newspapers. All of 'em, it seemed. Christina this, Christina that, Christina was friggin' *engaged* — how's that for a cosmic yuk-yuk? — and now he had to fix it, fix them, and if Princey-poo got in his way, Kurt was gonna knock him on his ass.

Nothing personal. But this was his future wife they were making off with. Chris was born to be Mrs. Carlson, not — jeez, the idea! — Queen Christina.

There was a rap at his shiny door (thing was probably solid gold, he thought uneasily) and then the prince stepped inside, followed by that super-tall dude, Edmund, and a guy not quite as tall, but sure broad through the shoulders. He had salt-and-pepper-colored hair, and his handshake swallowed up Kurt's hand; it was like being close to an aging quarterback, one who could still plow through the field if he had to. He had intense blue eyes, and — and looked a lot like an older, craggier version of Princey-poo, come to think of it.

"Hey, fellas," he said, retrieving his squashed hand with some difficulty. It was a lot like shaking hands with an old grizzly bear that had a few swipes left in his claws. "Hey, dude. You must be the king. Nice place you got here."

"Hello, Detective Car—"

"Dudes, dudes! I'm not on the job. My name's Kurt."

"Kurt, appreciate you coming back with my kid here."

"Oh, hey, no *problemo!* It was great to see Chris again. And great of the prince," he added with a nod at said prince fellow, who looked like he was chewing on lemon peel, "to invite me."

"Yeah. Well, listen, about that — where's your sidearm?"

"In my apartment back in L.A.," he said. "Don't worry, I didn't smuggle any firearms into your country."

"Dammit!"

Kurt blinked. The king turned to Edmund. "Get him fixed up."

"At once, Majesty."

Kurt's hand was swallowed again. "Nice meeting you, Kurt. You have any problems or questions, let me or Edmund know."

"Or even," Edmund said, "Edmund or me. If you wish to be grammatically correct."

"Uh, thanks, Mr. — uh — king."

With a wave, the king took off, leaving him with the skinny guy, and his archrival.

"Are your quarters satisfactory?" his evil nemesis asked politely.

"Yeah, dude, they're fine."

"This is a key card which will get you into the shooting range, anytime. A member of our security team will assist you in selecting a firearm. The king signed your carry permit this morning. All we ask is that when you're escorting Lady Christina —"

"Keep an eye out for the bad guys," Kurt said, instantly understanding everything. What luck! What total fucking luck! He practically snatched the key card. "No sweat. Hey, nobody's gonna mess with *my* ex-girlfriend, unless it's me."

Nobody laughed at his (admittedly lame) little joke.

"So you let me come back with you, and now you're giving me a gun and letting me practice on it, and letting me hang out with your — with Christina. You must really want us to get back together," he joked.

"Ah . . . well . . . I know you aren't here to try to win her back, so to speak, and —"

"Actually, dude, I kind of am," he said, half apologetically. He cursed his hippie mother for instilling him with a scrupulous sense of honesty. "I mean, you seem like a nice guy and all, but this whole palace gig — it's just not for the Chris I know. It's just not. And I'm hoping she'll remember that if we hang out enough."

"Detective Carlson, that is entirely inappropriate behavior," Edmund said.

"Damn right!" the prince yelped.

He shrugged. "Sorry, dudes. That's the way it is."

A bump as his rival's chest touched his. Hmm. The rival was pretty solidly built. And about three inches taller. "Shoot your mouth off all you like," he growled, "but be sure to keep your hands to yourself, or I'll cut them off."

"Oh, yeah? They still do that up here?"

"Edmund! Off with his head!"

181

"Sadly, Your Highness, I left my axe in my other pants."

"Well, start carrying one," the prince snapped, then stormed out.

"Uh . . . he was kidding, right? I mean, I read up on the guy. He's a marine biologist or a zookeeper or something."

"Yes, of course, sir. A marine biologist descended from a royal family known for cutting the Gordian knot as opposed to untying it."

"I don't know what that means."

"It means," Edmund said, just before his more restrained exit, "welcome to Alaska."


"How," Prince David demanded by way of greeting, "could your tattoo have escaped my notice?"

Christina paused in mid-chomp, then put her tomato sandwich back on the plate. She'd successfully seen Kurt tucked into his room and decided to treat herself to a snack. She was eating in one of the sunrooms, the one with the view of the ocean, today a mild slice of blue in the distance. The tomato was a rich, ripe red — a good trick for this time of the year — and drippy. She wiped her chin with her forearm and asked, "What bit you on the ass today?"

"Note how she didn't answer my question."

"What I'm noting is that you've picked up Eds's icky habit of referring to me in the third person. And it's a fine question — how *did* my tattoo escape your notice?"

"Well . . ." He sat down across from her, oblivious to the drenching beauty of the scene. As usual, she was momentarily distracted by his extreme yumminess. "We're usually in a hurry —"

"Because you never know when Nicky or Al or Alex or Alex or Jenny or Eds will burst in on us — so *not* conducive to horniness, by the way."

"— and it's usually dark —"

"And cramped," Christina added, smiling. "And sometimes furry. I still say we find that closet again."

He looked distracted, then shook himself. "So, where is it?"

"You're asking me? I still need a map to find the bathroom."

"I mean," he said through gritted teeth, "your tattoo."

"Oh, dear." She picked up her sandwich and took a bite. "After all those closet gropings, you have to ask?"

He slumped back in his chair and stared

out the window. "Well, if you don't *want* to tell me . . ."

"It's not so much that I don't want to tell you, it's that I think you should find out for your — yeeeek!" The plate went flying, her tomato slices parted ways with the bread, her chair slammed back onto the floor, her legs went over her head, and then he was nuzzling her neck and groping under her shirt. "Subtlety, thy name is not — that tickles!" Her legs sticking up in the air as they were, it was difficult to get leverage to fend him off. Not that she entirely wanted to. Still, her pride was at stake. "David, for God's sake, it's noon and the door to the sunroom's wide open and we're not exactly well — hidden — *God*, your fingers are cold!" A horrid thought crossed her mind. "You didn't come from the penguins to me, did you, you fucking pervert?"

He'd pulled her shirt over her head and seemed temporarily stymied by her bra — ha! Back clasps. "No," he said. "It's just chilly in here today."

Not for much longer! Yow. "David," she giggled into his throat, "will you cut it out? I'll tell you, all right?"

"Kurt knows," he muttered, peeking under a bra strap.

"Ancient history, Penguin Boy, and we already had this conversation, remember? What, it's my fault you've been in such a hurry to get some that you never bothered to look for distinctive markings?"

He scowled at her. "So you're saying it's my fault you went out and got yourself marked with permanent ink like some sort of biker lady?"

"Chick, David, biker chick, and no, but the only reason you're in here with your cold fingers is because you're mad at Kurt." She pushed her hair out of her face to give him a glare of her own. "Which is so totally dumb, by the way, I mean — why'd you invite him in the first place?"

He muttered something she couldn't quite catch, then they both froze when they heard footsteps. He kicked the chair, which wobbled back upright, snapped open the lock on the French door, and hauled her out onto the balcony. He glanced down, observed the four-foot drop, then booted her over.

"My sandwich!" she wailed on the way down.

He landed beside her in a crouch and tackled her. Cripes! At least the grass was warm. The few patches that had escaped the snow! Fucking ten-month Alaskan winters . . .

"Not to mention your shirt," he said, and whatever weird mood he'd been in seemed to have passed, because he was grinning at her. "Now let's hope whoever it is doesn't look out the window."

"They're gonna be too busy peeling tomato slices off the wall." She shivered in the chill spring air. "You owe me lunch, buckaroo."

"Done and done." He peeked into her cleavage.

"For God's sake." She sat up, shoved him away, presented her back to him, and unsnapped her bra.

There was a long silence, followed by his "Oh."

"See it?"

"Hmm."

"Happy now?"

"It's an albatross."

"Congratulations, Dr. Baranov, those years of college when you never had sex appear to have paid off." She snapped her bra again and started to stand, but he held her down with a hand. Weirdly, he was still frowning.

"An albatross, Christina."

"Yes, David, I know, I'm the one who

paid for it," she said patiently. Why was he looking at her so strangely? "Anybody who tells you tattoos don't hurt is a fucking liar, by the way. I figured, smack in the middle of my back, where my bra strap hides it, something small — and it still hurt!"

"A royal albatross, in fact."

"Now, don't go reading too much into this," she warned.

His eyes were faraway and he wasn't looking at her anymore, he was staring at the sea. "It's a large seabird that regularly circles the globe."

"Are you channeling Marlin Perkins now?"

He ignored her interruption. "In fact, it's a seabird famous for never lingering long in one place. In fact, it spends only about a tenth of its life on land . . . the rest of the time it's on the move."

"Also, it's pretty and I liked the black specks on the wings. David, will you lighten up?"

He blinked and looked at her. "Sure," he said. "I was just surprised. It's very pretty."

"Well, thanks."

He kissed her, his tongue tracing her lower lip before delving inside, and she slipped her arms around his broad shoulders. Boy oh boy, it was too bad they were out on the lawn where God and everybody could see them, because she —

"Ah-*hem!*"

They looked up. Edmund had the glass door open and was scowling down at them from the balcony. Prince Alex, looking *very* surprised, was standing beside him.

"That's it," David whispered in her ear. "My erection has utterly vanished."

She giggled as Edmund said, "Really, Your Highness. My lady."

Prince Alex cleared his throat.

"The quest for nookie
Has overtaken you two
I'm telling my dad."

"Alex, you're *so* odd," Christina sighed. "Shouldn't you be in a private screening of *Star Wars* or something?"

"I was on my way
I heard sounds of a struggle
The Dark Side had you."

She giggled in spite of herself. David, however, remained a stone. "Christina fell," he improvised. "I just came out to help her."

Edmund held up her shirt. "Quite a fall, since her shirt was on the chair inside."

"It was like — a whirlwind?" she guessed.

Alex snickered as Edmund went on implacably, like a majordomo Terminator. "Do tell. There is a slice of bread on the ceiling."

"I was saving it for later?"

David collapsed in laughter, actually rolling around the grass. She kicked him, then stood up, climbed the balcony, retrieved her shirt from a glacial Edmund, ignored Alex's leer, and set about cleaning up the room.

# Chapter 19

Christina sailed into Dr. Pohl's office, tossed her coat toward the coatrack (she missed, and it landed on the floor), then flopped onto the couch with a satisfying smack. She laced her fingers behind her head, stared at the ceiling, and said, "Ah, I can feel the sweet embrace of sanity already."

"Well, well, if it isn't the tattooed lady."

"Oh, *that's* nice," she said, then laughed. "It's impossible to keep a secret in that place, you know."

"You're in a good mood," Dr. Pohl observed. "Also, you're late."

"Hey, a princess-in-waiting has stuff to do, Doc. Don't take it personal. And why shouldn't I be in a good mood? Spring's here —"

"And with it, your wedding."

"— the grass has riz, I wonder where the flowers is? And all that. Also, did I tell you? Met a friend in Boston and David invited him to visit! We've been having gobs of fun."

"Have you decided on a ring yet, 'midst the gobs of fun?"

"You're such a buzz kill," Christina muttered. She sat up and swung her legs over the side of the couch. "Look, it's not as easy as all that."

"Really?" Dr. Pohl said, prominently displaying her own engagement and wedding rings.

"Get those rocks away from me. First of all, I had to nicely refuse Queen Dara's jewelry without hurting anybody's feelings, which was so *not* a walk in the park, believe me."

"They offered you the queen's wedding jewels?"

"She had, like, buckets of the stuff. Ropes of pearls. Piles of diamonds. So that was a mess, you know?"

"You had to call on all your powers of tact."

"Damn straight."

"Powers so secret and well hidden, most of us assumed they didn't exist."

"I hate you. Look, the idea of wearing a dead lady's — a dead *queen's* — jewelry creeps me out, okay? Tell the truth, wouldn't you feel a little funny wearing a dead monarch's rings?"

"I never thought about it," Dr. Pohl admitted.

"Well, think about it and get back to me. Anyway. So, we put that issue to bed, finally. But all the rings the jewelers have been bringing to the palace, they've just been — I dunno —"

"Not suitable?"

"Completely very much not suitable. Half of them, you need a crane to get 'em on your finger! Come on — who needs an eight-carat diamond? I could never put on another pair of pantyhose, not as long as I lived. And I'm a cook — anybody keep that in mind?" she griped. "A big-ass ring is just gonna get in my way. D'you know how hard it is to get butter out of jewelry settings?"

"Some people," Dr. Pohl said carefully, "might interpret your refusal —"

"Refusal!"

"— to choose a ring as evidence that you don't truly wish to get married, and make a life here."

"Well, those people ought to give it a rest. It's got nothing to do with David. That's not the important stuff — diamonds and gold and stuff like that — it's *not.* It's got nothing to do with David." Had she said that already? It was hard to remember. She'd been in a great mood two minutes ago, and now she was massively stressed out. Sweating, even!

"Really? Because an objective observer might jump to the conclusion that it has everything to do with David."

"Well, if he wants to marry me so bad, how come he keeps coming up with these rings that are so totally not me? Huh? Well, how come?"

"Are you going to hit me?" Dr. Pohl asked curiously.

"Not today. But listen. It's like, after all this time —"

"*What* time?" Pohl asked, her eyebrows arching like white wings. "You haven't even been here half a year yet."

"Regardless," Christina said stubbornly, "he doesn't know me at all. *He's* the one who doesn't know what's important," she finished triumphantly.

"And you've made how many trips to Penguin Hall since your engagement? In the interest of getting to know your future spouse?"

Sullen silence, followed by, "I'm getting to know him, Dr. Pohl, don't you worry about that."

"Oh, sex," she said, waving it away with her hand. "Sure. Real intimacy there."

"Well, there is! And shouldn't you be, I dunno, shocked or something?"

"That you've seen what you wanted and are going about getting it? Yes, very shocking, and terribly out of character."

"I'm sneaking around the Sitka Palace," she practically shouted, "boinking the heir to the crown!"

"Darling, I'm not your mother. I don't care. Listen, Christina, if gold and diamonds aren't important, then what is?"

"Family," she said promptly.

"But you're marrying into a group of strangers. Is that family? You've explained your motivations, and they're fine, if a little bloodless —"

"Hey!"

"— but isn't there at least a part of you who wants to marry Prince David because you want him for himself? In the way you hope he — and his family — wants *you* for *your*self?"

"I'm getting a headache." Then, grudgingly, "I like him, if that's what you mean."

"Just *like*? There's still time, you know," Dr. Pohl said gently. "You can call everything off, go back to your own life."

Horrified, Christina shook her head. "I'd never do that!"

"Never?"

"Besides, it's too late."

"Not until you say 'I do,' hon."

"Stop calling me that — I never know if you mean 'short for honey' or 'Attila the.' Besides . . . I'm — I'm getting kind of spoiled."

"Servants fighting to meet your every whim?"

"No! Yech! I broke 'em of that in a hurry, let me tell you. But . . . at least at the palace, I'm not so fucking lonesome all the time, you know? I mean, if David's not bugging me about reading his latest research paper on *Aptenodytes patagonicus* — that's Latin for king penguin, and don't I wish I didn't know that — then Nicky's hiding in my closet, or Alex — that's the Princess Alex, not the Prince Alex — is bugging me to come sketching with her, or the other Alex wants me to try my hand at haikus — d'you know he *only* talks in haiku? — or the king wants to take me fishing, or — well — it's kind of nice. I mean, even if David can't get my ring right, they've —"

"Accepted you."

"Well, yeah. I couldn't turn my back on them after they did that. Opened their home — and their family! — to a nobody like me."

"I understand you had a strong hand in planning the food for the wedding reception."

"Well, sure." Christina wrinkled her brow. "I'm a cook. I'm into food. So I wanted the food to be good — that's not such a big deal."

"Yes, that's true, but another way to look at it —"

"Oh, here we go."

"— is that you don't dare to care about the wedding — and subsequent marriage — too much because you can't afford to take it seriously."

She shifted in her chair. "What crap."

"So an impartial observer," Dr. Pohl said carefully, "would surmise you're involved in the food to give the illusion of being interested in the wedding, when really you're only protecting yourself."

"I don't think you heard me the first time," Christina said, "so listen up. What crap!"

"My lady —"

"Watch it with that."

"— I've never known someone so dumb and so smart at the same time."

"What?"

"And with that," Dr. Pohl said, "I think we're done with the week."

"Oh, come on! You can't say all that cryptic stuff and then refuse to explain it!"

"Sure I can, especially when it's not cryptic at all — you know exactly what I'm talking about. Arrive on time next week, and perhaps I will be able to elaborate."

"Fucking shrinks," she muttered.

"Yes, we're really annoying that way," Dr. Pohl said cheerfully. "Say hello to your ex-boyfriend for me."

Christina got up and grabbed her coat. "I said he was a friend — I never told you he was an ex. You've got spies everywhere, don't you, Doc?"

"All shrinks do. We get a pack of them when we graduate from medical school."

"You know, I really can't stand you." But she couldn't keep the smile off her face when she said it.

"I'm well aware, dear. See you next week."

Kurt was waiting for her in the lobby. *Me and my shadow,* Christina thought wryly. It was comforting that he thought it was as hilarious as she did.

"How'd it go, cutie?"

"Oh, the usual psychobabble bullshit. And don't call me 'cutie.' "

"Whatever you say, sugar."

"Apparently the fact that David keeps giving me rings that suck means I secretly don't want to be married."

"Oh. Well, uh —"

"Don't you start," she warned, shrugging into her coat. They stepped into the warm (for Alaska) spring day. "Listen, do you not actually have a job anymore? Because you've been here almost two weeks. Not that I don't love it, but I don't want you to get in trouble."

"I toldja. My boss thinks this is great P.R., so I'm here as long as the king wants me to play bodyguard. Besides," he added, slinging an arm companionably around her shoulders, "I'da stayed anyway. I think you might be in over your head."

"Tell me. It's —"

*Pop!*

"Don," she said patiently, "I've asked you not to do that."

"Back off with the camera," Kurt ordered, his left hand disappearing into his jacket as, with his right hand, he blocked the lens. "Right now."

"Whoa," she said, tugging on his arm until it came down. "Don't go all Sean Penn on me. This is Don Cook — he's a local news guy. And, inconceivably, taking pictures of me helps him feed his family."

"Everybody's gotta make a living," Don said, firing off another picture. "I couldn't help overhearing —"

"Our completely private conversation."

"Does this mean the wedding's off?"

"No," she said irritably. "It means I haven't found a ring I like yet. Write this down in your little book, Don-o — my promise to marry made me engaged, not a rock weighing down my finger."

"So it's still on?"

"Three weeks to go," she said, and managed to conceal the shudder. Three weeks . . . and she still didn't know the prince much better than the day she'd met him. Trouble was, she had a sneaking suspicion that was her fault more than his. "And FYI, your invitation really did get lost in the mail."

Don laughed. "Sure. Later, Lady Christina."

"See you around, Don."

Kurt was shaking his head as they walked toward the car. "Lady . . . man, I still can't get used to that."

"Wait 'til they start with the princess stuff."

"You know, Chris, it's not too late. Say the word, and we're on a plane to L.A."

"Thanks, Kurt, I appreciate that, but it

was my decision and I made it. And I'm sticking with it."

"It's just . . . sometimes you don't seem like an excited bride-to-be."

"Don't let my moody, depressive, bitchy exterior fool you. Inside, I'm crying with happiness."

"Ha!"

"Things will settle down," she said doubtfully, "after the wedding."

"Well. The offer still stands, you know."

"Is this 'get Chris off the hook' day? Did I miss a memo?"

"I figure the doctor and me are just worried about you, is all."

She studied him, her old friend, former lover, current cop and bodyguard. There had been a time when she would have stripped him of his sidearm and cheerfully shot him in the kneecap. Kurt was a California surfer-boy-turned-man to the nth degree; as far as she knew, he really *was* God's gift to women. Certainly he was one of the best-looking men she'd ever run across in her many travels.

And who knows what could have been, if he'd been able to keep his hands to himself? Or at least, only on her?

But she liked this better. It was so nice to have a friend nearby, one who knew her before she was (blare of trumpets, please) the Lady Christina. Although she knew intellectually that Kurt was yummier than a triple hot fudge sundae, she no longer felt it.

Instead, whenever she thought yummy thoughts, images of David popped up in her head. It was annoying and distracting, especially since she had no idea how he truly felt about her, and was too embarrassed to ask.

Dr. Pohl probably would have said it wasn't embarrassment, it was a poor sense of her own worth, and a fear of hearing an honest answer.

But what did a board-certified shrink with four degrees know? So the woman made a lucky guess once in a while. Now she was Christina's personal oracle? Uh-uh.

"I just want you to know," Kurt was saying, "that offer to take a plane to L.A. still stands, anytime. Day or night. You just say the word, we're out of here."

"Thanks." She squeezed his arm, then let go — it was his gun arm. "You're the best."

"Yup. Keep it in mind," he added with a grin.

# Chapter 20

Kurt walked her back to her room, dropped a brotherly kiss to her forehead, and disappeared for parts unknown after admonishing her to beep him when she wanted to go somewhere again. But the only place Chris wanted to go was bed . . . she had a splitting headache and needed a nap. Possibly two. She hadn't . . . well, she hadn't been sleeping well lately.

There was a black velvet ring box in the middle of her (made) bed.

"Dammit," she muttered. A) she'd been after the chambermaids to leave her room alone, and B) another ring.

She sighed and picked the box up. She ran through her litany of excuses: it's not me, it feels funny on my hand, I don't like the setting, I don't like the band, it's too expensive, it's —

Oh.

She'd popped the lid open and stared hungrily at the ring. It was — it was just fine. In fact, it was beautiful. A largish, light blue stone, set in a simple silver setting. After months of turning down rings, she knew good cut and clarity when she saw it. The blue stone — topaz? aquamarine? — was about two carats. A little larger than she would have liked, but not embarrassingly so.

She slid it on her finger. It fit perfectly. The stone caught the natural light in her room and seemed to wink at her.

Oh, it was . . . it was just . . .

Oh.

Two hours later, she sagged to a stop outside Al's office, then rapped on the door. For a wonder, he was in — usually he had snuck off to fish by this time of the day.

"What's up?" he asked, glumly signing paper after paper.

"You know what you need? You need a computer like on *Star Trek*. You know how the captain says, 'Computer, locate Commander Riker,' and the computer says, 'Commander Riker is boinking Troi in the holodeck,' or whatever? That's what this palace needs."

"Who can't you find?"

"Who d'you think? Your son! I've looked everywhere and I'm fucking exhausted!"

"Not just run-of-the-mill exhausted?"

the king asked, grinning a little. "Fucking exhausted?"

"I'm going to ignore that with the dignity it doesn't deserve. He's not in the penguin room, he's not in the gallery, the cooks told me he ate hours ago but he hasn't left the grounds, Edmund doesn't have a clue, Jenny just used the opportunity to bug me about shoe shopping, and Kurt doesn't know."

"He and his brothers and sisters are at the family plot," Al said. He capped his pen and ignored the overflowing in-bin. "Today is the anniversary of their mother's death."

"Oh." Shit. "Uh . . ." Shit. "Well . . ."

"It's all right. We should have told you. But you'd left to see Dr. Pohl and frankly, we didn't think hanging out at the family crypt was going to be your idea of a good time, so they went without you."

"Well . . . no . . . but . . ." Incredibly, stupidly, she was hurt that the prince hadn't asked her to come. She was going to be his wife. This was her dead future mother-in-law, after all. And he'd — they'd — left her. Gone off and left her. "Well. I'm sorry to barge in and all . . ."

"No prob, Chris. You're welcome in here anytime."

"Is there — how come you aren't there now?"

"I went this morning," the king said quietly.

"Oh." She could feel her face getting red; this was turning into one of the most painfully embarrassing scenes she'd ever been in the middle of. And she'd been in the middle of plenty. "Okay. Well . . . thanks for letting me know. Sorry to interrupt your work. What are you doing, anyway?"

"Signing bills into laws. You know, regular paperwork."

"Sure. Regular paperwork. Okay. Well, see ya later."

"Stay out of trouble," he said absently, already back at work.

"Too late," she muttered, closing the door behind her. Where she promptly ran into Edmund. "Geeyah! *Must* you sneak up on me like a goddamned ghoul all the time?"

"Yes, my lady. A moment of your time?"

"Why didn't you tell me the prince was hanging out by his mom's grave, fool?"

Edmund blinked in surprise. "I didn't think he still was." He glanced at his watch. "Hmm. Well, I'm sure he'll be back soon."

"Well, good. I need to talk to him. Check this out!" She proudly flashed her ring. "Isn't it great?"

"Praise the Lord — the lady has made a selection."

"I've told you a zillion times, stop talking about me in the third person. What do you want, anyway?"

"I'd like you to come along with me and approve your apartments."

"My what?" She fell into step beside him, which wasn't easy because he had a stride like an ostrich.

"Where you and His Highness will live after the wedding."

"Oh. We're living here? Is that what David wants?"

"I would imagine so, my lady, as he's the one who gave the orders for these apartments to be finished well before your wedding day."

"Thanks for asking, Dave," she mumbled.

"Beg pardon, my lady?"

"Nothing. So, we're gonna live here? All the time? Not that I mind, because this is a really nice place, and it's plenty big enough for all of us, but . . ."

"The prince also has homes in Boston, London, Prince Edward Island, and Rome."

"Coastal towns," she said.

"Well. His Highness *is* a marine biologist."

"Yeah, so I've heard."

"My ears are burning," someone said from behind them. Edmund didn't break stride, but Christina whirled.

"David! There you are. I've been looking all over the place for you. Literally, all over the place. What's this about living at the palace after we get married?"

"What's this about honeymooning in New York?"

"Well, I was gonna run it by you," she muttered.

"Ditto."

He fell into step beside her. Today, interestingly, he was wearing a black suit, which set off his dark hair superbly. He was freshly shaved and she caught the clean, sharp smell of his aftershave lotion.

"So, um, how'd it go at the cemetery?"

"As well as could be expected. I'm sorry, I thought you had our schedule for the day."

"I don't read them," she admitted.

"Ah."

"Hey, listen, Dave, I love the ring."

His brow furrowed. "Which one?"

"This one," she said, showing him her

hand. "It's the greatest. And the latest! Thanks a million. I hope it didn't — you know — it wasn't too much trouble to find."

"No." He smiled, took her hand, looked at it for a moment, squeezed it, let go. "It wasn't. I'm glad you like it. You're keeping this one, then?"

"You bet I am!"

"Wonderful. Did you show it to Kurt?"

"Not yet — I just got back and saw it. Well . . . just got back three hours ago, I mean. I've been looking *everywhere* for you." He was finally loosening up a bit; she was relieved to see it.

"I'm sorry you thought I was lost in the dungeons."

"Uh . . . you don't really have dungeons, do y —"

"Edmund is taking you to our apartments?"

"Yeah. I'm sure they'll be fine, but listen, we don't have to live here, like, three hundred and sixty-five days a year, do we?"

"No, of course not."

"Okay. Maybe you'll show me your house in Boston sometime."

"*Our* house," he corrected, and slipped an arm around her waist.

She rested her head on his shoulder. "I really love the ring."

"I'm really relieved."

"What's the stone? Blue topaz?"

"Blue diamond," he corrected. "I thought it would bring out your eyes. And the setting is platinum."

Whoa. So, instantly, ten times more expensive than her estimate. Well, okay. She loved the ring. All the more so because it meant David had finally started paying attention.

"I didn't know there were blue diamonds."

"They're rare. Like you."

"Oh, David, that's so . . . God, that's really . . . just so . . ." They stopped walking; his face was coming closer, his hand was sliding through her hair, gripping the back of her neck, his lips parted, she leaned toward him, and —

"Ah-*hem!*"

David jerked back. Christina glared. "What?"

"Your rooms, sir. My lady. As in, why don't you get a room. Well, here it is."

"Hilarious," she said sourly.

Big surprise, the rooms were huge, gorgeous, amazing, wonderful, blah-blah. She had a moment of blushing confusion when she looked at the king-sized bed — if she had to live with this sexual tension much longer, the prince was going to be raped on his wedding night. But overall the suite — "apartments," they called them — were terrific. There was a large bedroom the size of the average American's living room, a palatial bathroom done in golds and (sigh) a sealife motif, a small kitchen where she could whip up some snacks, two offices (what the hell she was expected to do in hers she had no idea), and a small living room with a fireplace and big, plush couches.

"Edmund, it's wonderful," David was saying. "You've outdone yourself."

"Then it's an ordinary day, Highness. I'm pleased you're pleased."

"Yeah, it's great . . . um, what am I supposed to do in my office?"

"Whatever you want," David said, looking surprised at the question.

"Uh-huh. And what are you going to do in yours?"

"My work," he replied seriously.

"An addendum to Nesting Habits of *Aptenodytes patagonicus?*"

"You remembered the name of my paper!" he cried, so delighted he gave her a squeeze.

"Duh. But y'know, David, it's great that you're doing all this research and stuff, and

I'm glad your papers are getting published because you work really hard on them, but what am I supposed to do? I don't have a job anymore, and you guys wouldn't let me cook for large numbers anyway . . . shit, I can barely get the cooks to let me make myself a sandwich. What's my job? There's got to be more to it than 'crown princess of Alaska.' Right?"

"Dad will probably start training both of us on the day-to-day running of the country."

She tried not to look appalled.

"The legislature does most of it," Edmund added. "But the sovereign — or sovereigns, in our case — has some duties, official and otherwise."

"Oh."

"Alaska is large," Edmund reminded her, "but its population is small. So you won't be christening boats or snipping ribbons on new buildings terribly often."

"It's nothing to worry about," David said. Then he frowned. "Okay, that's not exactly true. But it's nothing *you* can't handle — how's that?"

"Slightly less terrifying."

"My lady, trust me on this if in nothing else: you would not be marrying the prince in thirty-seven days if the king had found you wanting. The fact that you're still here bodes well . . . for all of us."

"Swell. I don't suppose I can fire the cook and take over his job, can I?"

"No. Besides, I hate to see a grown man cry," Edmund said, glancing at his watch. "Particularly before dinnertime."

Hours later, she found the family plot. It was set on the far eastern edge of the palace property, practically *in* the lake. It was, as she expected, beautiful. What in Alaska wasn't? Shoot, living in this place was like living in a glossy travel magazine.

She ignored the pressing feeling of not belonging. Like it or not (and she liked it . . . she was pretty sure . . . ), this was soon to be *her* family. She had as much right to be here as anybody. More, maybe.

Even if they hadn't invited her. Even if they'd gone off and left her — and was she a part of this family or wasn't she?

Maybe not.

Queen Dara's mausoleum was set between two soaring trees and, even with twilight coming on, looked sedate rather than scary.

Christina sat cross-legged on the small hill behind the stone building, and thought about dead queens.

*I must be out of my mind. One day I'll be queen and then I'll die and they'll stick me back here. What was I thinking about? This is no place for me.*

Then her forthright nature reasserted itself. To paraphrase JFK, if not her, who? Sure, she didn't have the pedigree for the job, but that didn't mean she couldn't be great.

Well, adequate.

"That's my goal," she said aloud, watching the grass wave. "Adequacy. All right, then."

She stayed by the mausoleum for a long time.

# Chapter 21

"*One*-two-three, *one*-two-three, *one*-two-three —"

"Ow!" Princess Alexandria complained. "You stomped my foot *again,* you klutzy cow!"

"One more bovine insult," Christina warned through gritted teeth — she was still counting in her head — "and you're the only Alaskan princess with dentures."

"Well, pay attention!"

"— two-three, *one*-two-three —"

"Owwwwww! Will you for Christ's sakes let me lead?"

"No."

"Edmund, why are you letting her lead?" Alexandria cried. "My brother's not going to let her lead, you can be damned sure of that."

"— two-three, *one* — because I like to live dangerously, Your Highness — two-three, *one*-two-three, *one*-two-three —"

"Edmund!"

"Stop bitching and count," Christina said.

"I can't count — I'm distracted by the fact that my shoes are filling up with blood."

"Look — I gotta learn to waltz. And if I danced with Edmund, I wouldn't be able to see past his belly button."

"Why isn't David in here teaching you?"

"*One*-two-three, *one*-two-three, *one*-two-three — because His Highness already knows how to waltz."

"Well, so does *my* Highness."

"Yeah," Christina said, "but I want to be able to surprise Dave with my waltzing virtuosity."

"So, you're using a stunt-waltzer?"

"Shut up and count."

"I hate you."

"*One*-two-three, *one*-two-three — we all do, Your Highness — *one*-two-three . . ."

Alex's dark blue eyes — so like David's — flashed dangerously. "It occurs to me that I outrank everyone in this room," she declared. "So I'm just about done with the tootsie torture."

"I can kick your ass and you know it." Christina swooped across the room with Alex. "Hey, I think I'm getting the hang of this!"

"You aren't. Trust me. Where's your bodyguard? Isn't it his job to enter into dangerous situations with you?"

"The last time I danced with Kurt, I kicked him in the balls."

"And . . . turn!"

"Get out!" Alex gasped. "Seriously?"

"Uh-huh. So he's understandably nervous about dancing with me again."

"He's gorgeous."

"He knows it, too, so watch out. Once you get past the 'I'm too sexy for my shirt' bush-wah, he's a pretty nice guy."

"Better friend than lover, huh?"

"Exactly."

"*One*-two-three, *one*-two-three, *one*-two-three — focus, ladies — *one*-two-three, *one*-two-three, *one*-two-three —"

It was, Christina mused, a little like gym class in hell. Certainly the ballroom was big enough, and although she didn't know the name of the waltz that was playing, the one-two-three beat was droning right through her head. Well, she would dare much for David. Waltzes and more!

"My lady? Ah! Here you are." Jenny hurried into the ballroom. The place was as big as a high school gym, and their voices echoed off the walls. Christina had stopped counting after half a dozen chandeliers.

As usual, Jenny was impeccably groomed and dressed in her Tuesday suit: the gray pinstripe with the white blouse, nude-colored pantyhose, black pumps. "Are you ready?"

"No. Go away. I'm busy."

"My lady . . ."

"No."

"My lady, be reasonable. Just this one time."

"Come on, quit bugging me. There's plenty of time."

"I beg to differ," Princess Alexandria said. "You're getting married a week from tomorrow. And don't hold me so tightly, or I'll get my pepper spray."

"You make it sound so damn dire. It's just shoe shopping. Shit, I can do it online in about ten seconds."

"But you haven't. And now we will take care of it ourselves. Be reasonable, my lady — it's one of my duties as a brides-maid."

"And mine, too," Alexandria said cheer-fully. "Kathryn's blowing us off, though — she's got riding lessons this afternoon."

"What's she riding? A Bengal tiger? Is he going to mind when she starts chucking rocks at his head?"

"An Arabian, and very funny. She's only throwing things at you right now."

"Oh, *very* comforting."

"*One*-two-three, *one*-two-three, *one*-two-three —"

Princess Kathryn's reputation preceded her. She was very much King Alexander's daughter. Except, of course, she hardly ever said a word, and tended to express herself by breaking things or throwing food. Chris felt sorry for her, a little . . . trapped in the middle of a rambunctious, larger-than-life family, with a to-die-for gorgeous older sister to boot . . . it was no wonder she expressed herself through mild violence.

But then, Christina thought, it was obvious they were all the king's kids, one way or the other.

"She trusts our selection," Jenny was blathering. "But we need to do it now, this morning."

"Why?"

"Because you're doing the tasting menu this afternoon," Princess Alex pointed out. "And tomorrow's booked with Dr. Pohl and the minister. And the day after, you and David are doing a coronation rehearsal."

"Why?" she whined.

"Because you don't want to look like a big dumb-ass up there when they plop the crown on your head, do you?"

"Oh, God help me," she muttered. She stopped waltzing. Alex immediately sat down on the highly polished floor, took off her tennis shoes, and rubbed her feet. She was wearing white socks, and Christina noted there wasn't a trace of blood anywhere.

"You're interrupting waltzing lessons to go buy footgear?"

"Yes," Jenny and Edmund said firmly.

Great. Sounded like it was going to be a real yawn-o-rama. "Fine, let's get it over with."

"That's the spirit!" Alex cried. She slipped her shoes back on and jumped to her feet. "With a positive attitude like that, you can't go wrong."

"Listen, how come there's a coronation? Aren't I automatically a princess when I marry your big brother?"

"Yup. By law, anyway. But the people like to see a ceremony, something concrete. And Dad always says, when at all possible, give the people what they want."

"*Your* dad says that?"

Alex ignored the sarcastic question. "But like I was saying when I was so rudely interrupted by a commoner, by law, the second you say 'I do', you're the crown princess of Alaska."

"Lovely."

"Relax. It'll be cake."

"Sure it will."

"You'll be a splendid princess," Jenny assured her. "Otherwise, His Highness would have — um — I'll go get the car."

"Otherwise His Highness would have tossed me out on my ass by now, huh?" Christina asked Alex, who nodded without a trace of a smile.

"Should we bring your bodyguards, or mine?"

"Mine," Chris said firmly. "Yours all look like they've been embalmed."

"They do not! They just take their jobs very seriously."

"Sure. So they got embalmed."

"I have the swatches right here," Jenny said, patting her tote bag, which bulged in all directions rather alarmingly.

"What the hell is a swatch?"

"We'll tell you," Alex said, slipping her arm through Christina's, "on the way."

# Chapter 22

Christina staggered into her room three hours later, utterly exhausted. Argh! A whole morning she would never, ever get back. Wasted on shopping. Shopping for *shoes.* Why not just hit her over the head until she lost consciousness? That would have been quicker. And kinder!

She opened her top drawer, intent on showering and changing to get the smell of Mall off her, and nearly shrieked. She caught movement out of the corner of her eye, leapt backward, and just managed to catch Prince Nicholas by the back of his hooded sweatshirt as he sprinted for the door.

She yanked. Nicky made a sound — Yark! — and she shook him like a maraca.

"Dammit, you little perv! You keep out of my drawers, understand? Stop. Rearranging. My. Clothes." Each word was punctuated by a shake.

"Awwww, Chris, come on! You can't keep your cottons with your silks. It's unnatural — yark!"

"I give a shit! And it's unnatural that a twelve-year-old boy should care about this stuff. I mean it, Nicky. At first I thought this strange obsession you had with my clothing was cute, but now I'm getting a first-class case of the creeps. How'd *you* like to have to go talk to Dr. Pohl every week?"

"I wouldn't," he admitted. "She looks like a nice grandma, but I think she's scary."

"Agreed. So cut. It. Out."

"You should be nicer to me," he burst out, his small, sneakered feet swinging a foot in the air. "My mom's dead."

"Join the club, pal," she said grimly. "No special treatment from *me*."

He stopped kicking his feet. "I forgot about your mama, Chris," he said, chastised. "I'm sorry."

"It's all right. But remember what I said. One more time, and I rat you out to the king and he makes you go talk to a shrink instead of going out fishing with the guys."

"Okay. Um . . . Chris . . . can I ask you something about your family?"

She set him down, but kept a grip on his sweatshirt hood, just in case. "Sure."

"Do you look like your mom or your dad?"

She blinked. "Neither. My mom was short and had long, straight dark hair, and brown eyes. My dad was a redhead with green eyes."

"*You* have green eyes. Except sometimes they're blue."

"Anyway, I look like my grandpa."

"Oh. Because I don't look like my fa— I mean, some people say I look like my mom's side of the family," he finished lamely.

"Well, 'some people' are idiots, Nicky. Do you know what a recessive gene is? No? Okay, it's why I look like my grandpa instead of my dad. And it's why you look like your grandma — or is it your great-grandma? I can never remember . . . anyway, it's why you look like her instead of your dad."

"Because . . . because I don't look anything like my brothers or sisters. They're all dark and I'm not."

She blinked down at him. It was obvious this was a big deal to him, but if *she* made it a big deal, that would be a mistake. So she let out an exasperated sigh and said, "Nicky, it's like I said. It's recessive genes. It doesn't mean anything. Besides, you think your dad cares if you're a blonde or a brunette? Got news, punk — he doesn't.

Not even a little bit. And I know plenty of people who would *kill* for your hair. Natural blond curls . . . it makes me mad just to look at you."

"Okay." He grinned. "You shouldn't call me a punk."

"I'll call you whatever the hell I want, you little —"

"Want me to shoot him?"

They both looked up. Kurt was leaning in the doorway, grinning.

"Can I see your gun?" Nicky asked, instantly distracted.

"Sure." Kurt pulled it from his shoulder holster, checked the safety, ejected the slide, ejected the bullet from the chamber, then handed the empty gun to the prince and bent to pick up the round on the carpet. "That's a Beretta, nine millimeter."

"I know. It's nice."

"You always said shoulder holsters were for TV," Chris commented. "Said it was impossible to get a quick draw from them."

"Well." Kurt shrugged. "I practiced. And that's not a problem anymore. D'you know the king gave that gun to me? He had that tall, skinny, scary guy —"

"Edmund," Nicky and Chris said in unison.

"— right, him. He had that guy check on

what I had back in L.A., and got me two new ones. One to carry, and a spare."

"Daddy said since we wrecked your vacation, you should get something nice out of it," Nicky volunteered. He handed the gun back to Kurt, butt-first. "It's nice, but I like the thirty-eights better."

Chris covered her eyes. "Oh, don't tell me."

"It's okay," Nicky said. "I'm only allowed to practice on the range, with my gun instructor."

"I feel *so* much better. I guess it's not in the king to let one of his kids take up a normal habit, like gardening."

Nicky snorted. "I'm going now."

"So go."

"Well, 'bye. 'Bye, Kurt."

"See ya, Nick." Once Nicholas had left, Kurt added, "Nice kid."

"In a mildly creepy way, yes. D'you know, yesterday he asked me to wait for him to grow up so *he* could marry me?"

"There's a lot of that going around."

"Oh, ha-ha. What are you doing up here?"

"Wondered if you wanted to go a few rounds in the gym. Figured you might need it after all that shopping."

"Oh, God," she said gratefully. "You have *no* idea."

"So I picked out a pair — unf! — right away, right? And they're perfectly *fine*. But nooooo, because they didn't cost six hundred bucks, they're unacceptable. Jenny's all — unf! — 'they're not suitable to your station,' whatever the hell that means."

"And Jenny — oof! — would be . . . ?"

"Protocol officer-slash-bridesmaid-slash-pain in my neck. Short, maybe up to your shoulders? Always wears severe suits? Looks weirdly like Shania Twain?"

"Oh! Right. The babe who looks kind of harassed all the time."

"That's her."

"She's cute."

"She's a pain. But yeah — cute, too. Want me to fix you up?"

"Naw. She looks a little too tense for me."

"She says she — unf! — loves her job," Chris said doubtfully. "But she goes through, like, a bottle of Advil a week."

Kurt swung; she ducked and socked a foot into his groin. He caught the blow on the outside of his thigh and his fist pistoned out. She sidestepped, and kicked his feet out from under him.

"You're not a brown belt anymore," he groaned after he hit the floor.

"Oh, did I forget to mention?" she asked oversolicitously. "Got my black two years ago."

"Bitch."

"Whiner."

She was too busy chortling over her little surprise to sidestep his sweeping kick, and now her butt was in the dirt. Well, on the gym mats.

"So then we go to this hoity-toity store in Juneau, a store so stuffy they don't even have their name on the door. There was a freaking chandelier on the ceiling — how's that for dumb?"

"I was there," Kurt reminded her.

"So what happens?" She braced her hands, rocked back, then flipped to her feet.

"I love that trick," Kurt said admiringly, still prone. "You look like Buffy the Vampire Slayer when you do that trick."

"Yeah, yeah." She bent to pull him up. "So what happens? Sixty-five pairs of shoes later, I pick out a pair that looked *exactly* like the pair at Payless, only these cost seven hundred bucks! And everyone's all, ooooooh, they're perfect, blah-blah, and I'm all, hello? What's the difference? And you know, you know what was *really* bad?"

"They told you," Kurt said, yanking her

forward so she collapsed on the mat beside him.

"I know! I heard more about seam stitching and hand-tooling than I ever wanted to know. Plus, they're not even the right color — they're white."

"I know. They're going to dye them to match your dress."

"Right. Frankly, I'm amazed they let me go with flats at all."

"That *is* amazing."

"I know! But I put my foot down on that one. Literally. No high heels. I'm going to be uncomfortable enough."

"You're so cute when you're all huffy and annoyed."

"Shut up," she said irritably, batting his hand away. "I was hoping for a little more sympathy."

"Babe, you got all my sympathy." He reached out again — weird! What was with him today? — and she jumped to her feet.

"Come on, let's finish up. I want a shower and then I have to do the tasting menu, God help me."

Kurt climbed slowly to his feet. "You know, Chris, you really don't seem very happy here."

"Eh? Well, I am. I mean, I'm stressed, sure, but I guess all brides are. There's a lot to do, and frankly, I'm not interested in very much of it."

"Exactly."

"What?"

His face was getting closer to hers. Kissing distance — how was that for weird? She stared as his face loomed like a moon, as it came closer, and when she finally figured out, yes, he really meant to do it, it was too late — she couldn't *believe* he was doing it, and was frozen to inaction, and then his mouth was on hers, and then she could move, did move.

"Owwwwwwww!"

"What. Do you think. You're doing."

"Shit, Chris, my fucking nose!"

She kicked him in the shin as hard as she could for good measure, then shoved. He went over like a bowling pin.

"Goddammit!"

"Don't you ever. *Ever.* Do that again."

"Jesus Christ!" He peered up at her from the floor, hands cupped below his nose to catch the blood. "How could you do that?"

"How could *I* do that? What the hell is wrong with you? You know I'm engaged, you know we're done — you're supposed to be my *friend,* and you put the moves on me in *my fiancé's own home?*"

"I just — I thought —"

"You didn't think. You never think when it comes to pussy. You just see what you want and you try to take it. And some-times — most times — it gets you into trouble. But you never learn, do you?" She tried to keep yelling, burst into tears instead. "How could you?"

She ran out, but didn't get far — her eyes were swelling and so teary she couldn't see, and was shocked when she banged into something hard.

Al's chest.

Worse, David was standing next to him.

Al took one look at her, one look at Kurt, thrust her aside, and started forward.

"Don't you dare," David said, and now *he* was pulling Al back, and starting for Kurt.

"Fuck that. My country, my house, my guest."

"My fiancée."

"Well, you can have the second shot."

"No."

"Stop!" she shrieked. "No more shots! I took care of it!"

"Hush, Chris," Al said absently.

"Never mind, Chris," David said, equally absently.

They bent as one man and hauled Kurt up. He went as easily as if he were made of helium. But then she was there, and tugging on their shoulders. "You guys, don't! I said, I took care of it. Look, he's sorry — see how he's sorry?"

"So, so sorry," Kurt added, then coughed and spat a sizeable glob of blood and mucous onto the mat.

"Not sorry enough," Al said, cocking a fist the size of a grapefruit.

"Quite right," David said. "He's still conscious. How sorry can he be?"

"I mean it, you two! Quit it, now!" Using every ounce of her strength, she managed to move them an inch or two away from a now-terrified Kurt. "It's my problem, my personal private problem, and I took care of it, now get lost!"

"Boy, have you lost your damned mind?" Al asked Kurt.

"Uh . . . yes. Yes, I have."

"Talking is one thing," David said. "Putting your lips on my girl, however, is entirely unacceptable."

"Yes," Kurt said, the flesh around his nose beginning to swell. "I see that now."

"It's not so much the kiss — although we'll be kicking your ass for that in a minute — it's making her cry." Al paused, then added, "I didn't think she *could* cry."

"No, it's the kiss," David said.

"Well, look. You work him over for the kiss, and then I'll work him over for making the kid cry. Deal?"

"Deal."

"Hold it!" Christina snapped. "Are either of you two going to bother to ask me what I want? Or are you too high on testosterone overload?"

"Uh . . ."

"Well . . ."

"I told you, but you *don't listen.* You never *listen.* I took care of it. Kurt's sorry. It won't happen again."

"*God,* no," Kurt added.

"And that's the end of it. Now — take your hands off him. *Right* now."

There was no denying the dry bark of authority in her tone; Al and David let go at once, Al looking faintly surprised, David expressionless.

"And you." Kurt flinched as she poked a finger toward his face. "This isn't fatal. I'm pissed, but will get over it . . . I just need some chocolate. And I don't want them to use this as a chance to kick you out of the country. I'd like you to stay, if you think you can behave yourself. If you can't, leave now. Tonight. Understand?"

"Yes," Kurt said, looking at her as if he'd never seen her before. He added, "I'm sorry. I guess I got my signals mixed up."

"Don't lie. You've been waiting for a chance, and you grabbed it as soon as you could."

"Uh . . . okay."

"Don't ever do it again, Kurt. Not ever."

"Okay."

She turned on her heel, and left.

"Uh . . . either of you guys know where I can get some ice?"

Later, David found her crying facedown on her ridiculously expensive bedspread, stuck a DO NOT DISTURB Post-It note on the outside of her door, blocked her doorknob with a chair for good measure, undressed, helped her undress, and held her for a long time. When the crying was done the kissing started, followed by the stroking, and the petting, and finally the thrusting.

They rode each other to orgasm, and never said a word, both deeply involved in their own thoughts.

David's: *She's mine. I'll kill him if he tries to take her away. I might kill him anyway, if she's still upset later.*

Christina's: *Stupid Kurt. Well, I guess he's learned, and at least David didn't shoot him or anything. I wonder if there's any of that chocolate fudge left?*

# PART THREE

# *Princess*

Ladies and gentlemen of the court, honored guests, may I present to you the bride and groom: His Highness, Prince David, and Her Highness, Princess Christina.

— Jennifer Smythe,
Court Protocol Officer

# Chapter 23

"This is so totally embarrassing," Kurt said, rubbing his eyes.

"Indeed, sir?"

"What am I doing here? I mean, she practically knocks my block off, makes it clear I'm on her shit list, and she's been *merciless* with the teasing. Not to mention the prince is giving me the ole hairy eyeball every time we run into each other. So why didn't I get on a plane and go back to L.A.?"

"Lady Christina did not wish it, sir."

"Yeah, yeah." He sighed. Sometimes he thought he'd gone as cuckoo as the royal family. If he'd half a brain he would have left as soon as the swelling went down. Instead, Chris insisted he stay, telling him the devil she knew was better, whatever the fuck that meant.

And . . . if he was going to be 100 percent truthful . . . he stayed to redeem himself. To prove that he wasn't what she'd said: a pussy hound with no conscience. That foxy Princess Alex had put a few moves on him, but he'd treated her like she was radioactive. Her father wasn't just a big guy, he could, like, bomb California or something.

So here he was, standing outside Christina's rooms with Edmund.

He knocked on the door.

Silence.

He knocked harder.

Silence.

Edmund said loudly, "We're coming in, my lady!" and — whoa! — opened the door and walked in. Brave dude!

Not knowing Chris as well as he thought he did, Edmund tiptoed over to the head of the bed. "My lady? It's time."

"Unffff, unfff," she muttered.

Kurt walked to the foot of the bed and pulled the comforter up, revealing Christina's sleep-lined face. "Aaggh! I mean, good morning."

"Go 'way," she grumped.

Edmund gingerly picked up the comforter on his end and gazed at her feet. "I think, first, a pedicure."

"S'not time t'get up yet."

"Oh, yes it is, sunshine!" Kurt flinched as her filmy gaze landed on him. "Uh . . . I forgot how . . . um . . . dewy fresh you look in the morning."

"Shut the hell up. Both of you pervs, get lost." She started to worm her way back under the bedclothes.

"Ah-ah-ah!" he sang. "You ignored your alarm clock, so Eds and I got the duty. It's time to get married!"

"Dammit."

"Quite so, my lady, but we all have distasteful tasks we must attend to. Now come along."

"Is it really," she sighed, "April second? Already?"

" 'Fraid so, cutie." From Kurt.

"It seems like I just got here."

"Really?" From Edmund. "It seems like you've been here an eternity. A joyful eternity."

"Shaddup. Where's David? Whyn't you go wake *him* up?"

"His Highness has been up for four hours, my lady."

"Figures. Kurt, what the hell? Are you in here waking me up because you carry a sidearm?"

"I was specifically recruited for this hideously dangerous mission, yes," Kurt admitted.

"Smart of 'em," she said grudgingly, and tossed back the bedclothes, and stood, and yawned.

Both men stepped back from the bed.

"What?" the future member of the royal family snapped.

"Nothing, my lady. You're as . . . refreshing . . . as always."

"Nothing," Kurt added, "except . . . could you go brush your teeth? Like, right now?"

"Assholes," she grumbled, and stumbled toward the bathroom.

Christina sat up abruptly, and the makeup artist nearly put her eye out with the eyeliner pencil. "Wow! Alex, Kath, Jenn . . . you guys look *awesome!*"

Kathryn and Alex, doubtless used to looking unbelievably, mouthwateringly gorgeous, just shrugged. Jenny blushed to her hairline. The dresses Horrance had designed set off the women's coloring superbly . . . all three had dark hair, and Kathryn and Alex had the Baranov blue eyes. Jenny's big, dark eyes seemed to swallow up half her face, and she was very white. Even for her.

"Jenn, why don't you sit down before you fall down? You okay?"

"Fine, my lady. It's just . . . there are several details . . . my list . . . I must find my list . . ."

"Siddown," Alex said, while Kathryn looked on with concern. "Naomi!"

A maid poked her head into the dressing room. "Highness?"

"Get Jenny something to drink and something for her stomach."

"At once, Highness."

"My lady . . . if you could *please* sit still . . ."

"Okay, okay." Christina slumped back. It was extremely weird to be fussed over by a stranger while she was sitting in her underwear. Well, at least Edmund wasn't doing her makeup. "I don't see why we have to do this, anyway. I'm perfectly capable of putting on my own makeup."

"Do you even know," Alex said, smirking, "which end of a mascara wand goes on your lashes?"

"Ohhhh, that's *so* funny I forgot to laugh."

"How old are you?" Alex muttered.

"The minister wants to talk to you," Kathryn added.

Christina nearly fell out of her chair. Kathyrn spoke! Without hurling eye shadow! It truly was a historic occasion. "Well, he can't. I'm in a damn bustier and panties and thigh-high stockings. He can just wait until I've got a few more clothes on."

"He's a man of God," Kathryn said. "He wouldn't give a shit if you had a rose in your teeth."

"Man of God, not eunuch. Besides, David gets weird about stuff like that. And your *father!* Cripes, don't get me started. And my, aren't we chatty today? What's gotten into you?"

"Well," Kathryn considered carefully, "it appears you're going to be here awhile."

"Oh, so now I'm worthy of speech, huh? That's just —"

"Close your mouth, please," the makeup gal said, and she obliged, and submitted to lip-liner. It gave her a chance to study Kathryn. Of all the royal siblings, she knew Kathryn and her brother, Alexander, the least. Because, of course, they were the most like David: stand-offish and cool. Pleasant (when she wasn't throwing pastries), but distant.

Kathryn was a smaller, slighter version of her sister Alexandria. Currently mired in her teens, she was a breath away from the promise of true gorgeousness. Once those braces came off, Chris figured the king would start stockpiling rifles. Meanwhile, it couldn't be much fun to be in Princess Alex's shadow. *Maybe that's why she didn't talk much,* Chris mused. *With everybody busy staring at her big sister, why bother?*

"And . . . done!"

"Thanks," she said, practically leaping up from the chair. "I can't remember the last time I had to sit still for so long. Oh, wait . . . yesterday. For rehearsal."

There was a rap at the door, and then Horrance was striding in, followed by three assistants, all lugging a flat black bag.

"Good morning, my lady! Your Highnesses," he added, bowing to Kathryn and Alex.

"Horrance, take a powder. I'm not dressed."

"Eh? No, of course not, I've got your dress right here."

"That looks like a body bag," she said suspiciously.

"I can assure you it isn't." He scooted behind Alex — he was a full four inches shorter — and did something to the back of her dress. Alex's neckline immediately straightened. "Ah . . . much better, Highness."

The dresses really were amazing, Christina thought. The deep blue brought out the princess's eyes (although, unfortunately, it was also accentuating Jenny's pallor), and the square necklines were very flattering.

"Nice jewelry," she commented. Her bridesmaids were all wearing square blue topazes on gold chains so fine, it seemed like the large stones were hovering in the hollow of their throats. Their earrings were smaller topazes.

"David designed them for us," Kathryn said absently.

"He did? Really?"

"Uh-huh. He's got something for you, too — ow!"

"Sorry," Alex said. "My elbow slipped."

"Right into my ribs, thanks very much." She glared at her big sister.

"Quit it, you guys," Chris ordered. "One bitch per wedding, that's the rule. And it's me, in case you didn't get the memo."

"At least we *read* the memos," Kathryn sniffed.

"Shaddup."

"You sounded exactly like my father when you said that."

"Awwww. Now you're gonna make me cry."

Kathryn dropped the faux world-weary pose and snickered. Horrance clapped his hands, which made Chris jump. Thank God the makeup lady had put the mascara wand away!

"Ladies! Step back, please, we need some room here. Ah, that's very good. Now, my lady, if you'll just stand and turn . . . like so . . . yes, a little more . . . uh-huh . . . okay . . ."

"Could you not get so close to me?" she whined. "I'm nearly naked, if you didn't notice."

"Eh? Oh, it doesn't matter."

"So . . . you *didn't* notice."

"Now turn — wait!" He slipped two impersonal fingers into her bodice and jerked it up, nearly pulling her off her feet. Day-amn! He was short, but he was strong. "Much better."

"Could you please," she asked politely, "get your hand off my boobs?"

"Yes, yes. Now turn . . . very good . . . and step . . . like so . . . yes . . . now stand still . . . ladies, some help, please . . . yes . . . no, not that one, the little button-hook . . ."

*"Buttonhook?"*

"You didn't think I was going to put a zipper into this dress, did you?" he replied, sounding aggrieved. She could feel him doing something behind her with his nimble fingers. It seemed she stood for an eternity until he finally said, "And . . .

*there*. Very good — turn around, please . . ."

He stepped back and looked her up and down with a critical eye.

"I feel like an extra in *Queer Eye for the Straight Guy*," she commented.

"Wonderful, wonderful show," Horrance said absently. "Yes. That will do."

"Wow!" Kathryn said, looking dazzled. "That is *wonderful!*"

"You think so? Really?"

"Chris, you look beautiful. The ice-blue really brings out your eyes."

Jenny looked up. "I thought your eyes were green."

"Never mind my eyes." Chris took a tentative step. Everything felt right. Nothing was too tight. She could breathe. Success!

Horrance pulled the matching cape from another body bag and flung it over her shoulders. "There!"

"Ooooooooh," the princesses oooohed.

"Outstanding. Horrance, really, you've outdone yourself."

"Thank you, Jenny." He rubbed his hands together. "I'm going to make a fucking fortune this year." Then he clapped a hand over his mouth, but Christina just laughed.

There was another knock on the door,

and Naomi entered with a tray. "I brought something for everyone," she said. Then she gasped when she saw Christina. "My lady! You look . . ."

"Like a big icicle?"

". . . wonderful!"

"Well, thanks," she said, pleased. "Thanks for the snacks, too."

"My lady, the minister would like to see you, if it's convenient."

"How'd you get out of having a bishop marry you guys?" Alex asked. "That's standard protocol for royal weddings, right?"

"Easy. Cray was the devil I knew, as opposed to . . . you know how it goes. I put my foot down about that one. Send him in. Jenny, have a sandwich. You do *not* look well, pardon me for saying so."

"Stage fright," she said weakly. "Forgive me, my lady. The spotlight isn't even on me, and —"

"Just eat already, willya? I keep expecting you to pitch face-first into the carpet. Or my cleavage."

Horrance and his assistants left, after admonishing everyone not to breathe or move or touch. There was a rap at the door and Minister Cray called, "May I come in?"

"C'mon in!"

He was, if possible, even paler than Jenny, except for the two hectic dots of color on his cheeks. There was a sheen of sweat on his forehead which he continually wiped away with a handkerchief. "Your Highnesses. Jennifer. My lady. You all look lovely."

"Thanks. Have a sandwich."

"No, I — I'd better not. My stomach — I'd better not. My lady, I just wanted to go over a few things with you. As in rehearsal, I will be asking you some questions, and then — then I'll — as we did yesterday, I'll —" He fumbled with his note cards and sprayed them all over the room.

"Whoa! Easy there, Cray, you look even more freaked out than I feel."

"I've never been on television before," he said weakly.

"You'll be fine. Come on, you've done this a million times."

"Not conduct an historical event, he hasn't," Kathryn commented with bright-eyed malice.

"Quit it, Kath. Go back to being mute — I mean it, now. And I meant weddings. You've done a million weddings."

"Yes, I — that's true. I — oh! I almost forgot! The prince asked me to give this to you." He held out the dark blue velvet box, and Christina took it.

"Thanks." *Now what the heck was this?* She opened the box and nearly gasped. It was a choker, set in platinum, with ice-blue diamonds as big as the first joint of her thumb set every two inches. "Oh my God! Sorry, Cray."

Alex was looking over her shoulder. "Huh. That turned out great."

"Turned out?"

"David designed all the jewelry."

"He *did?*"

"Well, sure. Did you think he just called a catalog and had them surprise him?"

"And my ring?"

"Yes. See, how it works is, when I said *all* the jewelry, I meant *all* the jewelry."

Christina put a hand over her eyes, then jerked it away, mindful of her makeup. "You mean all the rings I . . . I . . ."

"Cruelly rejected?"

"Oh, shit. Sorry, Cray."

Alex shrugged. "Eh, it was good for him. He needed a challenge."

Kathryn snickered.

Jenny had jumped up and taken the box. "Turn around, my lady, I'll put it on for you." She did so, and Chris felt the weight of the stones, cool at first, then warmed by her body.

*Tonight,* Chris thought, *I'll take every-*

*thing off except this.* The thought caused desire to bloom inside her like a black orchid.

"You okay, Chris? You look a little flushed."

"I'm fine." And with any luck, she soon would be.

# Chapter 24

From *The Queen of the Edge of the World*, by Edmund Dante III, © 2089, Harper Zebra and Schuster Publications.

Although Edmund Dante's notes are extensive, he of course could not know every detail, nor record every conversation, of the king and queen's (or prince and princess, as they were then) wedding day. Edmund's notes for that day are surprisingly succinct, ending with, She was as charming a bride as she was a houseguest.

This leaves us no choice but to speculate on what was going through Queen Christina's head in the moments before the wedding began. Was she thinking of her late mother? Or perhaps her future duties as sovereign? Could she truly grasp just how quickly her life would change, or was she merely concentrating on her first turn at center stage?

We will likely never know.

"Jenny, did you know you look an awful lot like Shania Twain?"

"Wh-what?"

"Shania Twain. You're, like, the spitting image of her."

Jenny blushed again. She'd been doing it with distressing regularity this morning. "The American singer? Oh, I — no. No, I don't. She's much prettier."

"Jenny — do you own a mirror?"

"Yes, of course." Jenny looked nervously at her watch. "Still ten minutes, my lady. I — uh — I had something I wanted to tell you, but I can't find my notes."

"You don't need notes to talk to me, you dark-eyed dork."

"Ah — yes. My lady — Christina — I just wanted — um — that is to say — well —"

"Spit it out — you're giving me the fidgets."

"Sorry. It's just — I wanted to thank you again for allowing me to be in your wedding party. My mother — my mother is very pleased. And very honored to be invited, as well," Jenny added.

"Jenn, seriously. We've been over this. It was no big deal."

"It *is* a big deal," she corrected sharply. Chris raised her eyebrows . . . she didn't know Jenny *could* be sharp. "My father died two years ago, and since then my mother hasn't been very interested in — well, anyway, the wedding is all she's been talking about for months. It's nice to see her excited about something again."

"Well, she got a good seat, right?"

"Oh, yes! Yes, she's in the third row, on the left. She's wearing a purple hat. She bought it especially for the occasion."

"Swell."

It was so nice to be out, not just on a lovely day like today, but also to be in attendance at a truly historic occasion. Mrs. Smythe, Jenny's mother, had only one wish: that her dear husband could have been there as well.

Jenny's wedding followed within a year, and soon Mrs. Smythe was enjoying the wonderful distraction of grandchildren. And until the end of her days, she told The Story over and over again. Jenny looked on but never demurred, and Jenny's children — particularly her twin girls — begged many times to hear The Story.

The Story went like this: "Well, I was sitting in the pew, waiting to get a glimpse of the queen — only she wasn't the queen then, don't you know? And when she came down the aisle, she looked almost as pretty as your mother did."

(Jenny would always break into The Story at this point: "Oh, Mother! You know that's not true. On my best day I could never have been as pretty as the queen." And Mrs. Smythe would always say, "Hush up, girl. Nobody's talking to you.")

"She was wearing a beautiful ice-blue gown, and a matching ice-blue cape, and a gorgeous blue choker, and a little crown of diamonds. And she was smiling. A little pale, but a lovely smile. And she found me! She looked in my little aisle, and looked at my hat, and looked at me, and she winked. The queen winked at me on her own wedding day! Why do you think she did that?"

And one of the grandchildren would say, "Because Mama told her you had come to see her get married, and bought a purple hat specially."

"That's right," Mrs. Smythe would say. "That's just right."

Kathryn and Alex had vanished for a final pee break before the big moment. Jenny had been called away to settle the matter of whether Prince Charles should be seated with the Spanish princess or Queen Noor.

So, for the moment — in fact, for the first time since Kurt and Edmund had gotten her up — she was alone.

Alone with her thoughts. Alone to sweat it out. Alone to realize she was in way, way over her head. Alone to . . .

"You believe this?" The king burst in. "Elizabeth didn't come, but she sent her kid. Well, we can talk about hunting at the reception. Too bad he didn't bring the little ones."

"The little ones," she said faintly, "are grown men and over six feet tall."

"Aw, they're punks. *Nice* punks, but still. Hey! Ready to face the enemy?" The king strolled toward her, chortling. "Damn! Kid, you look good enough to — what's wrong?"

"Oh, Al!"

"Jeez, what's the matter? Are you sick?" He hurried across the room and patted her ineffectually. She had time, even in the midst of her sudden, surprising onset of misery, to be amazed: the king was wearing a suit. He actually looked . . . well . . . kingly. "Did you eat something? You gotta eat something."

"It's not that. Oh, Al," she said, resting her face against his broad chest for a moment, then jerking back before she ruined his shirt with makeup. "I don't think I can do it. I really don't. All those people!"

"Bullshit. Christina Krabbe, you never ran away from anything in your life. You're not gonna start now."

"The 'e' is silent," she reminded him, "but thanks for the vote of confidence."

"I'm serious, kiddo. I know it's scary, but it's just an hour or so in front of the cameras, and then it's strictly fun stuff. You know — until I die," he joked.

"Okay. Sorry. I don't know what came over me."

"Hey, you wouldn't be human if you didn't get the fidgets once in a while. 'Specially today of all days. Shit, I was a wreck on my big day."

"You look great, by the way. Like a grown-up and everything."

"Fucking shirt collar is choking me. But thanks. You okay, then? You need anything?"

She managed a smile. "I'm fine. Thanks."

"Okay. See you out there. And Chris — really — David's a lucky boy. You look like a million bucks. In fact, you look like a queen."

She blanched. "Don't say that."

"Right. Sorry. But you do. Okay, sorry. 'Bye."

Mercifully, he left.

Jenny hurried back in, carrying her bouquet of light blue irises, and lugging Christina's bouquet of white and red roses, and dark purple irises. "I just got the word, Your Highness. We're on in three minutes."

"Don't start with that 'Your Highness' stuff," she warned, accepting the bouquet, which weighed approximately six tons.

"I'm well aware of your dislike of titles," Jenny said, smiling shyly. "I just wanted to be the first one to call you that."

"Jenn — get a life. I'm serious."

She laughed, which made Chris laugh. Unlike the demure young lady she presented to the world, Jenny had a whooping, infectious laugh. And for a moment, it was almost like an ordinary day.

"Ready, my lady?" Edmund whispered.

She was frozen, a deer in the headlights. She'd never seen so many people in one room — one enormous, cavernous room — in her life. And she hadn't even entered the room. She was still in the foyer, peeking in.

She knew she was supposed to start walking down the aisle. Everyone was waiting. More important, *David* was waiting.

She couldn't do it. She wouldn't do it. She'd run away. Leave now, today. Hike up into the wilderness . . . in Alaska, there was plenty of it. She knew how to hunt, she knew how to fish. She wouldn't be a princess; she would be a hermit. A smelly blond hermit who had narrowly escaped becoming royalty.

"My lady?" Edmund was looking at her with no small amount of concern.

"Ready," she whispered, with a smile that felt ghastly on her face. Stupid, pointless fantasy. Of course she would go through with it. She had promised, hadn't she? Not in so many words, but the ring she had accepted and wore on her finger was a promise — a promise set in platinum, with blue diamonds.

So — she would get married. And as for the rest of it, for her future job as queen or co-boss of Alaska, like Scarlett, she'd worry about that tomorrow.

The strains of Clarke's *Trumpet Voluntary* filled the air with their rich sweetness, and she started down the aisle. Suddenly there were too many things to look at; her brain struggled to process them all. And her smile felt frozen on her face.

First: the faces. Hundreds of them, all turned toward her. She thanked God she was wearing neither (a) pumps, nor (b) a train.

Then: cameras. All kinds of them. She spotted NBC, CBS, BBC, MSNBC, PBS, and ANB (Alaskan National Broadcasting), and that was just in one glance.

There were funny little flags hanging on the end of each pew . . . navy blue, with a big white letter. Some of them had a C, and some had a D.

Oh, right . . . David and Christina. Huh.

And flowers, flowers everywhere. Masses of roses, piles of irises. The church smelled like a garden. Or a funeral.

She walked, she walked, she would never get to the end of this aisle. She walked alone — that had been tricky. Al had offered to give her away and she'd used all of her tact (what there was of it) to turn him down nicely; she would not walk to her husband clinging like a vine to someone else. No matter how tempting it was. So — she walked alone.

Faces, faces, still more faces — how many people had they crammed in here? She'd thought the church on the palace grounds was enormous; it seemed far too cramped and crowded now. Faces . . . faces . . . hat. Hat. Purple hat. *Purple hat!* Jenny's mom was wearing a purple hat; Chris looked at her, observed that the older woman had Jenny's great dark eyes, and tipped her a wink. The purple hat bobbed in startled response.

She saw Kathryn, she saw Alex, she saw Jenny. She saw Prince Alexander, skinny as a blade in his tux — the boy really should lift weights or something, fill out — she saw the king, she saw Nicky, she saw . . . yes! There he was, at last: David, her groom. *Hers.* Very soon. Finally.

He looked unbelievable. He looked beautiful and kingly and wise and gorgeous and broad-shouldered and clean-shaven and kind and charming, all at once. He towered over nearly everyone, everyone but the king. His hands were clasped behind his back; he looked downright mouthwatering in his tuxedo. Who'da thunk it?

He was smiling at her.

She reached his side. He bent forward and said, for her ear alone, "You look *incredible.*"

She whispered back, "What time does your tux have to be back?"

*People* magazine's photographer caught them giggling at the altar; it was the lead in every entertainment magazine in the world.

# Chapter 25

She was wholly unprepared for the roar that greeted her and David as they entered the Sitka Palace's main ballroom: *"Long live the prince and princess!"*

"Well, thanks," she said. Under her breath, to David: "I assume they're talking about us?"

"Afraid so," David said, squeezing her hand. "Ready to run the gauntlet?"

"It can't be worse than getting married and crowned. No offense," she added.

"Of course not — who could find that offensive?" He rolled his eyes at her and brought her to the receiving line.

Where she shook hands for what seemed to be eight and a half hours. "Hello . . . thanks for coming . . . thank you very much . . . yes, thanks . . . hi . . . hello . . . thanks for coming . . . thanks, Horrance designed it for me . . . no, I wanted something besides white . . . never you mind . . ."

Jenny was on her left; David was on her

right. Jenny was doing both of her jobs —
bridesmaid and protocol officer — at once.
She would occasionally whisper the person's name to Christina, who would obedi-
ently repeat it.

"Queen Rania, Jordan," she muttered,
and Christina found herself eye to eye with
a woman pretty enough (and thin enough)
to be a Victoria's Secret model.

"Hi, Queen Rania . . . thanks . . . thanks
for coming . . . thanks, I wanted to try
something besides white . . ."

"Princess Elizabeth, Yugoslavia."

"Hi, Princess Elizabeth . . . that's so nice
of you to say . . . yes . . . thanks for
coming . . . hi . . . hello there . . ."

"Crown Prince Frederick, Denmark."

"Hi . . . thanks . . . yes, I *am* glad it's
over . . . yeah . . . well, it's only for one day,
right?"

"Crown Princess Mathilde, Belgium."

"Great dress . . . thank you . . . we appreciate you coming all this way . . ."

"King Juan Carlos, Spain."

"Hullo, King Juan . . . thanks . . . yes, I
picked them out myself . . . thank
you . . ."

"Charles, the Prince of Wales —"

"*Him* I know, Jenn." Still waiting patiently to wake up from this bizarre dream,

Christina was amazed to find herself shaking hands with Prince Charles. In person he seemed nice enough — he had the big ears caricaturists so loved to exaggerate, but his eyes were warm and kind, and he told her David was a lucky man.

"Well, thank you, Prince Charles." Jenny had told her it was entirely proper to refer to visiting royals by their titles and name. She knew Christina, as an American of no particular family, wasn't interested in referring to anyone else as "Your Highness." However, once she was married, like it or not, she would have rank equivalent to many of the royal guests. "I'm lucky, too. We appreciate you coming all this way."

"My mother regrets she was unable to be here," he offered smoothly.

"Well, I'm sure she's busy. Y'know, keeping an eye on England and all."

Prince Charles laughed. "That she is, Your Highness."

"Christina, please."

"Christina, then." He pressed her hand. He really *was* charming, in an urbane, geeky kind of way. His breath was minty fresh. "Congratulations again."

"Thank you, Prince Charles."

"Suzanne Somers," Jenny whispered.

"I know her, too," Chris said, exasperated. "Hi! I've got a Thighmaster and I just love it."

Ms. Somers made a gracious reply, looking like a million bucks in a bronze-colored dress that set off her hair and eyes superbly. Christina was amazed . . . she'd had no idea Suzanne's eyes were so big and blue and pretty.

"It was so nice of you to invite me," Ms. Somers was saying.

"Well, like I said. Love that Thighmaster. I hate my Buttmaster, though . . . that thing kills! I can barely walk the next day — I'm sincere!"

The famous blonde laughed. "Then you're doing it right, Princess Christina!"

"Great," she mock-grumbled. Then, "Hi, Dr. Pohl!"

"Your Highness," her shrink said demurely, then giggled. "Sorry, I couldn't resist. You look breathtaking." The doc kissed her on the cheek. "Nice work."

"Thanks. And thanks for coming."

"Frankly, I was amazed to receive an invitation."

"Oh, you shouldn't have been," Christina said seriously. "I really wanted you to come. I — I've enjoyed our talks."

Dr. Pohl laughed at her.

265

"Well, okay, they gave me something to think about, anyway. Listen, I'll catch you at the reception, okay?"

"I'm looking forward to it."

"Queen Beatrix, Netherlands," Jenny muttered.

"Good afternoon, Queen Beatrix . . . thank you . . . yes, it's been a long day, but a very good one . . . thanks . . ."

Christina let her attention wander for a moment, just in time to hear Prince Alex tell Suzanne Somers,

"I like to eat cake

My thighs must pay the price.

Hail the ButtMaster."

She rolled her eyes, which startled the British prime minister. Princess Alex swore up and down this was just a phase of her brother's . . . Chris fervently hoped it was true. Sure, the kid had lost a bet . . . a year ago! How long was he supposed to spout poetry? Poor bastard. Unless he secretly liked it. In which case, weird bastard.

"Crown Princess Victoria, Sweden."

"Hello . . . thanks for coming, Princess Victoria . . . did you like Yale?"

"Indeed I did," the princess replied with a kind smile. Another gorgeous brunette with brown eyes . . . and wearing pink!

"My friend Jenny says you're going to be

Sweden's first female sovereign in, like, a million years."

"Three hundred years, and yes."

"Well, good luck with *that* whole thing."

"And to you, Your Highness."

"Princess Stephanie, Monaco."

"Congratulations," Princess Stephanie said, shaking her hand.

"And to you, too," Christina replied. She'd read in *Newsweek* that Stephie got around . . . she'd just gotten married for the fourth? — fifth? — time.

"Thank you, Princess Christina."

"Just Christina," she said, "will be fine."

"So I hear," Stephanie replied, and her eyes twinkled merrily.

"Almost done," Jenny said in her ear.

"Thank God . . . hi, Ms. Beckinsale. I loved *Underworld.* You kicked ass."

"Thank you," Kate Beckinsale replied gravely. "I'm so glad you enjoyed it."

"Enjoyed it? I loved it! Great accent, by the way."

Beckinsale blinked. "I'm British."

"Oh. Well, then, no wonder."

"We just wrapped the sequel."

"Now that's the best news I've heard all year!" she cried, and people up and down the receiving line laughed. With her, not at her. Sometimes it could be hard to tell, but not today.

It was nice.

Christina was eating an open-faced cucumber sandwich with her salmon. Mmm! What was it about cukes and salmon that they went so well together? Who knew? It was one of those mysteries, like Stonehenge. But she meant to enjoy it all the same. And she chortled with delight every time she saw the guest favors . . . miniature wedding cakes exactly like her big one, except only two inches high, in a rainbow of pastels. Each table was littered with pink, or mint green, or baby blue, or cream.

"Thought you'd like those," David said beside her. His plate was clean, and he was watching her shovel it in, looking amused. "I'm sure there's more in the kitchen, darling wife."

"Ho-ho. I was too nervous to eat a *thing* today. Between Edmund nagging and Jenny hovering, I was, like, totally worried that hurling was imminent. On television, no less!"

"I'm glad you avoided it."

"And the food is *great*. As in couldn't-have-done-it-better-myself great. Although I certainly tried, but the chefs wouldn't let me near the kitchen as of seventy-two hours ago."

"They might have had instructions," Prince David admitted.

"Great. How come?"

"I wanted you to enjoy your wedding reception. Tough to do if you're obsessing over the number of egg yolks in the butter cream frosting."

"Shows what you know about butter cream," she grumbled, but she was pleased. "And is it me, or is Queen Rania a total babe?"

"It's not just you."

"Speaking of babes, or babies, rather —"

"Oh, were we?"

"— I threw away my birth control pills yesterday."

He quickly put his wineglass down before he choked. "All right. I, um, I'm not sure how I'm supposed to respond to that. Congratulations?"

"Well. All those classes on Alaskan history that Edmund gave me. They were endless, but mildly interesting. I learned a lot about your ancestors. And we talked about the succession and the royal family and that you need an heir to, y'know, be the boss of Alaska when we're worm food —"

"Yes, but you don't have to get pregnant this second."

"Well, good, because I'm not done with my cake."

He grinned at her. "I meant, you flighty creature, that we can certainly wait awhile."

"Oh. Really? I thought having babies was my job now."

This time he *did* choke on his wine. "Who told you *that?*"

"I figured it out on my own. Come on, don't pretend we're like a regular married couple." She crossed her legs and leaned forward, her cape tenting on the floor around her. "Don't you need babies, like, A.S.A.P.?"

"No, Christina. You're young, I'm young. We can wait awhile. If you like."

"Okay, well, I'll think about it." And she would. Most curious! She thought he'd be on board with the Insta-Baby program, but he clearly was in no rush.

Why was that heartening and disappointing at the same time?

"Speaking of jobs —"

"Oh, were we?" she asked sarcastically.

"— have you thought about writing a cookbook? You seem to have very strong opinions about, for instance, omelets —"

"It just makes me *crazy* when people dilute their eggs with milk!"

"— right, right, calm down and eat your cake. You could write a cookbook —"

"No. Not now I can't."

He blinked. "Why in the world not?"

"Because it would be a cinch to get it published, and there'd be a big print run — like, a zillion copies — but I'd never know if the book was a success because people liked my ideas and my recipes, or because I was — drumroll, please — Princess Christina! You see?"

"I . . . I do see."

She could see he, in fact, did *not* see. Since he had always been a prince, he had been able to take his fame and popularity at face value. It was always there, like the moon and the sun. She would never be able to do that. She was well aware that for the rest of her life, people would want to be her friend because she was (insert snicker here) a princess. It was stupid, but there you go.

"Let's talk about it later," she suggested. "It's our wedding reception — we should probably be having fun. Or something."

"I *am* having fun," he said mildly, and forked the last bite of cake off her plate.

"Creep. You — what's that?"

She heard a mild tumult and looked up to see Kurt's way being blocked by at least three security people.

"What the hell? Those guys know who Kurt is — what's with the 'can we see some I.D.' treatment?"

"Oh," the prince said casually, "I might have accidentally put Detective Carlson's name on a list somewhere."

"*Real* mature, Penguin Boy. Hey! Guys!" She waved. "Let him come over, it's all right."

"Hey, man," Kurt said to the head of security, exaggeratedly straightening his tux, "I knew the bride when she used to rock 'n' roll."

"Possibly more than one list," the prince added, downing the last of his wine in three gulps.

"Childish much?" she muttered, then gave Kurt a big smile. "Hey! Glad you could make it."

"I wasn't gonna miss the royal wedding of the century," he teased.

"Oh, don't start with that. We're barely even into the century. My God, I don't think I've ever seen you in a suit. You look great!"

"Edmund made me." Kurt ran a finger around his collar and grimaced. "I feel like a total fraud in this thing."

"Did you get enough to eat?"

"Relax, Chris. Food's first-rate. Listen, the reason I came over — me and Prince Alex and a couple of the guys are gonna go hit a few bars. I just wanted to say good night."

"Well, thanks for coming."

"You look great," he said, looking up and down in that old half-critical, half-admiring way. "Like a princess, for sure."

"Then my disguise is working."

He laughed and bent to kiss her cheek, then eyed the prince and shook her hand instead. "Well, best of luck and all that."

"Will you come tomorrow to see us off?"

"Sure. New York, right?"

"Uh-huh."

"Sure, I'll be there."

"Okay, great. See you."

" 'Bye. See you around, David."

"Good night," the prince said coolly.

"David," Christina said, watching Kurt walk away, "you've really got to let that go."

"It's faded into the mists of my memory."

She laughed. "Sure it has. Speaking of stuff fading into the mist . . ." She put down her fork and plucked at his sleeve. "I didn't get a chance earlier."

"It's too late to take it back," he said quickly.

"Very funny. Anyway, I didn't get a chance earlier, and I didn't *know* earlier. About the jewelry. The necklaces and the earrings and my engagement ring and the wedding bands. I didn't know you designed them yourself."

He looked puzzled. There was a bit of cream cheese at the corner of his mouth; she reached up and thumbed it away. "I told you I was going to take care of the jewelry."

"Yeah, but I thought that meant, 'Edmund, take care of the jewelry,' or something."

His mouth twitched on one side. "Well, it didn't. And if I ordered Edmund to 'take care of' anything, he'd likely laugh in my face."

"Still. All the same. I didn't know, and I'm sorry about all the ones I rejected."

"If you didn't like them, Chris, I'm glad you were up front about it."

"But I love the wedding band," she said fervently. Set in a platinum ring, the band was studded with a blue diamond for every two white diamonds. It went amazingly with her engagement ring. David's, she noted, was a simple platinum band. "I really do, David."

"Then that's worth a kiss," he said easily, and she laughed and bent toward him, and kissed the corner of his mouth, and in the background she heard clapping, and the king roaring with laughter.

"While we're on the topic of things we really liked," he continued, pulling back but resting his arm on her shoulder, "I thought the ice sculpture was a nice touch."

She shrugged. "Oh, it was no biggie. It's not like I chiseled the damn thing myself."

"No, but it's a very nice penguin couple."

She concealed a shudder. She'd said to the caterer, "Maybe something in penguins," and in return, he had created an eight-foot-high monstrosity: a pair of penguins, keeping the shrimp cool. It was nightmarish and hilarious at the same time.

"I'm glad you liked it. So, um . . ." She toyed with his sleeve. "How long do we have to stay?"

He grinned at her and started to answer, when she nudged him in the ribs hard enough to evoke a groan and said, "*Look* at that. It's a party, and Jenny's being bugged for, like, the millionth time."

"It's her job," he started to explain.

"Yeah, but everybody gets to quit for the day after a while. I mean, come on! It's . . . what? Almost ten o'clock at night?"

"Well . . . we're in a room full of visiting dignitaries, American celebrities, European royalty —"

"— and the royal protocol officer has been on her feet longer than I have. Don't go 'way."

"Christina, I'm begging you — no international incidents."

"Not on our wedding day, silly! Sheesh."

Cape flying, Christina charged over to a table in the far corner heaped with chocolate-covered strawberries, grabbed half a dozen and plunked them on a napkin, and hurried over to catch the tail end of Jenny's response.

". . . can certainly spend the night at the palace, although I believe His Majesty's security detail had already vetted the Marriott . . ."

"Stop!"

Jenny stopped, and looked at her. Edmund raised his eyebrows, and also looked at her. And the person bugging them, a balding man wearing horn-rimmed glasses and carrying a clipboard, actually cowered.

"You guys, give it a rest. It's a party. Hi," she said to Clipboard Boy.

"Actually, Your Highness," Edmund corrected, "it's a wedding reception."

"Whatever. You guys, take a break, for crying out loud. As of this second, you're officially off duty."

They spoke in alarmed unison. "Oh, Your Highness, I couldn't —"

"— entirely inappropriate —"

"— to be available to answer questions of —"

"— *never* really 'off duty,' as you so quaintly, yet idiotically, put it —"

"Stawwwwwwwp! Seriously! You guys! Enough already. You've been working like dogs —"

"That's true enough," Edmund said. Then, to Clipboard Boy, "That will be all, William."

"I want you guys to have some fun," Christina continued as he scuttled away. "In fact, take a vacation. Both of you."

"Your Highness, it's really out of the question —"

"Jenny, now quit it. I don't want to see your face — either of your faces — for a week."

"Twenty-four hours," Edmund said.

"Seven days, Edmund."

277

"Forty-eight hours."

"Seven. Days. Edmund."

His black-clad shoulders slumped in surrender. "As you wish, Your Highness. Seven days."

"Good. That's really good." *Holy shit! I won an argument with Ichabod Brain!* "Now go enjoy the party. I — I command it!"

"Yes, Your Highness," they chorused dutifully.

"And cut that shit out — you know I hate it."

"Yes, Your Highness," they chorused evilly.

# Chapter 26

From *The Queen of the Edge of the World*, by Edmund Dante III, © 2089, Harper Zebra and Schuster Publications.

By all accounts, the wedding of Prince David and Princess Christina was a charming, beautiful, and, yes, historic occasion. There was ample television coverage, and of course the famous Cook photograph of the prince and princess laughing together at the altar.

In its own way, the Cook photo was as famous as the 1939 photo of Judy Garland dipping her hands in cement at Grauman's Chinese Theater. The Cook photo was used again and again throughout the century because it so aptly summed up Alaskan royalty — the prince, grave but amused, and the princess, laughing with unashamed joy.

It was also at their wedding that

Prince David would suggest the now-famous book that would later become the international best-seller (over a hundred million copies in seventeen languages) Christina on Cooking: Favorite recipes of HRH Princess Christina of Alaska.

One assumes, however, that there were other things on the prince and princess's minds than cooking . . . or photographic opportunities. . . .

"David, for God's sake, will you put me down? You're gonna, like, rupture something."

David staggered to the bed — their new bed in their new apartments — and dropped her in the middle of it, then collapsed beside her.

"My, you're . . . you're a big girl," he said, clearly struggling not to gasp.

"And you're an ass." She propped herself up on her elbows and kicked off her shoes, watching as they flew across the room. The room was lit entirely by candles; there were at least a thousand of them. Which she supposed was supposed to be romantic, but frankly, it made her nervous. One thing she learned in her years of working cruise ships: fire is bad.

"I've said it before and I'll say it again: day-amn, this is a nice bunch of rooms! Say, blow those candles out, willya?"

He blew a few out, and she blew out the ones on her end table beside the bed — cripes, they were, like, two feet from the down comforter! Did feathers burn? They must. And they probably stunk like a bastard, too.

"This will be the first time I've slept in the palace in a place other than the apartments I've had since I was a baby," he said thoughtfully.

"Really?" She stopped in mid-blow. "You've never slept anywhere else? Don't you have, like, a cot in Allen Hall with the penguins?"

"Yes, but I don't *sleep* there."

She put a hand over her eyes. "Oh, my God, David. First of all, I was only kidding, and second of all, that's scary on at least five different levels."

"It's only so I can lie down and rest while observing their behavioral —"

"David. Seriously. Stop talking about the fucking penguins and kiss me."

"Can't I do both?" he teased, and bent over her, and kissed her for a lovely, long time.

". . . stupid cape . . ." She was wriggling

281

all over the bed. "Help me get this stuff off, willya?"

"A pleasure."

"Don't take this the wrong way or anything, but I've been wanting to jump your bones for the last six days."

"Likewise."

"Oh, that's so romantic! 'Likewise.' You should write for Harlequin."

"Sticks and stones. And Christina — shut up and kiss me back."

"A pleasure." With a wicked gleam in her eye, she grabbed him by the ears and kissed him. Then they were both wriggling and her cape was on the floor, followed by his suit jacket, and she yanked at his shirt and his blue diamond cufflinks went flying (she was later to find one of them had landed in her shoe), and then his pants were flying, and then one of his socks, and one of her stockings, and then —

"Christ! How many buttons are *on* this thing?"

"The designer guy had to use a buttonhook," she said anxiously, peering over her shoulder. "Can you get it undone?"

"Got an axe? Never mind. I'm very dexterous."

"Well, congratulations."

About half an hour later, the dress finally

slid off her shoulders. She kicked it away, relieved to be free of it at last. By now her hands were shaking; she'd waited *so* long and wanted him *so* badly, it was difficult to believe that the moment had come at last. She hoped David wasn't the type who suffered from performance anxiety.

"My God! Christina, you're — you're really quite lovely."

"That's just the lingerie. And seeing me in a bedroom as opposed to a closet." She grabbed her boobs and hoisted them up. "See? My boobs are not normally this high — it's the stupid corset."

"Ummm . . . yes, I see . . . fascinating . . . leave it on, would you?"

"Am I asking you to leave *your* underwear on?" she griped.

"I can, you know — these are boxers. Fly vent."

"Forget that. I've been wanting to grab your naked ass for, like, ever."

"Grab away," he said, choking on a laugh. He gasped as she squeezed — hard! — and pounced on him and rolled over, with him on top.

"I knew it," she said, deeply satisfied. "Those baggy shorts and those geeky suits didn't fool me. You have a fantastic ass."

"Likewise," he said, and ducked as she

swung a small fist at his ear.

"You're impossible!"

"Yes, I suppose I am," he said, and dipped his head, and found the soft sweetness of her cleavage. He nuzzled for a time while she sighed and stroked his thick black hair. She'd been longing to touch the silky-coarse strands for so long. The final, insane days leading up to the wedding had left them with very little — make that zero — time to sneak off for closet nookie.

It seemed unreal that he was here with her now, that he was her husband, he belonged to her, and she to him.

Just the thought — the belonging, the needing — brought such a wave of excitement that she could actually taste it — it was coppery and hot. She put her hands to good use and divested them of panties and boxers (she was later to find her panties had landed in her other shoe).

Then she was clasping that really fine ass and drawing him toward her, and he went to her, willingly enough, and sank into her — oh, Christ, she was ready for him, more than ready — and she wrapped her legs around his waist and pumped back at him as he began to stroke, stroke, stroke.

She thought she would die. Worse, she thought he might stop. His hands were fisted in her hair and he was whispering her name over and over again in her ear as he came into her, as he thrust and pushed and drove into her, hard and fast but it didn't matter, it felt wonderful, *he* felt wonderful; he was all smooth muscles and hard, hot length and she —

— she would —

— she was —

"Oh my *God!*" she cried at the ceiling, bucking beneath him — a new record, what was that, did she really come in, like, less than a minute? Cripes! She really *was* overdue.

"Did you?" he panted in her ear.

She nipped him on the shoulder and gasped an affirmative.

"Oh, thank God. Because I can't — not for another —" Then he stiffened above her, all his muscles locked, and then he collapsed over her with a satisfied sigh.

After a few minutes, when she had her breath back, she said, "Day-amn!"

"Likewise."

"Quit that, I mean it. I swear, that's a new record for me. I usually don't — uh —"

"Well, I usually *do*, but it's been a while for us." He smiled at her and patted her sweaty thigh. "I'll do better next time."

"*Better?* Then you'll probably kill me!"

He laughed and cuddled her into his side. "Oh, Christina. You're going to change my whole life, aren't you?"

"That's what I'm here for," she said. Then added hopefully, "Uh, when do you think you can do all that again?"

"I'll need a little more than thirty seconds," he said dryly, then snorted a laugh when she poked him in the ribs.

Later that night — or, rather, that morning — she was awakened out of a sound sleep by slow, sweet waves of pleasure, wakened to find his head between her thighs, his tongue in her and on her, his fingers dancing — he certainly *was* dexterous — and when she cried out, when she couldn't stand it a minute longer, he came to her, his chest settled against hers, his knee nudged hers apart, and he entered her with excruciating slowness.

She cried out and shook beneath him and dug her nails into his shoulders and rocked, rocked, rocked against him, with him, until her orgasm bloomed within her like a dark flower, until he shook and shuddered above her, until she was sighing and sinking into sleep again, until he was resting beside her, his hand against the small of her back, pressing her against him.

# Chapter 27

"I don't . . . you know . . . *feel* any different."

"No? Not at all?"

"Well . . . I feel well-laid —"

"Ah."

"And finally! In a proper bed without worrying about someone barging in on us. That's the great part. But I don't feel like somebody's wife. And sure as shit not like Her Royal Idiot, Christina — I s'pose it's too late to talk to you about keeping my own name?"

"I'm afraid so."

"Well, at least everybody around here seems to know how to pronounce Baranov. Your dad *still* gets my maiden name wrong. How many times do I haveta tell him? The 'e' is silent!"

She yawned and rolled over, burrowing under David's arm. He rubbed her back and she burrowed farther. "Ryy frr nnn ykkkk?"

"Ready for New York, did you say? Yes.

In fact, we'd best get going soon, or —"

A polite rap-rap on their door. "Your Highnesses! It's just about time to go!"

Christina's head popped up. "Piss off, J— wait a minute. That's not Jenny."

"You gave her the week off, remember?"

"You mean she actually listened? Too cool! Here, sit still, you're not decent."

"Look who's talking," David said, amused, as she flung the sheet over them. "Come in!"

Princess Alexandria poked her head in. "Well, you're awake, at least. Thank the gods I didn't walk in on some prefornication rituals."

"What are you doing here?"

"Jenny begged me — before she and Edmund were dragged away, protesting every second — to make sure you guys got up and out of the palace on time. Since I was coming to see you off anyway . . ." She shrugged. "No big."

"You're still wearing your bridesmaid's dress," the prince observed.

"Yeah, well." Another shrug. "Long night. And your friend Kurt can *really* put 'em away."

"You stay away from him," David snapped, sitting bolt upright.

"Bite me, your royal buttinsky. But get

dressed first. Nice rack," she added to Chris, then swung the door closed.

"Oh, very nice!" David exploded, leaping out of bed and pacing in a splendid nude rage. "Now that blast — that rat — that *person* is zooming in on *my* sister since it's patently obvious he can't have you!"

"Calm down," Chris said, amazed at the furor. Even his penis was trembling in rage. "Kurt's harmless — a little girl-crazy, but basically harmless — and your sister can snap his spine if he gets fresh."

"Well." David stopped and thought for a minute. Christina stopped and admired his form for a minute. "That's a valid point, Christina. Yes. She can — she's been studying for years — all right."

"Besides, Kurt knows your dad. You think he wants Al mad at him again?"

"Oh, to dream."

"FYI, you look pretty sexy in the morning, y'know, all scruffy and unshaved and stuff."

"Likewise."

"I am *not* scruffy. Slightly mussed, I'll grant you. And just for that, I get the window seat on the plane."

She started to flounce off the bed and he caught her with a lusty smack on her bare buttocks. "Ow! You'll keep your hands to yourself, you fucking pervert."

"Not a chance," he said smugly, and tried to smack her again, but she ran, shrieking, to the bathroom, and beat him by two feet.

"Which reminds me," she said, tucking her T-shirt (a wedding gift from the king: I'M THE CROWN PRINCESS, WHO THE HELL ARE YOU?) into her jeans. "Enough with people waking us up. Haven't you ever heard of alarm clocks?"

"Alarm clocks?" David said, as if saying, *Rattlesnakes?*

"Yeah. It's a fabulous new invention, champ. You set them for a certain time, they buzz or play music, bingo! You're up. Works great."

"Yes, but . . ."

"Where the hell are my tennis shoes?"

"Did you check the closet?"

"Why would they be *there?*" She checked. "Well, I'll be damned."

"Chris, about alarm clocks —"

"Anything's better than having a grown person shake another grown person awake, I mean, how old *are* we? I feel stupid, being woken up by somebody else."

"Yes, but," the prince said, trying not to

whine, "alarm clocks don't bring you breakfast and chat about the weather and press your suit and keep you up-to-date on current events."

"Or tuck you in or give you a kissy-kiss on your nosey-nose. Ech! David, really. Time to grow up."

"How about if you get an alarm clock and wake *me* up?"

"Fine. Loser."

"I get up rather early," he warned her, "to check on the residents of Allen Hall."

"Oh, the penguins can wait another hour or six for their fish heads. Come on, let's go, let's go, let's *go!* New York, here we come!"

"New York, watch out," David muttered, then dodged his wife's small fist, and pushed her out the door.

"Hi, everybody," the new princess said, blinking as about a zillion flashbulbs went off into her face.

"How's married life, Your Highness?"

"Is New York ready for Alaskan royals, Your Highness?"

"What are your plans, Your Highness?"

"Well, John," Christina said, recognizing the liaison for MSNBC, "my plan is to give all you losers the slip, get on this plane, and go far, far away. And cripes, how many pictures do you need?"

"Prince David, could you step back — there! Thanks." Another flashbulb popped. David looked resigned as the press corps descended on his wife. "So how was the wedding?"

"Don, you were *there*," she said patiently. "I saw you hiding behind the rosebushes. I told Jenny to bring you a slice of cake."

"Where *is* the press officer?"

"I gave her the week off. She works harder than all of us put together — she deserves a vacation."

"What's the itinerary in New York?"

"Oh, I've got it all printed up for you guys and David will be handing each of you a copy — *not!*" Over a wave of laughter, she continued. "Forget it, you pests. Our itinerary is our business."

"Just like your sex life, eh, Your Highness?"

"I heard that, Darrell. See if you get a Christmas card."

Kurt, responding to a signal from the prince, stepped up to the microphones, shouldering Christina aside so she nearly went sprawling into the wall. "Fun's over, kids. You can catch these guys on the way back."

"Good-bye," Chris said, before Kurt caught her elbow and dragged her toward the private room off the tarmac. "Real subtle," she said, once they were out of earshot.

"Hey, don't look at me, sunshine. Your hubby gave me the old hairy eyeball, so I grabbed you."

"Oh. David, I'm sorry about all the fuss — you're not mad, are you? Once I'm old news they'll forget about me and start bugging you again, I'm sure of it."

"Christ, I hope not," he said fervently. "The dumbest thing Prince Charles ever did — besides cheat on his wife — was re-sent the attention she got. Do you know how many more papers I can get done now? Think of my research!"

"Toldja he wouldn't be mad," Kurt said, blowing a bubble the size of his head. It smelled strongly of artificial grape.

"How can you chew gum this early? And you, would it kill you to be a little jealous of the whole 'hey, Princess Christina, over here' thing?" she asked, mildly disgruntled. "And where the hell are we?"

They were in a large, luxuriously ap-pointed room where the east wall was one big window. She could see planes coming in and taking off. In the distance, the plane the royals used to go here and there was slowly approaching. The press corps, locked out on the other side of the wall, was slowly dispersing.

"Hi!" Prince Nicholas said, dropping his chicken drummie and throwing his arms around her. "We wanted to see you off!"

"You're getting barbecue sauce all over my shirt. Bleah, how can you be eating at — what time *is* it, anyway?"

"It's ten-thirty," the king said with a yawn as he ambled over. He looked more like the groundskeeper than the country's reigning monarch in his baggy sweatshirt, drawstring-waist pants with dirt stains at the knees, sockless tennis shoes, unshaven cheeks and jowls, and bloodshot eyes. "You couldn't leave at, what? Noon?"

"Hey, it wasn't my idea." She gave him a hearty smack on the cheek, grinning to see the lip gloss mark she left. "I bet you're running on about thirty seconds of sleep. You look like a car wreck, old man."

"Hey, it was the first wedding in the family. Party time." The king yawned again. "Marriage looks like it agrees with both of you. David, I haven't seen you un-clench like this since you were out of diapers."

"Thanks, Dad," he said dryly.

"We're going to have a quick bite, and then you guys are going up, up, and away," Princess Alexandria said. Chris was amused to notice she'd changed into jeans and a sweatshirt. She might be comfortable telling David off, but she clearly had no intention of letting the king know she'd been out partying all night. "Heaven knows there's plenty of leftovers."

"Any chocolate-covered strawberries?" David asked, wandering over to the buffet table. "The cute ones that look like brides and grooms? That was a great trick."

"Dozens, sir."

"Awesome!" she said, joining him at the table. "Hi. I'm Christina."

"Yes, Your Highness, I know. I'm Devon — I'm filling in for Edmund and Jenny until they return. If there's anything you need, please don't hesitate to call on me."

"Relax, Devon, everything's fine." The guy was tall — not as tall as Edmund but, of course, no one was — and weirdly twitchy, with fuzzy blond brows that looked like tame caterpillars.

For someone who hung out at the Sitka Palace, he was a real wreck . . . most of them were formal, but relaxed. Devon looked like he was going to hurl into the punch bowl any second. Probably the pressure of his last-second promotion. Well, he'd relax when he realized none of them would bite.

"You guys want to check the plane for us?" the king asked, and the six-man security team obligingly trotted out the door.

"I'll stay here," Kurt called after them. "And guard the salmon."

"Check the plane for *what?*" Chris asked, although she suspected she knew.

"Bombs, guns, porn, bad food — you know," Princess Alex said, wolfing down a melon ball wrapped in prosciutto.

"Who'd care enough about us to blow us up?"

"Nobody *I* can think of."

"So where *were* you all night, anyway, Alex, hmmmmm?"

The princess threw a melon ball at her.

"Quit that," Christina said, ducking. "One princess tossing stuff I can handle — don't *you* start."

"Hey, Chris, your shoe is untied," Nicky said, and, before she could say anything, he quickly bent to tie it for her.

"You little weirdo, anything to touch —" *Zinnnnng-thump!* "— my clothes — huh?"

*Zinnnnng-thump?*

"Nicky!" Princess Alexandra screamed.

There was a muffled thump as she dropped her buffet plate and it hit the carpet, spilling melon balls like brightly colored pieces of spring.

*Zinnnnng-thump?*

Kurt, in the act of drawing his gun, suddenly crumpled out of sight in exact time with a loud, hollow, *Bonnnnnnng!*

Devon dropped the sterling silver serving tray (miniature wedding cakes had scattered everywhere), stepped over Kurt, corrected his aim, and —

"Nicky, *get down!*" the king roared, and his son dropped like a rock and rolled away. There was no mistaking the command in that yell — Christina nearly hit the bricks herself.

*Zinnnnng-thump, zinnnnng-thump!*

The king stared at the two small, red, feathered darts sticking out of his chest and slowly folded to the floor.

There was another *bonnnnnnng!* and Devon dropped his gun and clutched his wrist. Kurt was standing beside him, swaying. Blood trickled from his ear and dripped off his jaw. "Not s'fast without y'r pea shooter, eh?" he mumbled, then his eyes rolled up to the whites and he fell into the table.

"Y-you have to come with me, Prince

Nicholas," Devon said, trying a ghastly smile. He had the gall to stretch a hand toward the crouching boy. "Your place is with us."

Christina opened her mouth, and found herself shoved backward and to the side. Suddenly it was difficult to see; David had planted himself squarely in front of her.

"Get the hell out of here, you traitorous piece of shit," he ordered coldly. "If you leave now, our security team *might* not blow your head off."

"Us, sir?" Nicholas asked, slowly straightening. He was very white, and very polite.

"Your mother's family."

"Domonov," Christina hissed.

"Yes," Devon said, barely glancing at them. "Twice removed. On my mother's side. The queen is dead, long live the rightful king." And he looked at Nicholas — this was somehow more frightening than the shooting — with naked adoration.

*So fast,* Christina thought. She was too shocked by the sudden violence to feel horrified. That would come later. *It's all happening so fast — cripes, he only pulled his gun about thirty seconds ago! This is crazy, it was so easy for him, this is nuts, it's —*

"My father is the true king," Nicholas said, too young to know it was useless to reason with a fanatic. "You're — you're wrong. Your plan won't work. And if it wasn't my father, if he wasn't the king, it'd be —"

Chris tried to shove David aside. It was like trying to bully a redwood. "Devon!" Chris snapped, her voice cracking like a whip. The man actually jerked around at the sound. "You'll never get out of here. You've fucked up, it's done. You're done. Make yourself useful, and tell us what's in the darts." *And God help you, GOD HELP YOU, if the king is dead.*

"If Prince Nicholas will accompany me, I will show him to his true —"

*Ka-click.*

Christina, David, and Devon, equally surprised, looked. During their brief chat, Nicholas had crawled under the table, found Kurt's gun, crawled back, stood, aimed, cocked.

"You shot my daddy," he said, and although he looked like a boy who was having a bad day at school, he sounded infuriated. "You shot my king and my sovereign, and you hurt my friend. So I'm thinking, it's only fair if I shoot you. Except these aren't darts. Lieutenant Carlson carries a nine-millimeter Beretta and these bullets leave *big* holes. I know — he let me practice with it. It's okay, though." He grinned. He grinned like a king on a battlefield, one who sees victory in his grasp. He grinned like Alexander, like Edward I, like Henry VIII, like his forbear, Kaarl Baranov, who got pissed off one day and won himself a country. "You won't feel it for long."

"Your High —"

Then, the final puzzling sound, a muffled *whump-cra-thud!* Princess Alexandria had slipped out of her shoes and crept on cat feet behind her distant cousin, picking up a banquet chair on the way. While her brother distracted the traitor who'd shot their father, she swung the chair sidearm, putting every ounce of her one-fifty behind it.

Devon did not so much fall down as go flying. It wasn't like in the movies. In fact, Alex's arm took the shock of the blow and it would be days before she could raise her wrist above her shoulder. The chair didn't shatter.

Devon's skull, however, did.

Alexandria sprinted to the far door, yanked it open, and screamed, "Alaaaaaaaaaaaarm!" into the fair spring air. Meanwhile, David had reached his father, had plucked out the darts and was examining them. Christina bent and rested her head on the king's broad chest.

"These are animal tranqs," David said, puzzled. "I'm not sure exactly what kind, but they should just be enough to knock him out, or —"

"He's not — his heart — help me." She positioned herself and, as she had learned as an employee of the Carnival Cruise Line, began a closed-chest massage. One-and-two-and-three-and-four-and — "Breathe!"

David knelt by his father's face, eased his mouth open, blew a quick breath.

One-and-two-and-three-and — four-and — "Breathe!"

Another breath.

Most of her concentration was on the king, but faintly, on the far edge of her conscious mind, she heard Alexandria say, "Give me the gun, Nicky, okay?"

One-and-two-and-three-and — four-and — "Breathe! And somebody check on Kurt — that asshole clocked him pretty good."

She heard the click as Nicky popped the clip, as he ejected the bullet. Heard him slap the gun into his sister's hand. Heard Alex saying, "Oh, Nicky . . . Nick . . ."

Suddenly the room was crawling with security types — all the guys who'd been diverted to the plane. And why not? It was their honeymoon. Nobody had tried anything like this in four generations. And Kurt had been armed. And they had been a small group; they had thought they were safe.

And Devon was — was a member of — of the family.

"Your Highness, the ambulance is coming. Let me —"

"Leave." One and two and three — "Me." — four and — "Alone! Breathe!"

Nicholas and Alex were huddled above them, staring down, their Baranov blue eyes huge. "He shot Daddy," Nicholas was saying, pressing his face into Alex's stomach. "He shot him to grab me!"

"He paid for it, Nicky," Alex said, and though she was white to the lips, her words were cold. Christina, working up a sweat doing her closed-chest massage, shivered. "Anybody ever comes near you, they can say hello to a skull fracture, too."

"It's like this, Mrs. Baranov — Your Highness. Um, both Your Highnesses . . ." The doctor, though at the top of his field, had never met a member of the royal family before. Now the private room was filled with them. Alexander and Kathryn had arrived just after the rest of the party.

Prince Alex was gray-faced, but not too rattled to come up with,

"Sleep late for one day
Kidnapping attempts ensue,
What the hell's going on?"

"Not *now,* Alex," David snapped.

"Just give us the straight shit, Doc," Princess Christina said.

"Well, Prince David was correct — the kidnapper was using animal tranquilizers. A combination of chloral hydrate and ketamine. It seems he has a contact at the Juneau Zoo —"

"Yeah, another distant relative of our mother," Alexandria said bitterly. "Some vet or something. And she was soooo helpful when it came to silly-ass schemes. Her ass is in jail now, right?"

Carol, the head of the security team, nodded absently while listening in on her headset. The security team was jittery and slit-eyed and pissed. Recriminations could come later; right now, nobody was messing with them.

"Er . . . yes." The doctor coughed. "The tranquilizers themselves wouldn't have hurt Prince Nicholas and would have made him very easy to — um — transport."

"Not to mention, they weren't supposed to hurt anyone — kill anyone," Carol said, thinking aloud. "Because —"

"Because regicide is still punishable by beheading in this country — that law's been on the books for almost two hundred years," Prince David said pointedly. "Devon wouldn't have wanted to risk that."

"Fascinating," Chris said impatiently, "but why is the king still unconscious?"

"His Majesty had a severe allergic reaction to the chloral hydrate. He's in a coma."

Dead silence, broken by David's strangled, "For — for how long?"

Dr. Sarett shook his head. "He could come out of it tomorrow. Or a month from now. Or next year. Or . . ." He shrugged helplessly. "He's on a respirator for now, but we're hoping he'll start breathing on his own in . . . I mean . . . sometime."

Just when Christina thought she'd absorbed the sheer awfulness of the news, the magnitude of what had happened, Dr. Sarett hit her broadside all over again.

At first she thought he'd dropped his pen and was looking for it on the floor. But then he was — was he? He was! He was bowing to her, to David. And Nicky and Alexandria and Alex and Kathryn and the security gal were all bowing, too. To them. To *her.*

"Long live the king and queen," Dr. Sarett said.

"Oh, fuck," the queen said.

# PART FOUR

# *Queen*

A gold cage is still a cage.
— King David I

Oh, go cry in a bag of money.
— Queen Christina

# Chapter 28

From *The Queen of the Edge of the World*, by Edmund Dante III, © 2089, Harper Zebra and Schuster Publications.

Princess for one night; queen for . . . who knew? The Sitka Palace reeled from the attack, and not just because the king was gravely ill. Although the royal siblings all had genuine fondness for one another, none felt King David was ready. Not to mention Queen Christina.

Not only that, but Prince Nicholas's parentage was finally, formally, called into doubt. King Alexander had done his best to protect his son from slander and inquisitive gossip, but now the cat was, so to speak, out of the bag. The next day, the headline for the Juneau newspaper read DNA TEST, KING DAVID?

Lastly, both within and without the Sitka Palace, recriminations were flying far and fast. How had a Domonov been able to inflict such harm so suddenly? How long had the plot been in evidence? Worse, was there more to it?

Far, far worse: would King Alexander survive it?

These questions threw the royal family into its first crisis since the scandalous death of Queen Dara. Although, some historians argue, this latest crisis was just a result of that earlier one . . . the way sterility is often the result, years later, of German measles.

"It's my fault," Jenny said quietly.

"My dear Jennifer, don't be an idiot. It's *my* fault," Edmund said.

"Both of you, don't be idiots," Nicholas said gloomily. They were in the king's office on the north side of the building. They had been drawn there, royals and servants alike, to take comfort in a room so strongly stamped with the king's personality. There were dead animals covering nearly every square foot of wall. It was calming, yet morbid. "It's my fault. He was after *me.* He hurt Daddy because of me."

"It's my fault," Kurt said. "A pharmacist

took me out with a serving platter, for fuck's sake. Anybody mind if I shoot myself in the head?"

"Are you madder about the pharmacist, or the serving platter?" Princess Alexandria asked. She got a ghost of a smile for her efforts.

"It's my fault," King David said. "I should have knocked Dad out of the way."

"You were guarding the queen," Edmund pointed out. "Your hands were full."

"It's my fault," Carol, head of security, said. "We were so easily diverted to the plane! I should have left more men behind."

"Hey, the guy had a *serving platter*," Kurt said, slumping on the end of the couch so that his shoulders made a C-shape. "You can't do much against a serving platter."

"The fault is all ours
We would have kicked Devon's ass
But we chose to sleep."

Kathryn, seated beside her haiku-spouting brother, nodded. "Alex is right. If we'd been there, you would have had more help. We would have kicked Devon's ass up so high, people would have thought he had two heads. But we slept late."

Everyone stared at Kathryn, startled by such a long speech, then looked at Princess Alexandria, who glared back. "What? It's not *my* fault. I'm the one who took out the bad guy."

"Speaking of," King David said quietly, "how is Devon doing?"

"Deader than shit, Your Majesty," Carol said, not looking up from her Palm Pilot, across which a constant stream of data was running. "Want to send flowers?"

David snorted.

"Forgive me, but where is Her Majesty the queen?" Edmund asked. "Shouldn't she be here with us?"

"She's baking," David said absently. He squirmed in his father's chair.

Alexandria laughed. "You're like Goldilocks, Dave. 'This one's too small . . . this one's too big!' Sit still, you're making me nervous."

"This chair *is* too big," David said, and nobody commented.

The silence was broken by Kathryn's hopeful, "What's Chris baking?"

"A pie, she said."

"What kind of pie?"

"Jeez, Kath! You almost never talk, and when you do finally speak up, it's so you can find out when you can eat. Can you give your appetite a rest for five seconds?" Princess Alex snapped, smacking her just above the elbow. The outburst was so startling, several of the siblings stared at her.

Kathryn looked around for something to toss, gave up, and said in a small voice, "It's a national crisis. I have to keep my strength up." At everyone's stricken expression, she added, "That, uh, sounded a lot funnier in my head."

The door was thrown open and Christina walked in, carrying a steaming pie with the aid of two potholders shaped like pink salmon.

"Oh, good, the new caterer's here," Alexandria said sarcastically.

Prince Alex cleared his throat.

"Somebody's touchy
Today it's acceptable
Still: take it easy."

Christina set the pie down in the middle of the conference table and pulled a knife out of her back pocket, and a pile of napkins out of her other back pocket, which she set next to the pie.

Edmund and Jenny, of course, were on their feet the minute the queen entered. "Good afternoon, Your Majesty."

"Howdy, Jenny. Eds. Welcome back. Sorry your vacation got cut short."

"It's our fault this happened," Jenny began dolefully. Her lovely eyes were rimmed in red. Hers weren't the only ones, either. "I'm sure I would have recognized him . . . at least run him through our database . . . I know most of the Domonovs on sight . . . at the least I would have thrown myself in front of the darts . . ."

"Yeah, your eighty pounds would have made all the difference, Jenn. Listen up, everyone. Blame is a pie."

"Blame smells like blueberries?" Alexandria asked.

She ignored the interruption. "It's a pie. Everybody gets a slice. So here we go. First slice to me . . . I might be new to the royal game, but I've been cooking since I was eight. I ought to be able to spot a fake caterer . . . or a pharmacist posing as one. He wasn't just nervous because he was about to do a dirty deed. He was nervous because he didn't know dick about food, and he was afraid we'd — I'd — ask him something. In retrospect, duh." She cut herself a small slice; the room instantly filled with the smell of sugary crust and hot fruit. She set the wedge on a napkin and pushed it aside.

"Carol, front and center." Carol put her Palm away and slowly came forward.

"Needless to say, Security's been asking themselves some hard questions since this happened."

"Your Majesty, I can assure you, such a thing will *never* —"

"Yeah, yeah. Eat your pie. Alex."

"Which one?"

"Both. One for you, for sleeping late . . ." She sliced, plopped, handed the napkin to the prince. "Like *that's* a big crime, but we're all determined to take some of the blame, right? And you, Ms. Smug, you couldn't have taken the bad guy out forty seconds earlier?"

"I despise you," the princess said, but took her pie.

"Edmund and Jenny . . . for having the nerve to follow orders and actually take a vacation for once in your sad, sad lives . . ."

"Kathryn . . . and don't you *dare* toss this . . . and Nicky . . ."

"Because they think Daddy's not my — you know."

"Right. And because you're determined to share some blame. But Nick, I'm only giving this to you because you'd be mad if I didn't. It's really not —"

"Never mind," he said, and sighed, and ate his pie, a boy not old enough to shave, or even stay up past ten.

"Kurt . . ."

"I hate blueberries," he grumbled, but came forward.

"I don't think he should have a slice," Alexandria volunteered, her teeth blue.

"Bet your ass I should. That guy was twitching all over the place and I didn't see it until the king was down. Stupid. I know better."

"Where's my slice?" David asked quietly.

"Oh, you're being punished enough," Christina said humorously, looking at him over her shoulder. "*King* David. Or prince regent, or whatever we're supposed to call you. Don't you think? Besides, you couldn't be in two places at once. You decided to stay in front of me, and your dad paid for it."

"Hmph."

"There," she said, setting the knife into the near-empty plate. "Now we've all got our blame. Eat up, every bite. Yum-yum. Then maybe we can put this bullshit behind us and get focused, you know? I mean, what the fuck difference does it make who was here and who got hit and who grabbed a chair and who jumped in front of someone and who was scared and who got shot? We're dealing with the *now*.

So that's quite enough breast-beating. It's boring, and we don't have time."

Silence, broken only by chewing.

"Blueberry blame pie," Alexander said at last,

"Would be yummy with ice cream.

Such a tender crust."

"Yeah, yeah. Next time," muttered Chris.

There was a crash as Kathryn set her empty plate down, hard. "He's right. Blame has an incredibly flaky crust," she commented, her tongue flicking out to catch a blueberry perched on her lip.

"Thanks. Now — what's next?"

Edmund set his napkin down and clasped his hands behind his back. He addressed his remarks to the queen. This was a pattern, established the first full day of her reign, that would continue for decades. "The king is in serious, but stable, condition. No change in his comatose state. Parliament is meeting in a few hours to confirm that David is regent, but it's just a formality."

"How about the bad guy? Devon Domonov?"

"His last name is actually Stephenson," Jenny said. "He's a distant cousin, so his last name is different."

"Oh, yeah, that's how he fooled us — what a criminal mastermind," Christina snapped. "I don't care what his last name is. Is he in jail or the hospital or what?"

"He died at 10:48 a.m. Massive skull trauma."

Everyone looked at Princess Alex, who nibbled her crust and stared back.

"This does present a . . . a minor problem," Edmund began delicately.

"What problem?" David said sharply. "She defended her king and her prince. I was planning on giving her about a thousand medals."

"Forget it," she said with her mouth full. "They'll set off the metal detectors when I go shopping."

"Yes, but . . . Her Highness's motive must be called into question."

"Motive?" Christina asked. "I don't — what? What's going on? What's everybody else know that I don't?"

"I've got a master's in physics," Alex explained. "I knew the chair wouldn't break." At Christina's and Nicky's clueless expression, she elaborated. "Chairs never shatter spectacularly like on television. Most of them — particularly the ones around here — are made of hard wood. Very tough. It's like hitting someone with an anchor. You know the anchor won't break, but you damn sure know damage is going to be done. I did. I knew."

"At any rate," Edmund continued, "charges might be —"

"Absolutely not," David said, and looked, for the first time, like his father's chair might fit him. "My sister acted in defense of the royal family and, by extension, her country. The fact that the handiest weapon happened to be lethal, and she knew it, is irrelevant to this king and, I imagine, this family. Furthermore, I'm glad that treacherous fuck is dead, and if she hadn't taken care of it, I would have. *No* charges."

Edmund bowed his head. "As you wish, Majesty."

*Whoa,* Christina thought.

"Thanks," Princess Alex said quietly.

"No — thank *you.* Hand me that last slice of pie, will you, Chris?"

Wordlessly, she gave the last piece to her husband.

"What's next?" he asked with his mouth full.

"Parliament," Edmund said, and Chris suppressed a shiver.

# Chapter 29

From *The Queen of the Edge of the World*, by Edmund Dante III, © 2089, Harper Zebra and Schuster Publications.

Unlike most modern European royal families, the Alaskan royals actually held quite a bit of power when compared to the average citizen. The king and/or queen could declare war, end war, deploy the armed forces, declare states of emergency, grant pardons, sign death warrants (although the last time this had been done was 1897, when Jonas Weyers II was beheaded for smothering the infant prince Sergei Baranov), grant large sums of money to appropriate charities and/or persons, and sign bills into law. Parliament could and did do all these things, but it was all run by the reigning monarch as, for no other reason, an act of courtesy.

Past kings and queens had varied

from total indifference to government affairs, to micromanagement.

King Alexander II was known for his outwardly lackadaisical governing style, but he was careful to read every law, every proposal, every grant, and every declaration. He certainly never affixed the royal seal to anything he did not have a perfect understanding of. Parliament, of course, was used to this.

Of course, King Alexander was still alive (technically), so his son, David, and daughter-in-law, Christina, would actually be co-regents, with all the power those titles suggested.

And no one knew what the new regents' management style would be.

Christina was in her wedding dress again. "It's perfect," Jenny had assured her, fussing with her cape. "It's the opening of Parliament, which is always a special occasion. It's also a — a significant occasion. And it's not a traditional wedding gown — it's more like a formal. It'll show your respect, but it'll also pop their eyes out and remind them you're a queen."

"Great. Because I want eyes popping out."

"You really do, you know," Edmund advised quietly. "It's important to establish your and David's fitness for the throne."

"*Mine* and David's? Whatever happened to all the 'you're automatically royal when you get hitched, don't sweat it' stuff?"

"It's called hedging our bets," Edmund replied, giving her a slight push.

She started down the aisle, and was again weirdly reminded of her wedding day. Except this was a whole lot scarier. Today they actually expected her to *do* something.

David was already sitting on the throne at the head of the room. Normally they would have entered together, but she'd gotten her cape caught on the edge of the stove in the west kitchen, engendering hysteria in both the kitchen staff *and* the housekeeping staff. She herself had been inclined to just leave the cape behind, but no one would hear of it.

She walked past what appeared to be a thousand members of Parliament and carefully sat on the throne (the throne! the *throne!*) at David's right.

"Sorry I'm late," she said out of the corner of her mouth. "Cape disaster."

"So I heard," he muttered back. He was deathly pale, but managed a small smile for her. "Thanks for showing up. I bet

Edmund a thousand dollars that we'd find you on the docks, looking for the next ship out."

"Don't tempt me."

"Ladies and gentlemen," someone she couldn't see announced, "Their Majesties, King David and Queen Christina. Please rise for this, the one hundred forty-second opening of the Alaskan Parliament."

She started to get up, but David's hand shot out and grabbed her forearm, so she stayed put. Everybody *else* got up, and bowed.

"Thank you," David said.

"You're welcome," she replied.

"I wasn't talking to you," he muttered. Then, louder, "Be seated."

They sat, rustling like a giant flock of crows. Come to think of it, most of them *were* in black. She herself felt like a fraud, and for more than the obvious reasons. She felt like she should be wearing somber colors instead of jewel tones, because Al was so sick, but on the other hand, he wasn't dead (yet) so mourning was inappropriate.

And speaking of inappropriate, what was she doing sitting on a throne?

". . . this Parliament does on this day, the fourth of April, two thousand and four, accept David and Christina Baranov as co-regents of Alaska. So noted."

"Thank you," David said. Christina was amazed he could speak. She was amazed she herself hadn't wet her cape. "Please note that We expect this to be temporary and will only assume this duty until Our father regains his health."

*That must be the royal We,* she thought. *And memo to me — I'm never, ever referring to myself as "We." It sounds stupid. Not when David does it. He can actually pull it off. But I'd sound like a retard. Plus, everybody would laugh, and who could blame them?*

"So noted, Sire. May we proceed with the agenda?"

"Proceed."

Later, Christina would sum up Parliament in a single phrase: blah, blah, blah. There was some interest when they were talking about the Domonov plot, but it turned out that since Devon was dead, the others were singing in order to reduce their sentences.

There had been a total of four people arrested. The vet for the Juneau Zoo had supplied the tranqs; the vet's supervisor had signed off on the tranqs, one of them had driven Devon to the airport and had been waiting to spirit him and Nicky away, and of course Devon himself had initiated the attack.

There was no mention of charges being brought against Princess Alexandria.

When the question of beheading the conspirators came up, David shelved it for next time.

When the question of a DNA test for Nicholas rose, Christina said, before David could open his mouth, "Prince Nicholas is the son of the king and fifth in line to the throne. Period."

"Fourth," David coughed into his fist.

"Right. Fourth."

There was a long pause, followed by that unseen fellow saying, "So noted."

Christina was too nervous to doze, which was torture, because it was really pretty boring. She didn't even watch CNN, for crying out loud; what was she doing here? But her boredom disappeared when David said, "I have an item for this afternoon, if you please."

*Divorce,* she thought. *He's had enough. I've driven him over the edge. It was bound to happen, but I thought we might last a week, at least.*

"Proceed, Sire."

"My father never meant for me to rule

Alaska alone . . . or even with a queen. Regent," he corrected himself.

*Eh?*

"In fact, he wanted to have my sisters and brothers rule as kings and queens, with my queen and myself as high king and queen over them. In that way, we could all share the burden of the crown, and if anything happened to my queen or me before an heir was produced, the succession would continue with a minimum of strife."

*Interesting,* Christina thought, *but futile. The succession order seems pretty clear. But if it's what Al wanted . . .*

"Is Your Majesty suggesting we implement this?"

"I'm suggesting we shelve it, and think about it for next time. I will consider your arguments, ladies and gentlemen, but I must also consider my father's wishes."

And that, as they say, was that.

# Chapter 30

"Dad really meant all that High King crap?" Alexander said, waiting for them outside the hall. "Or are you drunk again?" Christina was amazed. No haiku! That made the nightmare seem, weirdly, more real.

"You'll see. Are the others ready?"

"Ready, Sire."

"What's going on?" Christina asked, picking up her skirt and hurrying to keep pace with David and Alexander's long strides.

"My father left a tape. He had instructions for the heir to the throne to watch it first and then have everybody else take a look. We're going now. There wasn't time," he added apologetically, "for the rest of you to see it before Parliament started."

"Oh. Is it, um, private? Maybe between your brothers and sisters? Because I don't want to inter —"

He grasped her elbow. His hand was warm and comforting. "You're part of the family now, Chris. He wanted — wants — you to see it, too."

Again, they assembled in the king's office: all the royal siblings, Jennifer, Edmund. Kurt was missing, prowling the grounds looking for a bad guy — any bad guy — to shoot. He'd checked himself out of the hospital AMA, and no one argued with him.

"Nice work in Parliament today," Princess Alex said by way of greeting, and Kathryn nodded and smiled at her. Christina knew how rare that was; Kathryn was morbidly self-conscious of her braces.

"Thanks," David replied.

"I was talking to your wife. Seriously, Chris, I was expecting a swoon or a dirty joke or something. Many congrats on not humiliating yourself in front of our national government."

"I was so petrified, I forgot the joke I was going to tell," she admitted. "Ooch over, Nicky, make room. Gah, my feet are killing me."

Nicky obligingly scooted to the end of the couch and she sat down with a sigh and kicked off her flats.

Jenny's eyes narrowed suspiciously. "Those aren't your wedding slippers."

"Oh, who was going to notice?" she

snapped. "We're sort of having a country crisis, if you haven't noticed. No one is interested in my feet."

"I'm interested in your feet," Nicholas teased.

"Your Majesty, it is unseemly —"

"Hush," David ordered absently. "Edmund's got the tape going."

The seventy-two-inch screen brightened, revealing King Al sitting right where David was. He was wearing a green flannel shirt frayed at the cuffs, and hadn't shaved in about three days. He yawned, then grinned at the camera and Christina saw Alexandria put her hand briefly over her eyes, as if she couldn't bear to see him looking hale and healthy.

"Hey, boy. Hey, kids. If you're watching this, I'm up shit creek. I'm either worm food, and I hope you didn't bury me — cremation, remember? — or so out of it David's running the country.

"Well, that's all right. I don't mind being done with the king gig, but I sure would have liked to have had more time with you guys. And Christina," he added thoughtfully. He pulled a small penknife out of his pocket, unfolded it, and started cleaning his nails. "Chris, I would have liked to have watched you get used to being a princess. Now you'll be queen — or queen regnant — and you're probably pretty pissed at me. Well, no one is ever really ready for the crown . . . not even people who wage wars for one. But, in this country at least, it never goes to someone who doesn't deserve it.

"Which brings me to my point. You kids might remember me reading you the *Chronicles of Narnia* when you were little. Man, I loved those books. Anyway, the thing I liked best about them — after the talking animals and the kick-ass lion — was the fact that Peter, the Narnian King, was High King over his brother and sisters. And they all helped each other rule Narnia. If Peter had to go up north and kick some ass — the giants lived in the north, you'll remember — his brothers and sisters stayed behind at Cair Paravel so the subjects didn't get nervous. In fact, King Peter was gone once when Narnia was attacked by the Calormenes, but King Edmund and Queen Lucy handled it.

"You'll recall your European history . . ."

"We will," Princess Alex said. "I didn't think *you* would."

Kathryn giggled, and elbowed her.

". . . when King Richard went off to fight the Crusades he damn near didn't have a throne to come back to. I don't want that to happen, and I don't want the burden of running the country to fall on David and Christina. It's nothing against Chris or David . . . I'd just like you guys to be able to share the work. It's not all christenings and ribbon cuttings, as I'm sure you've found out by now.

"I'm not signing anything, I'm not making it an order — although legally you wouldn't have to follow it, now that I'm kaput and David's king — but I do want you to consider it.

"You're all Baranovs, which means you're quick, intelligent, ruthless, and loyal. You could do worse than help each other make Alaska the greatest country in the world.

"That's all, except . . . David, you can do it. You were, in fact, born to it. And you picked yourself a helluva wife. Alexandria, use that big brain of yours to help your brother instead of give him shit 24/7. Alexander, ditto . . . and your days of sleeping late might be over for a while. Also, boy, seriously — enough with the poetry already. Kathryn, I know deep down — way, way deep down — you like your new sister-in-law. Consider showing it once in a while.

"And Nicky, I know you're going to hate

this, but you're still my baby boy. I update this tape every six months or so, which means you're still a kid. Stay a kid a little longer, for your old dad." He winked at the camera. "Edmund, Jenn, I know you two are hovering like damn ghouls . . . I don't have to ask you to help the kids out, but I will ask you to take it easy on them." He paused, and put the knife away. "Okay, I'm done. Done, and I love you gobs, and all that mushy stuff. Now get back to work."

The screen went dark.

# Chapter 31

"What . . . a . . . day . . ." Christina sighed, staggering into their apartments and tossing her cape over a chair in the corner. Someone had turned the lights on low, had remade their bed, had the stereo playing softly, had vacuumed. It was like living in a really nice hotel. Every day. "Seriously! The hospital, then Parliament, then that gruesome tape of your dad . . ." She trailed off. The day had been so long, and depressing, and as far as honeymoons went, this one sucked the root.

And it *was* her honeymoon! She should be naked, just about all the time, possibly experimenting with flavored oils and whipped cream, but noooooo, she had to open Parliament, for the love of God, and it'd be too weird to put the moves on David, not to mention the fact that he was probably so not in the mood, and —

She turned and he was there, right there, and then his mouth was on hers, his hands were in her hair, pulling the pins out, massaging her neck, and as the tension left her muscles she groaned into his mouth.

They staggered toward the bed, hands all over each other, pulling, tearing, ripping, and she heard him growl, "Fuck the buttonhook," and fell onto the bed with her, and then his hand was up her skirt, groping, pulling, and then her panties were flying through the air with the greatest of ease —

"Bare legs? Bare legs and ten-dollar shoes?"

"Like anybody cares," she grumbled, nibbling on his throat where she could reach it past his shirt collar. Then she was reaching down and fumbling for his trousers, groping for his zipper, then cupping his hot, hard shaft.

"Ummmm," she said, or something equally inane. Then her skirt was pushed up to around chin-level and he surged forward, burying himself within her. It was tight and mildly painful but sweet at the same time, and she sighed.

"Sorry," he panted in her ear. "I can't — I need you — next time will —"

"Shut up and fuck me," she replied, as politely as she could under the circumstances.

Delighted, he obliged. His hands were on her shoulders, his face was tucked into the side of her neck, and he shoved, shoved, shoved, and the headboard kept merry time with his strokes. She could feel his raw need, his urgency, and wrapped her legs around his ass (the better to go deeper, my dear), and then his mouth was on hers, his tongue was in her mouth, and she sucked on it, and he groaned wildly, and then he was done.

"Oh, God," he groaned, and collapsed over her.

"Horrance is *not* going to like what you've done to his dress."

"It's your dress."

"Not to hear him tell it," she said, and kissed his ear.

He pulled back slightly and propped himself up on one elbow. "I'm s —"

"Don't you dare apologize. We're married now."

He smiled and traced the curve of her lips with his fingertip. "I wasn't apologizing for making love — I'm sorry it was so fast. I know you didn't come. It's just — I've been thinking about this all day, and the pressure kept mounting, and you looked so beautiful I couldn't — couldn't wait anymore."

"Well, that works out nicely, because I was looking forward to jumping your bones, too. And the king, God love him, isn't here to stop us." She realized what she had said, then added carefully, "I didn't mean that I don't think of you as the king, because I —"

"No, you're right. The king's not here to stop us. I didn't know my mother very well."

"Okay," she said, because she had to say something, and hello, did *that* come out of nowhere or what?

"She wasn't a very — a very involved parent. So when she died, I barely felt it. But this — but my father —"

Then he leaned over, pressed his face into the side of her neck, and wept. She was appalled, both at her tactlessness and the raw emotion coming from a man who was usually tightly controlled, or at least indifferent. She didn't know what to say, and she was afraid if she did say something, she'd just fuck it up worse. So she held him, and stroked his hair, and waited for him to be done.

She stared at the ceiling and wondered what would become of them all.

*Three weeks later . . .*

"And if you could sign here, Sire . . . and here . . . and here . . ." Edmund gathered up each paper as David signed. They were ordinary-looking eight-and-a-half-by-eleven pages, but very stiff . . . they didn't curve or bend at all. Christina was curled up on the far sofa, watching them and wondering how much wood stock was in that paper. "Very good, Majesty."

"What else?" David said, rubbing his eyes. He looked ghastly, and no fucking wonder. It was eleven o'clock at night, he'd been up since five a.m., and the day wasn't over yet.

"Just a minor household matter, Sire —"

"Let me do it," Christina said. Both men looked at her with surprise, as if they'd forgotten she was there.

"Why are you still up?" David asked.

"Ask another dumb question, O mighty ruler of Alaska. It's my job, too, you know."

"Chris, there's no reason for both of us to be sleep-deprived," David pointed out reasonably. "Go to bed. I'll be up in a bit."

"Like yesterday? When you stumbled in at three a.m.?"

"There was some legislation I had serious questions about —"

"Look, Dave, I'm not bitching, okay? I mean, I am, but I don't mean anything by it. I understand you've got big-time responsibilities now. But so do I. I want to share in the work. You're saying it's not fair for us both to stay up late, but it's not fair for me to go to bed whenever and you stumble in when Fuckface here finally lets you go."

"Fuckface resents the term, Madam," said Edmund.

"Don't blame Edmund," David said.

"I don't," Christina said, glaring at Edmund.

"I've been trying to spare you the late hours."

"Well, don't. But thanks."

"It's my choice to stay up. There's a lot of ground to cover. I'm kind of learning on the run. And I — I have a lot to do."

Christina knew he'd almost made a slip and admitted his deepest fear: *And I'm afraid of screwing up.* She said nothing; it was something they'd discussed in the privacy of their chambers, and she wasn't about to betray his confidence.

"Look, Eds here said it was a minor household matter, right? Well, let me take it."

"Okay."

"That was quick," she muttered.

"I *am* tired," he replied, giving her a ghost of a grin.

"It can wait until the morrow," Eds said.

He gathered up all the paperwork. "I will retire, with Your Majesties' leave."

"No, let's make him stay up all night doing something he hates. Trying on blue jeans! We can make him give us a fashion show."

"Tempting, but then we'd have to stay up, too. This way we can actually get to bed before midnight."

"I would die before wearing dungarees," Eds said stiffly. "Your Majesties could throw me in the dungeon."

"Okay!" Christina said cheerfully. "Do we have one of those?"

"Come along, beautiful," the king said, standing, crossing the room, holding out a hand to her. "Let's get going before he changes his mind."

"Done and done," she replied, taking his hand. She stuck her tongue out at Eds while David wasn't looking and, to her complete amazement, he stuck his out in return. Only for a nanosecond, and she wondered if she'd really seen it. It was quick. Like a lizard.

"Eight a.m. tomorrow, Queen Christina. Jenny and I will discuss the household matter with you."

"I wonder," David said thoughtfully, leading her up the stairs, "what constitutes a minor household matter?"

"Beats the hell out of me, but I want you to sleep in tomorrow."

"I can't. I have to see to the penguins."

"David, you're the king, for crying out loud. Hire someone to take care of the fucking things."

"Oh, I couldn't do that," he said, shocked. "They're my responsibility."

"Overextend yourself much?" But she didn't bait him anymore. At least he looked relaxed whenever he returned from Allen Hall, even if he was slightly fishy-smelling. He sure didn't look relaxed when he was doing king paperwork. Half the time he looked constipated. "Fine, have it your way."

"Well," he said modestly, "I *am* King Regent."

"Sure, ride that one a little longer."

"I'd rather," he whispered in her ear, "ride you."

"Mister, you've got yourself a date."

Later, after love, he took her hand and said, "I couldn't do this without you, you know."

"That's not true, but thanks anyway."

Then she waited, hoping. She waited a long time, and assumed he had drifted off, when he finally said, with great difficulty, "I love you."

"That works out nicely," she said, "because I love you, too."

"Do you really?" He sounded honestly surprised.

"No, I married you because you were the only guy who asked. And because I'm a power-mad whore who likes being the goddamned Queen of Alaska."

"Oh, Christina," he said, "that's so touching. You're going to make me cry."

"Probably not for the last time, chum," she replied, and tickled his ribs, and unsuccessfully fought him off as he tickled her back.

# Chapter 32

"Minor household matter?" she nearly screamed.

"Now, Your Majesty," Jenny said, looking more anxious than usual. "There are only two hundred forty-eight thousand, six hundred seventy of them."

"I'm supposed to write two hundred fifty-eight, two hundred forty-two . . ."

"Now, Queen Christina —"

*"Jenny."*

"— er — Your — um — Majesty —"

"How about if Jenny and I write the thank-you notes," Edmund suggested, looking especially cadaverous in a white shirt and cream-colored jacket — "and you sign them?"

She nearly pounced on the idea, then came to her senses. "No. Thanks, but no. Those eighty zillion people liked us enough to send wedding presents, so I guess I better get around to thanking them."

"You also have —"

"Oh, God." She covered her eyes. "Don't tell me."

"Eighteen thousand, three hundred twenty-six sympathy notes regarding King Alexander. So far."

"Argh!"

"Of course," he added with perfect straight-faced malice, "the daily mail hasn't arrived yet."

"But we have freshly made ice cream," Jenny said. "With sprinkles. You can snack while you work."

"You guys! You can't just wave ice cream under my nose and expect me to — what kind of ice cream?"

"Chocolate," they said in unison.

"Okay, okay. I said I'd do it, and I'm a woman of my word. But you guys. Cripes! Minor household matter, my big white butt. You guys are on drugs. What the hell is a *major* household matter? And what's this?" She peered suspiciously at the boxes and boxes of stationery. The paper was light blue, heavy stock, with *HRM Christina Baranov* in dark print at the top. "Ech. Queen stationery."

"We had to rush the printing," Edmund said quietly.

"Oh," she said, understanding. "Sure." There had of course been boxes and boxes of stationery, which were probably stashed in the basement somewhere, with Her Royal Highness. Princess paper. Which she couldn't use anymore. Son of a *bitch.*

She tried to lighten the subject, and went about it badly. "Can't I wait until Al wakes up and make *him* write thank-yous?"

"Sure you can," Jenny said, cutting Edmund off — probably for the first time in her life. "Sure. He'll wake up and then . . . and then he can — can write them." Then, shockingly, she burst into tears.

"Jenny!" Christina took her in her arms and hugged her. "Don't cry, Jenny, you'll get us all started."

"There, there," Edmund said ineffectually, patting her shoulder with long, skeletal fingers.

"I'm sorry," she sobbed. "I'm glad you're the queen regnant and I really like David . . . but I miss the king . . . he was really nice to me . . . and he's so sick . . . and he was so nice . . . and he's in so much trouble because he was nice — a good dad — and — and —"

"Jeez, will you stop? He'll be all right. He's too obnoxious to die."

"Why don't you take the morning, Jenny,

344

and take some personal time?" Edmund suggested. "With Her Majesty's leave, of course. It's been a stressful time for all of us."

"No, I can't do that," she said, calming. "I have too much work. We all do." Then she stiffened, doubtless freshly realizing the queen was holding her. "I must beg Your Majesty's pardon. I — I forgot myself and I'm so —"

"Jenny. For the love of God. When are you going to lighten up?"

She sniffed and wiped her face with her palms. It hurt Christina's heart a bit to see that gesture, so childlike. "Well, again. I apologize."

"It's a stressful time," Edmund commented, possibly the understatement of the decade.

"Yeah, well, you can make it up to me by licking envelopes."

"Blurgh," Jenny said, and the three of them laughed.

From the Alaskan Royal Archives.
Museum of Alaskan History, Juneau,
 Alaska.
From the Baranov collection; donated
 by HRH Prince David III, prince of
 Alaska, 2080.

This note, on HRM's personal stationery, is a typical example of Queen Christina's style of correspondence. It is a thank-you note for an original Picasso, given to the queen on the occasion of her wedding to David, the then-crown prince of Alaska, and donated to the museum by her grandson, Prince David III.

May 8, 2005

Dear Mr. Gates,

Thank you very much for the painting. It's really amazing. We hung it in Allen Hall, a wing of the castle very important to the king, and where he can see it every day. I try to get in there and look at it when I can. Those are some pretty amazing colors.

I'm sorry you couldn't come to the wedding, but I wish you the best of luck with your lawsuit.

Sincerely yours,<br>Christina K. Baranov

P.S. I have some of your software, and it works great. Good work.

From the private papers of HRM
Christina Baranov

April 9, 2004

My dearest Christina,

I just finished watching CNN; you looked beautiful and poised. Well done.

I wanted to take a moment to drop you a line to tell you how sorry I am about what happened to King Alexander. Although I'm certain you were personally and professionally horrified by the recent turn of events, I'm equally certain you are up to the task of helping the new king regent run the country.

Many times when we talked in my office I could see your fondness for King Alexander and Prince David, and your anxiety that you would be unable to be an asset to his son when the time came.

Christina, if no one has mentioned this, then I will do so now: you're more than capable of the task set before you. No one has a bigger heart or (beneath the swearing) a kinder disposition. I can think of no better woman to be queen, for Alaska and for myself.

Please don't hesitate to call on me at any time if you want to talk; I would dearly love to see you again, although I understand there are now many demands on your time. Now that you are married, you no longer need me, but I miss our talks. I am at your disposal and will come to the palace whenever you require.

Until we meet again, I remain,

Your friend,
Dr. Elinor Pohl

# Chapter 33

"David?" She opened the door, grimacing at the smell. "You in here?" She walked inside, trying to ignore the penguins, half of which had stopped whatever they were doing to stare at her. Ick. And that weird-ass Picasso, the one that looked like a bar floor after the drunks overindulged. Double ick. What had Bill Gates been thinking? "Helloooooo? I'm going buggy writing thank-yous and wanted a kiss. And possibly a quickie. Dave?"

Nothing. Well, shit. She backed out of the room, never taking her eyes off the weird birds. She shut the door, turned, and nearly fell over the penguin that had somehow snuck around and gotten outside the room.

"Ack!" She skipped clumsily to avoid stepping on it, lunging a few feet to the side and fetching up painfully against the wall.

It stared at her.

She opened the door.

It stared at her.

"Go back inside, now."

It clucked. Was it hungry? Thirsty? Preparing to attack?

"Okay, go inside now."

It totally ignored her.

"Fucking thing," she muttered.

It clucked louder.

"Sorry." She edged a few more feet to the left. It followed her. She edged faster. It followed faster. "Quit that, now. Quit. Quit! Stop it! Help!"

Chris came rocketing around the corner, nearly knocking David off his feet. She grabbed him like a life preserver and said, "It's after me, it's after me!"

"What? Who? Is Kurt —"

"No, fool! It's coming to eat me or kill me or whatever! It's like a Terminator with wings — it won't stop!"

David looked down in time to see a young penguin just past its first molting hurry around the corner. "For heaven's sake, Christina, you shouldn't let them out. They —"

"Am I not speaking English, King Dumb-ass? It stalked me! It tricked me and snuck out and now I can't get rid of it. It's after me!"

He tried very hard not to laugh. It was obvious from her wide eyes and flushed face that she was not remotely amused. "I'll take care of it, Chris. Don't —" He coughed into his fist and prayed she wouldn't notice his watering eyes. "Don't be frightened."

She peered at him suspiciously. "Are you laughing at me, buddy boy?"

"No."

"You better not be."

"I love you," he said spontaneously. It was getting a bit easier to tell her each time. She never laughed, at least. Not about that. In fact, she claimed to love him in return.

"Why?" Still suspicious.

"Oh, several indefinable reasons." He kissed her on the nose.

"Yech, get a room." They turned to see Kurt smirking at them. He was wearing khakis, loafers without socks, his shoulder holster, and a T-shirt with the logo I'M A GOOD THING. "Or at least a palace. What's up, royal dudes?"

"Christina is making friends," David said.

"Very funny. I'm glad to see you, Kurt. Can you take care of it?" she asked, gesturing down to the penguin, which had edged closer while they talked.

"What do you want me to do?" he asked doubtfully. "Shoot it?"

"For heaven's sake," David said, before Christina could incriminate herself. "I'll take care of it. Kurt, make sure she doesn't get into any more trouble."

"Got a hypo of Thorazine?" he called after David, who laughed in reply.

"Well, well," she said, still annoyed. "Aren't you two best pals these days." Actually, it was kind of nice . . . gone was the underlying resentment and me-Tarzan-she-Jane vibe the men would give off whenever they were in the same room.

"Aw, he's a good guy." Kurt lowered his voice. "I feel sorry for him, you know. What happened to his dad, and then that big-ass promotion. And, of course, being married to you. When it comes to talking to Parliament and visiting orphans, you're not what I'd call an asset."

"Well, we both appreciate you staying around, asshole. David even said so the other day."

Kurt shrugged. He was more relaxed than she could recall seeing him, and he and Princess Alex were getting quite chummy these days. He appeared to be in no rush to return to L.A. She was glad.

Alex had confided that he lingered because he still felt guilty about the king getting shot. It was a bad reason to stay, but a good man was staying, so it worked out. Sort of.

"What are you doing here, anyway?"

"Jenny sent me to get you."

"What a slave driver! I just wanted to take a break from interminable thank-you notes."

"Yeah. She said you left four hours ago."

"It's a big palace," she said defensively. "I was looking for David again."

"Excuses, excuses. Come on, I promised Jenny I'd drag you back."

"Who exactly *is* in charge around here? Because it isn't me."

"Ask Edmund," he suggested, and walked her to the elevator.

# Chapter 34

"Really?" David asked for about the hundredth time. "It's not one of your, um, unusual jokes?"

"For the billionth time — it's not a joke."

"Really?" He grinned.

"Yes, David. Good work. I'm not joking about that, either. I mean, whoof! *Good* work. Yum."

He slung an arm around her hips as they walked down the hospital corridor. They had talked briefly to the press outside and, in a tit for tat, the press had stayed outside. Tension was still high, but the country hadn't imploded or melted since David assumed the crown, so the press and pundits had adopted a wait-and-see attitude.

As for today's goings-on, she and David had been summoned to the king's hospital room by an urgent call from Princess Kathryn.

"That's — I can't believe it. I really can't."

"Then you haven't been paying attention to the extent of our extracurricular activities, Penguin Boy. Or should I say Penis Boy?" Then, a little nervously, she added, "Are you — do you mind? I mean, do you like it?"

"Are you kidding? It's wonderful news." He chortled. "Edmund's going to have kittens!"

"Thanks for a truly disturbing visual — oh, here we are." They walked into the private room, where Dr. Sarett and Princess Alex were waiting for them. "Where's everybody else?"

"Nicky's got riding lessons — I didn't want to interrupt. I know Dave wants the kid's life to stay as normal as possible under the circumstances — the other Alex is touring a new battered-men's shelter, and Kathryn is meeting with the COCS."

Christina giggled. The Coalition of Cruise Services had the worst acronym ever. She knew it was immature, but hearing it out loud always slayed her.

David went to his father, straightened the blanket, and kissed the man's forehead. He didn't look deathly ill — in fact, David was paler. King Alexander merely looked like he'd fallen asleep after a hard day. Possibly one where heavy drinking was involved. "Is there news, Doctor? My sister said it was urgent."

"Well. I don't know that it's what you'd call urgent . . ." Weeks of frequent meetings and medical updates with the royal family had helped him loosen up a bit. He still dressed too stiffly for a doctor; Christina imagined hospital administration insisted he wear a dark suit under his lab coat, and his mahogany-colored shaved head gleamed under the fluorescent lights. He'd be downright scrumptious, she thought, if he'd lose the big, clunky glasses and switch to contacts. His brown eyes swam behind the large lenses, making him look constantly near tears. "It's definitely promising, howev—"

"He's starting to wake up!" Princess Alex interrupted. "He talked!"

"No way," Christina said, utterly flabbergasted.

"Way, my queen. He said 'ham and . . . ' That was it. Like ham and eggs."

"Dr. Sarett, how many times do I have to tell you? It was salmon. My dad's a fisherman. Trust me, wherever he is in his head, he's thinking about fish, not eggs."

"What happens next?" David said.

"Well, we'll keep monitoring him closely, of course, but his brain waves are already shifting and he does appear to be —"

"English, remember," Alex warned.

"It's like he's in the deep end of the pool, and he's swimming toward the shallow end."

"That's awesome!"

"Yes, Your Majesty. Her Highness thought you and the king should know right away."

"Her Highness knows her shit."

"Awwwww," the princess said mockingly. "That's so nice."

"So, can we hang around and wait for him to wake up?" Chris asked eagerly.

"Your Majesties are welcome to wait, but it could take him another month to come all the way back. However, studies have shown that comatose patients can hear and even see — you've noticed his eyes open occasionally — so if you'd like to speak to him, it might facilitate —"

Christina bent until her mouth was level with the king's ear. "Hey, dickhead! Your kid knocked me up! So rise and shine, because I'm not doing this by myself! Now get up before I put my foot up your lazy ass!" She straightened and cleared her throat. "How's that?"

Dr. Sarett's eyes were bigger than usual behind his glasses. "That will probably do the trick, Your Majesty." He clutched the king's chart protectively to his chest. Chris and Alex grinned at each other, each imagining the notes the guy was going to add later. David merely looked pained. "Congratulations, by the way," the doctor added.

"Yeah, that's so great, you guys!" Alex hugged Christina, then grabbed her brother and squeezed him so hard he gasped. "When did you find out?"

"About ten minutes ago," David said.

"This morning," Christina said. "The stick was blue. But chill out, we're not telling the planet for at least another couple weeks."

"Boy," the princess said, impressed, "you guys didn't waste any time. Honestly, David, I thought you were a monk or something."

"Ha!" Christina chortled.

"I'm not having this discussion," David said.

"Thank Christ," King Alexander II said.

# Chapter 35

She opened the door of Allen Hall and spotted "her" penguin at once; it was getting disgustingly fat. She really had to stop sneaking up here and feeding it. Just because David told her it was an orphan didn't mean she, like, had to bond with it or anything.

"Hey, guess what, Fred?" she asked as it came toward her as fast as its nonexistent legs could carry it. "Al woke up! Isn't that the coolest? Now . . ."

She crossed the room, opened the feeding closet, rummaged, then grabbed a bucket of fish out of the fridge. "Okay," she said, turning back, "I can't give you the whole bucket this time, because that book of David's I read said too much wasn't —"

The door to Allen Hall opened, and in came Edmund. Carrying a bucket.

He saw her and started in surprise.

*Best defense: good offense.* "What are *you* doing here?" she snapped.

"Surely Your Majesty has greater demands on her time," was his frosty reply. Fred had totally forgotten about her and was now hopping up and down in front of Edmund.

*The two-timing little creep!* Fred. Not Edmund.

"Perhaps I should bring this up with the king."

"Which one? Never mind. Look, let's just put all our cards on the table, all right? I won't tell if you won't, okay?"

". . . as you wish."

"Yeah. Consider that, like, a royal command. Or something."

Edmund reached into the bucket, withdrew a smelt in his long, white fingers, and dropped it. Fred made it vanish. "Or something, yes, ma'am."

She narrowed her eyes at him, but all he did was look innocent (as much as he could, anyway) and keep feeding Fred.

"All right, then," she said at last.

"Her Majesty is quite right," Edmund said suddenly. "They are inordinately smelly birds."

"And annoying."

"Can't even fly."

"Can't keep them full!"

"All in all, quite aggravating."

"Okay, so we're agreed."

"Yes, ma'am."

"Okay. Well, 'bye."

"It's merely that I felt the king regent had enough demands on his —"

"Eds — don't even bother."

He sighed and dropped another smelt. "Yes, ma'am."


"Now don't get me wrong, Al —"

"Oh, man, here we go." The king was sitting up in his hospital bed, wolfing down green Jell-O. His hospital gown kept slipping, revealing formerly tanned skin that had paled during his hospital stay. "All aboard for the ingrate train."

"— because I'm glad you're awake and all —"

"I'll bet, *Queen Regnant* Christina."

"— but cripes! Talk about a heart attack! I nearly fell out the window."

"You were nowhere near the window. This Jell-O sucks. Somebody get me a steak. *Two* steaks."

"No steaks for you, Coma Boy. Not for a while, at least."

"No steak, my ass! Who's in charge around here?"

"Neither one of *us*, I'll tell you that much."

"Congratulations. Once you realize that,

you're ready to be queen."

"No, thanks. Did you see David? He aged about twenty years in six minutes."

"Cry me a river. Kid's gonna have to suck it up again sometime . . . longer than a few weeks, too. *God,* this Jell-O is terrible."

"Stop your whining." Christina raised the shades and squinted out at the sunny day. "So when can you start running Alaska again?"

"I dunno. Doc says I'm here for at least another week. And I could use a vacation."

Christina nearly fell out the window again. "Vacation! You've been asleep for almost two months!"

Edmund rapped discreetly and crept into the room. Al and Christina stared; Edmund never crept. There were rumors that he snuck, but he'd never been caught. "Good afternoon, Your Majesty. Your Majesty."

"Oh, come *on,*" she groaned.

"I feel your pain, my queen. But technically you're still co-regent until Parliament relieves you."

"And they can't un-king *me,*" Al said with a remarkable lack of smugness.

"The queen of England is here to see you, Sire."

"Uh-huh. Pull the other one. And get me a steak. And find out when I can go fishing again. And where's the mail? I can at least go through my mail while I'm trapped in this cotton hellhole."

"No mail!" Chris said loudly. "You're supposed to take it easy. Believe me, *believe me,* no one wants you up and around more than I do. But you gotta do it slowly. By the way, stay away from animal tranquilizers in the future."

"Yeah," the king said dryly. "I hear they make me sick."

"King Alexander, Queen Christina," Edmund said loudly, startling them both . . . he usually slipped away during an argument, disappearing like Batman. "Her Royal Majesty, Queen Elizabeth of Great Britain."

Queen Elizabeth walked in. For a record third time in two hours, Christina nearly fell out the window. Even the king looked stunned; a scrap of green Jell-O clung to his beard and his mouth was open. He hastily adjusted his hospital gown.

"Good afternoon," the queen said.

"Buh," Christina said.

"Hi, Liz. Thanks for coming by."

Queen Elizabeth's regal brow wrinkled momentarily, then smoothed out. "It is my pleasure, Alex. I am so pleased to see you've begun your recovery."

She was a small woman, surprisingly small, but she stood ramrod-straight in her blue tweed suit. Her hat was also blue, with a tiny veil she could peek through. Her gloves were white, and immaculate. Her shoes were low-heeled, dark, and sensible. Her dark gray hair looked perfect; nothing was out of place. A white purse with a white strap dangled from her forearm.

Her eyes, the color of faded denim, missed nothing.

"This is my daughter-in-law," Al was saying, "the protem queen of Alaska. Chris, this is Liz. She runs England. 'Scuse me if I don't get up," he added, then hee-hawed.

"It's nice to meet you, Queen Elizabeth," she said through numb lips. It was extremely nerve-wracking to be talking to the Queen of England, even if she did look like someone's stiff-and-proper grandma. Which she was. "It was really nice of you to come all this way."

"The pleasure is mine, Queen Christina." Elizabeth extended a gloved hand. Christina shook it, wishing she hadn't chewed off most of her nails waiting for the stick to turn blue. "My son told me your wedding was lovely."

"He was really nice. It was nice to meet him. It's nice of you to come visit — I'm sure you're super-busy." Was she saying "nice" too often? She wanted to wipe her forehead, but didn't dare. "You look very nice." Argh!

"Yeah, Liz, you're looking good. Y'know, I could use a private duty nurse," the king leered. Then, "Ow, dammit!"

"I'm so sorry, Al," Christina said. "Was that your foot? I should have been watching where I dropped your chart."

"Goddamned right," the king muttered.

Queen Elizabeth smiled, and Christina could have sworn those blue eyes twinkled at her. "Your Majesty is welcome to Buckingham Palace anytime. I hope you will find time in your busy schedule to visit us." She cast an appraising glance at Christina's waistline, which was unbelievably weird, because Chris figured she'd been pregnant for maybe a day and a half. "Although I suspect you'll have your hands full in the year to come."

"Yeah, well, maybe we will," the king said, completely ignoring the fact that Elizabeth hadn't been talking to him. "Good hunting over there. Maybe we could go to your Scottish place."

"Perhaps," the queen said.

"And, uh, sorry about what happened with the dog. But how the hell was I supposed to know it wasn't a crazed, rabid skunk — *owwwwww!*"

"I'm so sorry, Al."

"I must be going," Elizabeth said, a tiny curl of a smile tugging at the left side of her mouth. "I do hope you'll consider my invitation, Queen Christina."

"Thanks, ma'am. That sounds really nice."

"I would wish for you to feel better soon, Alex," the queen added thinly, "but you appear to be back to your old self."

"Awwww, Lizzie. Don't be cold. Hop in here with me. I'll warm you up!"

*Oh God, oh God, ohgodohgodohgod . . .*

" 'Bye," Chris said hastily, practically hustling the queen out the door. She rounded on the king as soon as the door hissed shut. "I can't believe you were coming on to the queen of England!"

"She wants me," the king said, picking the piece of Jell-O out of his beard and popping it in his mouth. "I can tell."

Christina checked back once more before retiring to the palace for the night. She wanted to make sure Al wasn't overdoing, maybe sneaking peeks at one of his bags of get-well cards. She wouldn't put it past him, but she — they — were all going to be merciless. It was vital he recover fully, and not just for political reasons. They had all missed the big lug, and that was a fact.

But nothing of the sort was going on. Instead, she found Al snoring, and curled against his side like a puppy, also sound asleep, was Prince Nicholas. They looked like Lost Boys who had fallen asleep after a long day of deviling Captain Hook.

In a chair by the window sat Edmund, head back, mouth open, snoring lightly.

*Asleep at the wheel,* Christina thought gleefully. *Finally! Proof he's human! Oh, wait'll I tell the others!*

Christina left them where they were, informed the nursing staff that the prince could stay the night, and confirmed the same with the security staff.

Then she went home to the rest of her family.

# Chapter 36

"Back to being a lowly princess," Christina said. "Yippee!"

"And a lowly crown prince," David added. They were nude, slightly sweaty after a bout of lovemaking. His chin was resting on her stomach. "I can't wait."

"Tell me. Although you realize we still have to write all those thank-yous for the wedding presents."

"I thought you took on that little task."

"They tricked me," she admitted, giggling as his breath tickled her belly button. "Minor household matter . . . shyeah!"

"Speaking of minor household matters, when are you due again?"

"Cripes, do I have to write it on my forehead? February first."

"Hmph." He kissed her stomach. "I wish he could be born tomorrow."

"*She'll* be here soon enough."

"Oh, so that's how it'll be?"

"Honest? I don't give a shit, as long as she's healthy. And less than eleven pounds."

"Christina is a nice name," he said.

She ran her fingers through his hair. "So is David. But you know which one I really like?"

"I'm bracing myself."

"Nicholas."

He groaned.

"No, really! I really like that name. I just wanted to, you know, get my picks on the board."

"There's plenty of time."

"Yes," she said, satisfied, bringing him up for another kiss. "There's plenty of time."

# Epilogue

From *The Queen of the Edge of the World*, by Edmund Dante III, © 2089, Harper Zebra and Schuster Publications.

## Author's Note

Although Queen Christina's first reign was brief — sixty-seven days — she and King David acquitted themselves well during a period of tremendous stress for the country, something that was never forgotten.

King Alexander II was, of course, welcomed back with open arms once he had completed his recovery, and went on to rule for many years. He soon had a new hobby to add to fishing, hunting, governing, and deviling the House of Windsor . . . doting on his grandchildren.

Although enormously stressful, and certainly not something to be wished for, years later King David admitted that the attack on his father and their subsequent elevation to ruling monarchs had brought him and the queen much closer, much faster, than they might have been under more sedate circumstances. She found new respect for his position, and he was able to see what a true asset she could be to the royal family in general, and the king in particular.

Queen Christina, with time and experience, did learn caution and was even noted to bite her tongue on occasion. But Her Majesty never forgot her roots, and never responded well to bullying. Years later, when Parliament demanded she cease her requests for an increase in her annual allowance (Her Majesty wished to increase her donations to various children's charities by no less than seventy percent), the queen's verbatim reply was: "I'm the wife of a king, and the mother of kings. And I'm not asking you, I'm telling you. So fuck off, Jack."

Her Majesty got the increase.

Edmund Dante III
Juneau, Alaska
In this, the third year of Her Royal Majesty's reign, Queen Christina III, 2086.

We hope you have enjoyed this Large Print book. Other Thorndike, Wheeler or Chivers Press Large Print books are available at your library or directly from the publishers.

For more information about current and upcoming titles, please call or write, without obligation, to:

Publisher
Thorndike Press
295 Kennedy Memorial Drive
Waterville, ME    04901
Tel. (800) 223-1244

Or visit our Web site at:
www.gale.com/thorndike
www.gale.com/wheeler

OR

Chivers Large Print
published by BBC Audiobooks Ltd
St James House, The Square
Lower Bristol Road
Bath BA2 3BH
England
Tel.  +44(0) 800 136919
email: bbcaudiobooks@bbc.co.uk
www.bbcaudiobooks.co.uk

All our Large Print titles are designed for easy reading, and all our books are made to last.